THE DIADEM SANG,

flowing in phantom splendor on the blue-black hair while in her head fragmented images of cool wary black eyes flickered hazily at the rim of mental vision, triggering confusion and a ravening curiosity in her.

Her body moved, clumsily at first, then with a swift sureness that startled and delighted her. For the first time since the diadem had started taking her body she wasn't wholly pushed aside, a helpless prisoner in her own skull. She shared the grafted skill, and the pleasure she found in it added to the confusion that wheeled in her head.

Stavver's strained face, Maissa's hate-ugly one reflected the phantom sparks of flickering colors from the jeweled centers of the diadem flowers as they caught the light and reflected it back.

"Let her go."

Her voice sounded strange to her as if it struggled toward a resonant baritone an octave below her normal tones. . . .

LAMARCHOS

Jo Clayton

DAW BOOKS, INC.

DONALD A. WOLLHEIM, PUBLISHER

1301 Avenue of the Americas
New York, N.Y.   10019

FIRST PRINTING, JANUARY 1978

1 2 3 4 5 6 7 8 9

PRINTED IN U.S.A.

PART I

Chapter I

"Still raining?" Stavver ducked into the lock and knelt beside her, eyes on the rain which fell in a depressing, grey curtain.

Aleytys brushed her hands over her black-dyed hair, breaking up the clinging drops of mist that had drifted in from the rain, then glanced briefly at the moisture beaded on her forearms. "Not a break yet."

"Maissa will be spitting like a cat. She hates getting wet."

"I can't get the feel of her." She waited for a response. "Sometimes she actually frightens me." More silence. "So much anger . . ." Still no answer. Flicking a hand upwards, she said, "What about up there?"

"A Karkesh skimmer went by a minute ago. Still no sign they know we're here." He relaxed against the far side of the lock and smiled at her. "You don't look like yourself."

Aleytys glanced down at her altered body. Her breasts were bare, except for pale blue tattoos of butterflies fluttering in a line to her shoulders. A wide coarsely woven batik, printed in pale blue, wound twice around her hips and pinned with a silver wire brooch. Her skin was darkened to a warm russet. "Each time I look in a mirror I get a shock." She ran her eyes over him, assessing his changes as well: white hair dyed black, pale blue eyes now deep brown, skin dyed darker than her own, finally, the bold blue lines of tattooing on face, arms, and shoulders. "Each time I look at you . . ." She chuckled. "I woke up last night and nearly had a fit when I saw the stranger in my bed." She yawned and stretched. "What about you, Miks?"

"Standard tactic in my profession, Leyta."

"Well I haven't your vast experience with all this changing about. This is only the third world I've seen and Maissa wouldn't let me off ship to see more than a snatch of the place where we picked up Kale."

He wrapped his fingers around her ankle and waggled her foot back and forth, ignoring her protests. "Poor, innocent, little mountain girl." He chuckled. "I've seen you in action."

"That wasn't me, idiot. Let go." She pulled her foot free and feinted a kick at him. "You of all people—you should remember the diadem. You stole it." She touched her head and made a face at him when the faint chime sang through the hiss of the downpour outside. "It's let me alone since we left Jaydugar, thank the Madar."

The grin on his face dissolved. He got onto his knees and leaned across her to stare at the ceaseless, dreary rain. "Damn this weather. We've got things to do."

Aleytys watched him settle back, arms circling his knees, face pulled into a brooding frown. The pervading, dull hiss of the falling water pounded on the sensitivity which made him a brilliant thief and was also his major flaw. A quiet tension quivered in the beaded air while she waited silently for the return of the sardonic mask he used to hide this weakness from the world's malevolent eyes. She studied him, sensing a peculiar unease; curious because she could discover nothing in their present circumstances to justify his anxiety. Feeling about to find what was troubling him, she voiced a thought that lay like a wrinkle under the surface.

"Are we really supposed to fool anyone into thinking we're natives of this soggy . . . ?" She shrugged and jerked a thumb out the lock where the rain had begun to thin. Ghost images of several trees were developing in the greyness.

Stavver blinked slowly and lifted his head, the somber frown flowing into blandness. "Maissa explained all that."

"I still don't believe we'd convince a blind baby we belong."

Stroking the darkened skin beside the jutting beak of his nose, Stavver said patiently, "People see what they expect.

Would the nomads on Jaydugar know Maissa wasn't a caravanner?"

Aleytys rubbed her shoulders against the ridged metal of the ship, frowning thoughtfully. "Isn't this different? You said there aren't as many physical types on this world as we had at home."

"You're the key, Leyta. If they accept you as genuine— and why shouldn't they, aren't you a genuine healer?—you cover any slips we make. You're to be gikena, healer and worker of small miracles. We're merely humble nonentities attached to your service." He dipped his head in a servile bow. "Who would look twice at us?"

"It only takes one. The right one."

"So we're all from across the sea. Strangers. That should explain any oddities. If the natives accept us, the Kark-iskya certainly will. From what Kale told us, his people have very little contact with them." He grinned at her. "Kale says you've got the language down better than any of us."

Aleytys heard the dry note in his voice and turned her face away. "One of my talents."

Outside, the rain was only a trickle of wetness, the shimmering, orange circle of the sun visible through the thinning clouds as it hesitated just above the western horizon. Swinging around so her legs hung out the lock, she gazed thoughtfully at the dark, steaming earth with its thin patches of short, prickly grass, debating whether to say what she had to say or leave it till Maissa returned. She walked her fingertips over the heavy, batik material, drawing a measure of reassurance from the familiar feel of herself. "Maissa puzzles me," she said slowly.

Stavver's long back was curved into a section of lock-side, while his thin, wiry legs stretched out over the black, rubberoid flooring. He ran lazy eyes over her body, the smiling mask back on his face again. "No doubt."

"My skin crawls when she's around you or Kale." She waited for an answer. When he stared past her out the lock, saying nothing, she gave an impatient exclamation. "Dammit, Miks, this isn't idle chatting."

"She doesn't like men," he said reluctantly. "I don't want to talk about her, Leyta."

"I guessed that," she said dryly. "All men?"

"Yes."

"And you said she hates getting wet?"

"Yes."

"Mmmhh." Aleytys slicked the mist off her knees and stared thoughtfully at the rain pools below. Silence spread through the lock, vibrating tensely against the irregular pattering of the breaking rain. The warm, humid air made their lungs labor and their nerves tighten but neither made a gesture toward the more temperate atmosphere of the ship. The shadows of the grey half-light deepened their facial lines and occluded their eyes, obscuring expression and giving a somber harshness to both faces.

"She's due back about sundown. How long is that from now?"

"The 'phemer lists the day length as nineteen hours. That leaves her about two to play with."

"She went to get caravans with horses. She didn't say how she planned to acquire them. Do you know, Miks?"

"What difference does it make?" His mouth tightened repressively. "Let's not discuss it, Leyta."

She glanced around at him, eyes moving over his curved shoulders and forbidding face. "Why not?"

"You won't like the answer."

Aleytys reached back and set her hand on his leg, feeling the hardness of the long, wiry muscles in his calf. "She's a killer?"

He nodded. "It's how she gets her kicks."

"You called her to us."

"You remember how close we came to getting snatched by the Rmoahl Hounds? She was the only one I could reach that day."

"I'm not blaming you, Miks. But I also have to remember the price we pay for her help. Stealing the treasures of the Karkiskya for her. I don't like being a part of slaughtering the innocent."

"The Karkiskya are far from innocent." The next words came out slowly, painfully. "Keep clear of Maissa. Don't question what she does; do what she says, don't get underfoot, and you'll stay alive."

"If she's so dangerous—"

"Leyta, believe me, Maissa in a fury is capable of anything."

"Am I so helpless? Even without the diadem I crossed a world alone and pregnant."

"Aleytys, my Lee, my innocent, healthy-souled mountain girl—you'll never understand Maissa. Never. To know her you'd have to walk in her shoes, and I wouldn't wish that on anyone." He sighed and moved to sit beside her, his long legs dangling out the lock. "She was born on Iblis. Her mother was a two-obol whore on Star Street in Shaol. Her father—who knows?" He stared gloomily at his bare feet. "She was raised to the infant trade. Knifed her mother when she was seven and took to the streets."

"Knifed her mother?" Aleytys felt a sick horror clutch at her stomach.

"Her mother. The woman who rented her child to anybody who'd give her the price of a drink. Maissa was two years old the first time."

"Madar." Aleytys shut her eyes, a sour taste in her mouth. "Two years old."

Stavver shifted slightly, his skin squeaking across the metal. "Right. Since then—well, she's survived."

"You're right, Miks. I'll never empathize with the result of that life. Madar! I won't try." She shuddered.

"So walk lightly around Maissa until this game is over."

"Isn't there some way to help her?"

Stavver made a brief, impatient sound. "She doesn't want help. Let it lie, Aleytys. Don't interfere in what's none of your business."

Aleytys wrenched her thoughts from the sickening images in her mind. "Well," she said briskly. "All that being true, then you'd better know this right away. If this world doesn't welcome me, you can forget about my being gikena."

"What the hell are you talking about?"

Aleytys smiled tightly and watched her toes wiggle. "Exactly what I said, Miks. If the natives don't accept me, they can make it impossible for me to do any of my 'tricks.' Better put the ladder down so I can ask them to let me play the game." She glanced up at the dark grey blanket of clouds. "At least the rain has stopped for a while."

"Superstitious nonsense. Wake up, mountain girl. You left your witches and demons behind on Jaydugar." With his narrow face pulled together in a frown, he jerked her around and glared into her face. "God, woman, if you spoil Maissa's plan . . ."

She caught hold of his thin wrists and pulled his hands away from her. "Can I fly a starship? Can I walk into a fortress like you and steal the teeth off the guardians without disturbing their sleep? No, and I'd never try it. I haven't the training or the wish. So, don't you question me, Miks, when I tell you what I know of my own skills."

"All right." He dropped his hands to his knees. "Explain."

"Each world has . . ." She hesitated, searching for the right words. "The shemqyatwe. Remember them?"

"The witches. I remember. When we rode with the wagons of the nomads. Khateyat and her girls. So?"

"They called the ones I'm trying to explain the R'nenawatalawa."

"I've heard the word—some kind of native gods."

"No. Not gods. They who *are*."

"They? What th' hell . . ."

"They who are the essence of each world."

"Some kind of elementals?" His voice vibrated with skepticism.

"Yes, I think so." She shrugged impatiently. "What does a name matter? They are . . . they."

"So?"

Aleytys nodded at the scene outside. "So this: let down the ladder, I need to touch the earth. If this world is hostile to me, it will fight everything I try to do. Let down the ladder and you can see for yourself."

Face skeptical, Stavver got cautiously to his feet, keeping his head down, his back bent so he wouldn't hit his head on the curving top. He thumbed the touch plate, waking a faint hum as the ladder extended downward. "Make it fast. I don't think Maissa will be very understanding." He sat back down, legs dangling over the rim of the lock.

Mouth twisted into an unhappy smile, Aleytys pulled the cloth from her waist, stabbing the brooch through the folds so it wouldn't get lost. "Wish me luck, my friend."

"Luck, Aleytys." He touched her ankle briefly.

She dropped down the extruded ladder until her feet squelched into the earth the rain had churned into a semiliquid mud. After paddling through water and mud to a grassy hillock several meters from the base of the ship, she knelt in silence, feeling for the elemental forces that had their ambiance in this particular conglomeration of matter. Then she bent over and placed her hands, palm down, flat against the soil.

She could smell the dark brown richness of the wet dirt, the sharp green peaks of the grass and leaves. A cool-warm breeze coiled around her flanks while a living warmth crept up through her arms and filled her. At peace, she settled, legs crossed, hands resting lightly on her knees. Her breath slid in and out in gentle serenity while she waited for them to come closer.

She felt a probing. Fingertips rippling through her body: exploring, curious, excited. She felt like laughing; like leaping joyously to her feet to dance a maenad dance. As it pulsed through her, she felt the different aura these had. Unlike those of Jaydugar, these were not slow, vast, immensely wise, these were sprite-like. Somehow younger. Given to practical jokes and rippling laughter. Feelings of exuberance and joyous abandon. She felt their excitement racing through her quiescent body.

Softness brushed against her knee. Tilting her head down she looked into bright, black eyes that examined her with disconcerting intelligence. A small animal, fur a bright russet brown, sat on rabbit-like hind legs, fore limbs ending in agile black three-fingered hands held crossed over a cascading ruff of white fur. She smiled affectionately down at the small one. "I greet you, friend."

The pointed ears that stood tulip fine over the small dome of his skull twitched amiably as he scrambled onto her knee, the nails of his narrow nervous feet pricking rapidly over her skin. Fluffing his fur to shake off lingering traces of rain, he settled contentedly into the curve of her hand. "Sister."

Aleytys blinked, a little startled under the surface of her calm, to find an animal speaking to her. "Yes?"

"I am speaker. The voice of Lakoe-heai."

"Ah." The words in the high voice were clear and distinct. She gazed into the bright, black eyes and understood that the speaker was the means of communication they had chosen on this world. They. Lakoe-heai they called themselves here. Addressing the intelligence behind the black eyes, she said softly, "You know we come as thieves?"

The animal moved restlessly, shifting against her palm.

Aleytys cautiously lifted her free hand and scratched him behind the ear. He sighed plaintively as her searching fingers found a nerve complex where their probing brought delight to his small body. Joy bubbled feverishly through her. A fluttering laughter fell on her senses like rose petals while a bright, beaming interest surrounded her, vibrating the air until it tickled her skin.

"You don't care about that. You have a purpose we serve?"

The small head moved once again against her palm. "Not one but four."

She chuckled. "Four out of one. Thrifty." Then she sobered. "One of us—one will kill."

"We hear. It is known. There is already blood."

"Ah." The pleasure soured in her. "I feel there will be more. It sickens me."

"Not your doing, forget it. Life and death are both parts of the whole, one flowing into the other, death and life." The speaker smoothed his small, black hands over his stiff, springing whiskers.

"Ah." She sucked a breath deep into her, expanding her stomach, then let the air slip out in small bundles until no more would come. Sitting in silence she felt warm in the energetic approval of the Lakoe-heai. Warm in spite of the thickening mist that threatened to break into rain again, and happy to be out of the artificial womb of the ship, happy to be in touch with the earth and the world's life. Once again, she grew aware of the complex hierarchy of smells that matched the interweaving of life sparks. They rose in a glistening crescendo even to the clouds where unseen birds circled and soared among the drifting minutiae of the aerial bacteria that spread across the sky in brightly colored swirls.

After a dreamy, timeless time she sighed and stirred. "Then I may play at being gikena?"

"Sister." The small voice gleamed silver in her ears. "Be what you are."

She frowned. "I don't understand."

Laughter circled joyously around her, hidden in thunder that boomed through the clouds, filled with a whooping amusement that brought images to her mind of soap bubbles bouncing wildly through bright spring air. The speaker animal snuggled against her stomach, ears

flickflicking in response to the forces whirling wildly
around them. The small voice spoke again, filled with
amusement. "Sister, you are gikena born."

"But I'm not born of this world."

"Sister."

The word suddenly had meaning for her. "You call me
kin?"

"Sister."

Aleytys looked dreamily down at the tiny beast curled
in a ball of white and russet fur against her stomach, his
head tilted back so the black eyes met hers, the look of intelligence startling in his beast face. She sighed and slid
her hands under him to lift him back on the ground.

Tiny, black fingers closed around her thumb. "Keep the
speaker. He is necessary to the gikena. Keep him with you
while you walk our paths."

"I thank you, Lakoe-heai." She stumbled a little over
the word, repeated it. "Lakoe-heai. I bless you for your
friendship." Cuddling the speaker against her breast, she
lurched to her feet on stiffened legs, feeling the presences
circling proprietorally around her, then retreating gradually as she stumbled toward the ship, shivering with sudden chill. When she put her foot on the lowest rung of the
ladder they were only a vague ripple in her awareness, an
intimation of an interest so distant she could sense it only
when she threw her own awareness out toward the horizon.

Quietly happy, almost tranced, she clambered heavily
up the ladder, hampered by the speaker until he moved up
onto her shoulder and clung to her hair so that her hands
were free. As she stepped into the lock the rain came
down again in impenetrable sheets that played on the
nerves like clumsy, hurtful hands.

Stavver thumbed the plate, starting the ladder sliding
home. "Well?"

"Yes." She drifted past him, tapped open the inner lock,
and ducked into the interior of the ship.

Stavver picked up her abandoned batik and shut the
outer iris. He caught up with her in the cabin as she bent
over her son's improvised crib, letting the small furry beast
settle himself beside the sleeping baby.

"Are you crazy?" He stepped past her and reached for

the speaker. "That's a wild animal. No telling what diseases it carries."

She stopped him. "Don't be silly, Miks. I wouldn't harm my little one." She yawned and moved toward the shower. "Madar, I'm tired. And filthy."

Smiling at the bemused expression on his face, she added quietly, "I know some things very well, Miks. I might not have your experience in the murky places of the universe, but wild things belong to me." She yawned suddenly, startling herself. "I'll explain, Miks, as soon as I wash this mud off."

Stavver shrugged. "It's your baby." He sat on the bed to wait for her.

Aleytys stepped into the shower alcove and let the hard driven needle spray wash the caked mud off her body, washing her fatigue away with it. When she stepped out, Stavver held the batik for her while she wheeled around wrapping herself firmly in it. She pinned the brooch at her waist, driving the pin through the triple layer of cloth. Then she dropped onto the bed, patting the hard mattress beside her. "Come sit down, Miks. Tell me what's bothering you."

"Is it so damn obvious then?" He collapsed beside her, leaning back against the wall, hands clasped behind his head.

"To me. You relax with me, Miks. You let your guard down."

He moved his shoulders restlessly. "I work alone, Leyta. I always work alone."

"You don't trust Maissa."

"She comes through on contracts."

"That's not what I mean. You don't trust her to manage this thing."

"I trust my own skills, Leyta. I know them." He shrugged. "You compound trouble when you take a partner. And these. . . ." He jerked abruptly, impatiently, to his feet and began pacing back and forth across the narrow width of the cabin. "I know Maissa too well to depend on her. Her mind is good. But her obsessions ride her too hard. The whole business can fall apart in a minute if she blows. Then there's Kale. He's some kind of outcast on this world. What a recommendation! The whole thing's a disaster already. I don't think it's going to work,

Leyta. There's too much about it I can't control." His long, thin hands closed into tight fists, then opened helplessly. "But we owe passage. We'll have to make it work."

"Miks." Her quiet voice pulled him around to face her. "Come sit down and relax. The Lakoe-heai are on our side. At least, they're friendly."

He frowned at her. "What are you talking about?"

"Come." She waited until he slumped beside her. "Put your head on my lap and let me work the tension out of you."

Stavver sighed and stretched his long, thin body out along the mattress. "Magic fingers."

"Mmm. Come now, relax, best of all thieves. . . ." She smoothed her fingers gently over his forehead a while then slid her hands down and kneaded the tense, hard muscles in his neck and shoulders. He sighed, this time with deep pleasure, eyes closing, hands falling limp and relaxed.

Aleytys chuckled, a warm, slow sound that slid like honey over his nerves. "Poor thief . . . let your planning go . . . don't worry your head about Maissa. We're all caught in the web of another's weaving, we're on this world to their purpose, puppets with strings in strange hands. . . . But that's not so bad, that means they'll help us, help things go smoothly. . . ."

He opened his eyes, still calm under the soothing effect of her smoothing hands. "You're talking riddles again, Lee."

"I mean the Lakoe-heai of this world have taken us into their own plotting, my love. We don't have to give up what we came for, but they've got us marked for their own purposes, so relax."

"'Walk into my parlor' said the spider to the fly—relax?"

"Speaking of spiders, I haven't dreamed the Hounds since we left Jaydugar."

He pulled away from her hands and sat up. "Thanks, Lee." He stretched and yawned then leaned against the wall, eyes searching her face. "We're still broken loose of them?"

"Mmmmh." She tapped a forefinger against her temple evoking the ghost chimes. "I think as long as I wear the diadem they'll sniff me out."

"Pleasant thought."

"I'll just have to keep running fast."

"One comes." The reedy, small voice cut into the conversation, pulling both pairs of eyes to the crib. "And one other." The speaker's small head, alert ears wiggling erratically, dark eyes glittering, nestled between tiny, black paws clutching at the foot of the crib.

Aleytys ran her fingers through her tangled hair. "Maissa . . ." She yawned and rubbed her face. "So it begins."

Stavver stood up, his face drawn in an intent inward look, radiating a feeling of unease and diffused anger. Anger at himself, at Maissa, at the whole situation which forced him to submit himself to the caprice of others, and anger at Aleytys for arousing feelings in him that imposed a responsibility for her safety on his reluctant shoulders.

The strip of batik around his hips began to unwind as it slid down beneath the wide leather belt. Muttering a complex curse in a language Aleytys had never heard, he jerked it taut, resettling the belt to keep it in place. "Maissa will expect us in the lock waiting for her," he growled. "Lee, you remember what I said? Don't contradict her in any way. Just do what she says, all right?"

Aleytys shrugged. The elaborate, blue markings on her breasts drifted and jiggled with the movement. "I hear," she said shortly. "You don't have to keep reminding me."

He eyed her unhappily. "You've got a temper, Lee. I— oh hell." He stalked out of the room without looking to see if she followed.

Aleytys sighed and smoothed the cloth over her hips.

"Take me with you." At the sound of the speaker's voice, Aleytys started and turned around. The three-fingered, black paws were waving excitedly in the air. She picked him up, then checked to see if Sharl were still asleep. She touched her son's soft cheek with love flooding through her body, forgetting briefly the complicated and dangerous situation waiting for her.

Sighing, she shifted the speaker to her shoulder and reluctantly left the cabin. Out in the corridor she rubbed her fingers up and down his spine, laughing as his contented humming rumbled in her ears. "Do you have a name, little one?"

"Name?" His breath was warm against her ear.

"No name? Then I'll call you Olelo. You're Olelo. Do you understand?"

"Olelo." The speaker tried the sound out, pleased with it. "Olelo. Me, Olelo. Olelo." The syllables turned over in his mouth as if he found them tasty. "Speaker say thank you for the naming, Sister."

Aleytys jumped slightly, almost dislodging the beast, startled by the sudden change of timbre in the small voice.

"Ahai! I suppose I'll get used to this. No thanks necessary, Lakoe-heai. It's only a matter of convenience. A very little thing."

"Naming is no small thing, Sister. A name given sends ripples through time like a stone thrown into water. Never name lightly." She heard a tiny chuckle from the speaker, echoed by the boom of thunder outside the ship. "But you have named well, nonetheless, and we thank you for the gift."

The sense of presence receded until, once again, Aleytys heard the beast purring in her ear. She pulled her mind from this new puzzlement and marched resolutely down the corridor toward the lock.

Hand on the cold metal above the fingerplate, she paused. "Olelo?"

"One hears."

"The rain. Can one do something about that? I ask because she who comes will be difficult enough without the added burden."

A tiny chuckle rustled in her ear. "One can."

Smiling in her amusement with the buoyant elementals inhabiting this world, Aleytys tapped the plate and stepped into the lock.

Chapter II

The horses stood head down, tails twitching desultorily over their wet sides. They had a hard-driven look that kindled anger deep inside her. She walked to Maissa's team and touched the long, rain-sleeked hair that steamed faintly in the humid heat of the sun which was sinking like a squashed orange behind the vermilion-touched haze at the western edge of the world. The animal jerked nervously away, then quieted under her hands.

Aleytys gentled the horses, crooned to them, anger bubbling hotter as her fingers moved over welts and ragged cuts, healing them, taking the hurt away. Lips pressed together, she watched the empty mouth of the lock with its pendant ladder waiting for Maissa to appear; thinking of what Stavver had told her. Sensing her disturbance, the horses pawed at the coarse soil and nickered uneasily. She turned abruptly to face Kale. "Why?"

He shrugged and stepped down from the driving bench on the other caravan, his blocky body moving with the taut control of a hunting cat. "The captain doesn't like the wet."

"And you?"

He rested a broad, strong hand on the flank of the left-hand horse of his own team. "Would I lash my own feet?" Then he jerked rigidly upright, his eyes on a level with hers, flat, dark, suddenly angry. Everything about him looked time-polished, compacted by will and use into a gloss that shed punishment almost casually. The stylized pattern of hunting cats that climbed up arms and chest, the blue cat faces snarling on his broad, high cheek bones suited his feral aura even though they weren't his clan signs but skillful fakes like those she and the rest of the party wore. He stared at the side of her face, a rising anger struggling out from behind the mask. "Let it go," he said.

Aleytys frowned. "What?"

A hiss exploded into a spitting sound. He took a step toward her, his body poised forward on his toes while his arm came up, a tautly trembling finger jabbing at the animal sitting on her shoulder. "The speaker. That." The finger jabbed again. "I don't know how you caught it, woman, but only a gikena—a *real* gikena, woman—can keep it. Fool!" His hand jerked in a crooked circle compassing the ship, wagons, and the distant rim of the horizon. "Do you want to wreck everything?" His eyelids came down, hooding his eyes. "Let it go."

"You call me fool?" Aleytys snorted. "Use your eyes, Kale. Why didn't you tell us about these animals and their connection with the gikena?"

He dropped his arm. "Why say anything when there's nothing we can do about it?" Thrusting his thumbs aggressively behind the wide belt resting on his hips, he watched her through slitted eyes.

The silence grew taut between them, a wordless confrontation that was a clash for dominance between the two. Like a stench in her nostrils, Aleytys sensed treachery in him. A closely guarded set of ends that he was using the rest of them as ladder rungs to reach. She felt distrust bloom cold in her and held her icy, blue-green eyes hard on him, thrusting at him her certainty and power. After a minute he cursed and looked away.

"No," she said softly. "You didn't tell us. That was stupid, Kale. Maissa would have done something. What were you trying? Who would believe I was gikena without the speaker? Stupid!"

The long muscles in his neck swelled but he kept his eyes sullenly on the ground.

"Look at me!" she commanded. "You've got eyes in your head." She nudged Olelo out away from her ear until he was clinging to the point of her shoulder, obviously unfettered.

Kale stared at the ground.

"Look!" she repeated, throwing her anger at him.

Reluctantly he lifted his eyes and fixed her with a bitter, hating stare. "I'm looking, woman." He sneered the word, the scorn for females inherent in his culture boiling up through the crust of sophistication he had acquired rambling around a dozen worlds.

"But you don't see. Hunh! Look at the speaker, man. What holds the little one where he is?"

Kale shifted his gaze, saw the speaker sitting free on her shoulder. He gasped, his dark skin turning dull ash.

"Lakoe-heai," she said softly.

He twitched like a nervous horse, flinching repeatedly as she went on. "Lakoe-heai sent the speaker to me. Olelo, tell him."

The animal edged back to her head and straightened, keeping his balance by wrapping small hands in her hair. He focused brilliant black eyes on Kale. "The woman is gikena and more. Sister to us and under our protection. We lay this command on you, man. Until you have what you seek, you will aid, protect, and obey the woman." Olelo broke off and cuddled against Aleytys.

Still grey in the face, Kale stumbled a few steps backward. "I hear," he said hoarsely. "Aid. Protect. Obey."

"Aleytys!"

She swung around to face the lock. Maissa leaned impatiently out. "Get your kid," she snapped. "We're leaving."

"Now?" Aleytys glanced at the vanishing sun.

"Now. Soon as Stavver has the Vryhh-box installed. The rain's quit so we need to put distance between us and the ship." She looked nervously around. "Don't just stand there."

Aleytys took a step toward the ship then glanced over her shoulder at a silent and thoughtful Kale. "If you can help it," she said quietly, "don't let Maissa drive."

He jerked his head up as if waking from a not too pleasant dream, stared blankly at her, then nodded his understanding, a fugitive flicker of awe struggling through the black chill of his eyes.

Chapter III

"What lies ahead?" Aleytys flipped her free hand at the rutted road unreeling beneath the horses' plodding hooves. Abruptly she yawned, eyes widening in surprise at the effect of the clear, cold morning air.

"This road goes along the edge of the lakelands," Kale said gravely. After their confrontation the night before, he had thawed considerably, treating her now with a dignified courtesy that she found rather charming. He leaned against the slatted back of the driver's bench, relaxed and enjoying the fresh feel of the new day.

"The lakelands. Tell me about them. Did you live there?"

"No. My clan . . ." His mouth tightened. "We live close to the sea. On the far side of the mountains."

"Oh."

"The lakelands . . . mmmm . . . They raise our finest horses there."

"Anything else?"

"Pihayo. A meat animal with long hair and a strong tink. Vegetables near the towns. On the lake islands, fruit trees. A rich land. Seas of grass. Much water. Streams. Hundreds of lakes. They have a good life, the lakelanders."

Aleytys nodded. "I can imagine. My people lived in much the same style, though we have a harsher range, valleys high in the mountains with winters longer than your whole year. A good life, though."

He slanted a glance at her, his unspoken questions loud in the silence. Why had she left? Why had she abandoned her people to chance her luck in this ill-matched crew? After a minute he turned his head so that his eyes followed the road as kilometer after identical kilometer slid toward them through the gently undulating hills. "Was it the thief?" he asked, a hint of sneer back in his voice.

Aleytys sighed in exasperation but knew enough to let it go. "They called me a witch. An aunt of mine was arranging to have me burned at the stake. So I left. Stavver came later."

"Then we're both exiles." His hand settled on her arm. She felt the heat in him.

Shaking the hand off, she said coolly, "It doesn't make us kin."

"Woman, you have no courtesy."

"Man, I walk my own road and you'd better learn that now." Though the words were a challenge in their content, her voice was slow and thoughtful as if she were exploring something in herself rather than answering him.

"I don't understand you. You have the form of a woman, but . . ."

"Different people, different ways. You should know that by now." She shook the hair out of her eyes. "After the Lakelands, what then?"

"The stonelands and the wind gods. Then the killing posts."

"Killing posts?"

"Aye. Boundary posts of the Karkiskya holding. I saw a man burned to ash when he tried to cross between them outside truce time."

"Truce time?" She shivered. "Is this truce time?"

"Yes. The time of fall fairing." He grunted and hooked

his thumbs behind his belt. "Karkiskya don't like prying eyes. They keep the road closed except at spring and fall fairing. Then the posts flanking the road have their kill-force turned aside." He took the knife from the sheath slotted on the leather belt, pulling it free with quiet pride. "This is a Karkesh blade." He turned the blued steel so it caught the golden light of the morning sun coming up behind them. "Not mine. I had mine at my bloodfrom. It cost my father the poaku ikawakiho my mother brought as part of her dowry. And, in a way, it cost me an uncle" His voice slowed until the last words dragged out like stones.

Aleytys flicked a glance at his brooding face. "Poaku? That's another word for rock. You mean someone took a rock as payment for a knife?"

He shifted restlessly on the hard, wooden seat, fingers absently stroking the smooth metal of the knife blade. "Poaku ikawakiho. An Old Stone. Not one of the Very Old. Still, it had its power. Blue, this one, with cream-white veining. Carved with summer bloom."

"Ah." She sucked in a deep breath delighting in the silken feel of the air, refusing to let his absorption in some nameless tragedy from his past spoil her pleasure in the beautiful morning. "How many days to the city? Will we be meeting other travellers? Or stopping any place before then?"

He slid the knife gently back in the sheath. "Si'a gikena, given good faring, six days by this road will bring us to Karkys. We may indeed meet others. And certainly we will when we reach the city. As we get near the dust will reach the heavens; the roar of voices, the shriek of wheels, the thunder of hooves will drown out thought itself. As to stopping before then, that lies in her hands." He jerked a thumb at the caravan behind them, brought thumb and forefinger together in a circle, and touched the circle to his lips. "And in their hands."

"As you say." A wail came from inside the caravan. "Kale?"

"Si'a gikena?"

"Take the reins a while, will you? There's a small, hungry person summoning me."

The day rolled placidly on, the hours as alike as the curves of the road. Stop for nooning. Go on. The only difference visible in the world the changing angle the sun made with the earth. Inside the caravan Aleytys sank into a memory-haunted lethargy.

Qumri's hate-filled face swam out of the sinks of memory, shouting at her: "Bitch! Witch-woman's daughter, whoring after any man. You'll burn, I'll see you burning. . . ."

She fled the hate and the threat, surfacing at the gates of the Raqsidan, seated on the back of a russet mare, looking down into the moon-shadowed face of the dreamsinger. "Vajd, I don't want to leave."

His long, mobile mouth curved into a smile. "You do."

She reached down and he wrapped his fingers around hers, the touch warm, comforting, full of tenderness. "You know me too well," she said ruefully. "Come with me."

"I can't." The smile faded from his face, his dark eyes grew larger and larger until she swam in them in the agony of parting from him. "Go to your mother, Leyta, you'll be safe there."

Once again she fled the pain, flipping through the pages of memory—lying in the light of the double sun on a wide, flat stone, the heat baking the tiredness out of her body. Lying beside the lazy, black form of the tars. "Daimon," she murmured with pleasure. She buried her hands in the long, soft fur at his throat, scratching vigorously until his fang-lined mouth opened into a heart stopping yawn. She laughed softly, revelling in his pleasure. "Daimon . . ."

A page flipped. The tars was gone, whipping like black death across the meadow to kill the herdsman, her nemesis, as the herdsman's victim crumpled, spurting blood around three arrow wounds. She ran to him. His lips moved painfully. "Bad luck piece from . . . Raqsidan. . . ."

A third time she drove herself frantically away from the hurting memory but out of the chaos of images she pulled Tarnsian's bloated face bending toward her, black wings of obscene power beating the air behind him; smothering her; defeating her; driving her out, out of her body until her spirit shattered under the burden of her terror and her loathing. She tried to break free from the sick horror of that hideous time but she was caught by the hot, tranquil afternoon, transmuting memory into nightmare.

Like a fly fighting from the prison of a web she

struggled until an intangible something gave a little and she was fleeing again. Riding madly, drowned in dust, black stallion's feet pounding, pounding beneath her. . . .

She dreamed the relentless pursuit, the mind pressure like a goad driving her beyond her strength . . . anything to get away . . . away. The word throbbed in her head driving out caution, prudence, forethought; driving out anything but the mindless will to escape. Without rest, choking down a mouthful of dry bread, a gulp of water, on and on, up over the mountain, over the pass called the tangra Suzan, with Tarnsian clinging doggedly behind— crazily behind, abandoning all he had gained for this relentless pursuit. Over the tangra Suzan, weaving with fatigue, then down and down; endlessly down, switchback coiling on switchback until her mind reeled and fear ate at her—in the frustration of the necessarily slow progress. Down and down and down . . . twist and turn . . .

Despair. The tijarat place, meeting place of nomad and caravanner, spread out flat, dry, deserted. There should have been herds and herders, gaudy caravans with gaudy caravanners peddling anything that would bring a profit no matter how meager. Too early. Another week. Just another week . . . hope died in her. She pulled the saddle from the black stallion's back and sent him off to fill his gaunted stomach, then settled in a hopeless huddle to watch the river flow past her feet.

The black miasma thickened as it neared, spreading a stain of evil over her then—strangely, a feeling of affection touched her. Khateyat's strong square face broke through the stinking cloud of terror, driving it back with the hammer of her calm good sense.

Sturdy red-brown hands held out a dusky velvet bag whose dull black seemed to suck in the light around it. Out of the pouch Khateyat poured the shimmering beauty into her hands, a circle of flowers spun from gold wire with glittering jewel centers, each a different color. *The diadem*. She stroked her fingers over the beauty, evoking a ripple of clear, pure chimes; each stone center singing its own note. Enchanted, she set the supple circlet on her head, smoothing down the flyaway red-gold hair, blowing gently in the river breeze. Then she plummeted headlong into strangeness. The diadem. Older than the oldest memories. Prisoned by the Rmoahl, freed by the thief

Miks Stavver, brought to Aleytys in the hands of the nomad witch Khateyat. She couldn't take it off, it wouldn't
come off, it sank roots into her brain, burned unendurably
when she tried to tear it from her head—then it melted
into her . . . somehow . . . melted. Vanished—yet stayed.
Oh god, it stayed. . . .

And Tarnsian came riding out of the trees—caught up
with her at last. Himself as much a victim of his ob-
sessive evil as she was. As he leaped from his horse the diadem chimed, and his feet slowed, slowed . . . took eons
to reach the ground. He leaped at her, knife a bitter tooth
in his reaching hand, mouth screaming obscenities that
moved so slowly they died before reaching her.

Her body moved. Without her willing it, her body
moved. The diadem sang to her, sweet whispering chimes
that deepened, deepened. . . . She watched. Prisoner in
her own skull. Watched in terror as her hands came up,
clasped themselves together and slammed down on his
neck as his terrible, slow leap took him past her. Heard
the sharp, cracking sound . . . like a twig breaking. . . .

She jerked away and fled into her memory. Fled past
the slow, sweet images of the pleasant days trekking with
the herds across the Great Green to winter sanctuary in
the western mountains; fled past the joy of holding her
newborn son in her arms; fled on in memory until horror
meshed around her again.

Stavver rode before her down the deepening ravine, his
mount like hers the lanky, cat-like sesmat. Ahead . . . excitement and expectation rose in her. Ahead the ship, her
way off Jaydugar, her way to finding her mother, her first
step on the long journey to the legended world of
Vrithian. She scratched the mare's arching neck, then
moved from side to side in the saddle to ease sore and
aching muscles. A small murmur sent her hand into the
folds of the baby sling to comfort her son.

A spear whipped by her so close it dragged away her
headcloth. Before it struck the sidewall of the ravine she
was tumbling off the sesmat, clutching her baby to her
breast and scrambling into the shelter of one of the huge
boulders lining the path.

In her uneasy sleep Aleytys huddled, knees against her
breasts, head rolling back and forth on the coarse cloth
covering the thin mattress. "No," she moaned. "No. . . ."

They drove her from the rocks, faces grinning and sweating in their lust for her death. Drove her to Myawo her enemy.

And then the diadem chimed. She watched her hands hold a short spear and push-pull it again and again into the hard muscled chests of men who couldn't even know they were dead until the time spell lifted. Saw her hands drop the spear and turn to the men in front of her. Saw her hands pull a knife from unresisting fingers and carve new mouths in four more necks. Heard the diadem chime again. Heard dead men fall around her. She screamed. One, two, three, four. Screamed. One, two, three, four. . . .

"Aleytys!" Kale bent over her, his hand leaving her shoulder. "You were dreaming."

She sat up, eyes heavy, head aching from the harrowing of the nightmare memories. "Thanks," she muttered. The air inside the caravan pressed around her, hot, stifling, used up. She blinked repeatedly and pushed her hands through her sweaty hair. "Do we stop here?"

"No. But you were making so much noise. . . ."

"Oh." She staggered to her feet. "Let me drive a while. I need to clear my head." She moved clumsily through the curtains, swung around the seat, and dumped herself down. As soon as she was settled, she looked around at the wagon stopped behind. Stavver seemed half asleep himself, his long, thin body bowed forward over the reins, following her lead without comment.

She sighed and leaned against the age-polished slats, grateful for the fugitive current of air flowing past her sticky face. "What about Maissa?" Lazily she watched Kale stretch out his legs and lean back. "Didn't she have something to say about us stopping?"

Kale yawned. "She's probably asleep. She's drugged."

"Oh."

"Better get going." Kale folded his arms across his chest then sent a sliding glance at her. "What were you dreaming about?" As she sent the horses into a steady walk he stared at her, dark eyes glinting with curiosity. "At the end you were counting. Loud enough to wake the dead."

"The dead." Aleytys swallowed painfully. "A good choice of words. I was counting the ghosts I drag behind me."

His face paled and a shiver ran through his body. With a sudden, swift gesture he touched eyes, nose, mouth with middle finger pressed on top of forefinger. "Riding the nightmare. Bad luck when the sun's still high."

Shaking off the lingering wisps of the dreams, Aleytys laughed raggedly. "Bad luck anytime, Kale, for the one who suffers them. Poor Miks. He's had to deal with my dreams a dozen times. Ahai, I wish I could forget. . . ."

Lids lowered over heavy eyes, she settled into the rhythms of the drive as the hours passed.

The sun shone almost flat into her eyes when the caravan tilted up a gentle slope. Black specks circling in front of the color streaks ahead caught her eye. "Kale?"

He broke a snore in half and came reluctantly awake. "What is it?"

"Those birds." She pointed. "What are they doing?"

He looked blearily along her arm. "Ah. I see. Scavengers. They wait for something to die."

"I thought so." As the horses moved steadily along toward the hovering birds, she said sharply, "It's still alive?"

"As long as they stay up there."

The caravan tilted down then curved around a sandy hillock covered with sparse clumps of dusty grass. Beside the road ahead a bony, sway-backed nag stood head down, cropping with soremouthed care at tough, spindly grass that half obscured a narrow form lying face down.

Aleytys pulled herself onto her feet, clutching with her free hand at the carving along the side of the caravan to steady herself. "That's a man!" She dropped the reins and started to jump down.

"Wait." Kale caught at her arm and pulled her back. "Let me look."

She frowned. "Ahai, Kale. I'm no fragile flower."

"Aleytys," he said patiently, "this is my world."

She looked silently at him for a minute then sat down on the edge of the seat, pulling the horses to a stop beside the scrawny nag. Still silent, she watched as he swung down and strode to the recumbent figure.

He stopped short, stared a minute, then walked rapidly back. Without a waste motion he pulled himself onto the seat. "Go on."

She looked at the circling cloud of scavengers. "Is he still alive? Or are we keeping them from their feast?"

"Forget it. Drive on."

"No. Answer me. Is he dead?"

"Yes. Drive."

She shook her head. "You can't lie to me, Kale. He's alive."

"All right," he said impatiently. "So he's alive now. He won't be for long. Better for him if he dies."

"Dead is never better than living!" She swung around.

"No!" He caught her arm in a bruising grip. "He's pariah. Leave him."

"My god—you *mean* that!" She pushed at his hand. "Let me go."

"No. Keep away from him. If you touch him, we're all pariah. You hear me?" His fingers tightened further until she gasped with pain. Anger exploded in her.

"Take your hand off me." Her eyes glittered. "Now."

The Karkesh blade whispered out of the sheath. "Send the horses forward," he said tensely.

"Kale, I told you. . . ."

"Drive!"

"Kale." Stavver stood loose limbed and casual on Aleytys' side of the caravan, watching coolly as they clashed.

Kale glanced up briefly. "Keep out of this, thief."

"I warn you, groundling. You'd better take your hand away."

"So." The sneer was heavy on Kale's dark face. "You plan to make me?"

"Me?" Stavver shrugged, amused contempt on his narrow face. "I don't give a damn how you ruin yourself, but Maissa seems to think we still need you. Let Aleytys loose or she'll kill you. I've seen her work, little man."

Kale snorted his disbelief. Turning back to Aleytys, he touched the point of his knife to her throat, then pulled it down between her breasts maneuvering it so delicately that he never broke the skin. "Drive."

A whisper of chimes broke the taut silence. Once again Aleytys felt the air congeal against her face while the single dominant note slid down-octave until it was a blurred vibration barely above the threshold of hearing. Prisoner again in her skull as the diadem took her body,

Aleytys crouched in terror whispering soundless pleas—no, don't kill him, there's no need, no more killing, please, please. . . .

Her hands fluttered up and plucked the knife from Kale's hand. The pale, featureless landscape swung past her eyes, then she saw the knife released to hang floating in mid-air, close to Stavver's face. The grassy knolls flickered past again and she was looking at Kale. The hands reached out and pushed.

Slowly . . . slowly . . . painfully slowly, like a stone dropping through gelatin, Kale toppled off the seat and sank towards the ground. The diadem waited, Aleytys waited. An eon passed and passed again and at long last Kale's stiff body touched the ground. His arms and legs unfolded slowly, slowly like the petals of a flower in a time-lapse sequence, until he was starred out on the ground. Aleytys whispered: "Thank you, thank you whoever you are, ah God I couldn't take any more killing. . . ."

The diadem chimed again. As the note slid up to its normal range, Aleytys thought she saw amber eyes open and smiling at her, then she forgot it as Kale leaped to his feet, his face contorted with terror.

"Kale." She stood up, snapping, "Kale!"

Intelligence flowed back to replace the animal fear. He rubbed a trembling hand across his face and straightened slowly.

"Stavver warned you. I could have killed you. Don't try me again."

"Si'a gikena," he said, his voice hoarse with sincerity, "Believe me, I won't." He glanced uneasily over his shoulder at the body. "But . . ." After hesitating a minute he went on doggedly. "The boy is pariah. As are all who speak to him, feed him, help him in any way. Even a touch. Do you understand? If you try to help him, and I swear it's probably too late already, then we might as well get back to the ship and leave."

"Sister." The shrill, small voice startled all of them. "Take away the curse. You are gikena." The speaker had crawled out of the caravan and sat perched precariously on the back of the driving bench. "Heal the boy and restore him to his people. That is your first task for Lakoe-heai."

"So be it," Aleytys said quietly. She turned cool eyes on Kale "You hear?"

Kale looked startled. "I forgot, woman. I forgot you were true gikena and kept thinking of you as offworlder." He bowed his head stiffly. "I ask your forgiveness for my stupidity."

"Yes, of course." As she spoke Aleytys swung down from the seat. Without waiting for his answer she ran to the boy and knelt beside him. A quiet relief spread through her as she saw his skeletal body still moving as he struggled to breathe. She swallowed painfully as she saw the broken stump of an arrow protruding from his back just under the shoulder blade, the skin around it swollen and yellow with ominous red streaks running like a star of death from the central wound.

Carefully she laid her hands on his back drawing a moan of pain from him in spite of the gentleness of her touch. She spread her hands around the arrow so that it was the center of a rough triangle formed by her thumbs and forefingers. Gladness warmed in her as she felt the strong steady pulse of life in him. He was badly hurt and nearly starved but the will to live burned so strong in him that he was far from dying.

Aleytys sucked in the hot, dusty air and let it out in small discrete bundles, sucked in another breath, and let it out, her body slowing into tranquility. Into a quiet oneness with the air and earth. She closed her eyes and reached for the river of black water winding between the stars, her symbolic image of the power that fed her talents. Tapping into the river she sent the power flowing through her arms into the shuddering body beneath her hands. Time passed, how long she had no idea, then she knew the healing was done.

With a sigh she lifted leaden arms and straightened her aching back. The boy was sleeping heavily, the wound a pale pink star, vivid against the sun-bronzed skin of his back. Lying flat beside the wound the broken arrow moved gently up and down with the boy's breathing, gummy with blood and pus, having worked itself free as the wound healed behind it.

She picked it up and tossed it aside into the grass. "Why is his head shaved?"

Kale stared down at the boy. "He will live?"

"Why not? I'm a damn good healer. Why is his head shaved?" She cupped her hand tenderly over the short bright stubble.

"Before his people cast him out, they shaved the hair off his head and body to mark him." He shifted uneasily. "The stealing . . . what we plan . . . it doesn't bother you?"

"The Lakoe-heai know we come as thieves. I don't like it, but what can I do?" She sensed his growing uneasiness around her. "Relax, Kale. They've got some kind of plan to use us. They won't interfere."

"Oh." He glanced at the boy again, chewed a minute on his full lower lip, then walked nervously away to look down the road. "There's no need for a guide," he muttered half to himself. "The road's clear."

Aleytys stretched and laughed. "All right. All right, Kale. You change places with Stavver if it makes you feel better. The boy can ride with Sharl."

Maissa came striding around the caravan, her delicate, pointed face drawn into an angry scowl. "What's holding us up?" she demanded.

Aleytys met the cold glare with a quiet smile. "We stopped to help the boy."

"Well?" The small woman came mincing across the rough soil with its sharp stubs of last year's grass, not yet accustomed to walking barefoot. She stopped beside the boy's body and thrust an impatient toe into his protruding ribs. "A waste of time. You finished?"

"The healing's done. When he wakes, he comes with us."

"Nonsense! Get back on the wagon and let's get going. We don't need a strange pair of eyes to spy on us."

Aleytys sighed. "Maissa, if I'm supposed to be gikena, let me be. If we go off and leave him, we'll be outcast ourselves. To take the curse off him, he has to serve me for a time. Anyway, he's a guarantee the others will accept us as what we pretend to be."

"I'm sure you thought of that all the time. Huh!" She turned and picked her way carefully back to her caravan. She paused at the big wheel and looked back at Aleytys, her dark eyes glinting hardly. "I boss this job—you remember that."

Behind her Aleytys heard a rustle in the grass and

turned around to find the boy sitting up staring at her, his brown eyes huge in his thin face. "Welcome back to the living," she said briskly. "How'd you get in this mess?"

His white-caked tongue moved painfully over cracked lips. "Pariah," he muttered hoarsely.

"Miks."

"What?"

"Bring the waterskin, will you. Our new friend's got a big thirst."

"Right." The thief came around the back end of the caravan, swinging the well filled waterskin from its wide, leather strap.

The boy watched the dripping, cool bladder with desperate burning eyes, then he held up trembling hands palm out warning them off. "Pariah," he repeated, his voice breaking painfully.

Aleytys smiled at him and took his shaking hand in hers despite his attempt to avoid her touch. "I am gikena, boy. When you've had the water, we'll see about taking away the curse on your head. Do you understand? I've already cured the wound in your back. Have you forgotten that?"

Stavver handed him the waterskin and helped him drink. The boy took a mouthful of water then pushed the skin away. His face drawn in lines of fatigue and suffering, he held the cool liquid in his mouth, working it around and around. Then he spat it out and took another drink, a small one. He swallowed. Fascinated, Aleytys watched his throat working, appreciating the stern discipline that controlled his desperate need for water. He drank twice again, then pushed the waterskin away though his eyes followed it greedily.

"I thank you, si'a gikena."

"Will you tell me your name?" Once again Aleytys smiled at him, warming inside as the wary suspicion left his eyes.

"Loahn, si'a gikena."

"You will serve me as required?"

He startled her by bowing swiftly until his head touched the earth in front of him. As quickly as he sat up, dark eyes bright with renewed hope. "I serve as long as you want—till the end of my life, si'a gikena."

She laughed and stood up, reaching out for his hand. It felt warm and dry and curiously strong. "It won't be that

long, Loahn. Not nearly." She mounted the steps at back
of the caravan. "Come in, but be quiet. My son is asleep."

The interior of the caravan was hot and close. Loahn
looked curiously around. The inside was neatly made, the
wide, flat bunks doubling as seating in the day, the
mattresses covered with coarse ticking. Below these a
series of deep drawers marched in neat rows. One was
pulled out and turned into a nest for the placidly sleeping
baby. Aleytys stopped to touch him, feeling as always the
warm outpouring of love he evoked in her. When she
looked up she found the boy looking hungrily at her. He
blushed and turned away.

"You lost your mother?"

His thin body stiffened, then he nodded. "When I was a
child."

"Well, sit down. You'd better ride in here. We'll be going on till light fails. Rest and think what to tell me when
we camp for the night." A smile twitched the corners of
her mouth upward. "I need to know just what to do about
you."

"Yes, si'a gikena," he said with careful politeness, the
wary look back on his face.

"Olelo, come here." She smiled at the boy, amused by
his skepticism. "I need you to speak for me again, little
one."

The speaker swung through the front curtains. Loahn's
eyes widened then he relaxed, his suddenly shaky knees
dumping him onto the bunk.

Aleytys chuckled. "So you're convinced at last."

"Pardon, si'a gikena," he stammered.

"Nonsense. A little skepticism's a healthy thing. I'd
think you foolish if you believed everything anyone told
you."

His mouth curved into a tired smile, his eyes dropping
heavily as fatigue flooded over him.

"Unroll the quilt and go to sleep. If you need water, the
man and I will be outside. Call. You understand?"

He nodded sleepily.

"When you ride with us, you'll see things—things that
may seem strange. If you find yourself puzzled, come to
me. Don't talk to outsiders about what troubles you. Understand?"

He settled himself on the mattress, wadding the quilt

into a pillow for his head. "No," he said quietly. "How can I?" He stretched out, laced his fingers together behind his head. "Only that I come to you and accept what you tell me."

She eyed him coolly, then burst out laughing. "No fool, indeed. You'll accept what I tell you even if you suspect it's not quite the truth?"

He grinned sleepily at her. "When I got my life back, when I saw your beautiful and wonderful and kind face, I gave my soul into your keeping as long as you want it." He yawned, then waved a hand. "You needn't bother asking, gikena. Just tell me and I'll do it."

Aleytys crawled through the curtains and joined Stavver on the seat. "That's a sharp one in there."

"Dangerous?"

"I don't think so. I could always put the curse back." She glanced at the sky. The streaks of color were beginning to thicken, leaving patches of clear blue sky. "Let's get started," she said crisply.

Chapter IV

"They're offworlders, aren't they." The boy's voice came out of the warm darkness behind Aleytys. She swung around and examined him silently, trying to read the set of his too-thin face, the complex mixture of emotions radiating from him. What she sensed most was a calm curiosity which surprised her almost as much as his words.

"What do you know of offworlders?"

The boy sank beside her, resting his thin arms on his knees. A broad smile split his dark face. "My father took me to Karkys the year of my blooding to get my blade."

"And?"

"We didn't get along well. My father and I." The boy spoke slowly, his eyes fixed on her, the whites glowing palely in the light of the low hanging moon. "So he ignored me while he did his trading. I sneaked through the Karkesh quarter and out into Star Street. Nobody paid any attention to a scruffy kid or bothered to mind their talk. I watched the starships come and go and saw the strange ones and heard them talking to the hooded Kark-iskya."

"The year of your blooding."

"I've always been small, looked younger than I am."

Aleytys tapped her lips with her forefinger. After a while she said, "I told you we came from across the sea, Loahn."

He snorted softly. "Then you come from across the sea. But you better teach the woman not to give orders like a man." He nodded at the figures walking around the dying fire.

"Her name is Leyilli." Aleytys spoke softly. "The long man is called Keon, the other Kale. I am called La-hela." She lay back on the grass, face turned to the moonlit sky, studying the huge pale circle that floated majestically between the false thunderheads. "One moon seems so lonely," she murmured. "Where I was born we have two." She smiled as she heard the boy gasp. "Very perceptive, Loahn. We are all offworlders. Except Kale."

"The speaker?"

"Don't worry about your curse. Lakoe-heai proclaimed me gikena born and sent me Olelo as a sign of their approval."

"Why did you all come here, then?"

"To steal, young friend. We're thieves. Name me Lahela if you please. I need to become accustomed to the sound of it."

"Why tell me, Lahela? What if I betray you first chance I get?" He shifted on the grass coming to bend over her, his thin face grave and questioning in the moonlight.

"You won't," she said quietly. Then she chuckled. "Don't I have your soul?"

"Tchah! That's a stupidity."

"Seriously, I do have a lien on your soul. Remember? I am gikena." She reached up and touched his cheek. "Besides, my dear, I don't say it's impossible for a man to make me believe a lie, at least when I've my wits about me, but so far it hasn't happened. An unkind gift, one I'd sometimes rather do without." She patted the cheek gently feeling the harsh, dry skin resulting from his recent ordeal. "Do you understand that at all, young friend?"

"Are you so much older than me, Lahela?" He sounded

annoyed, jerked his head away from her touch. "I've seen a full eighteen winters."

"And I've seen only eight." She chuckled at his exclamation of disbelief. "But it's true, Loahn. On the world where I was born our years are three of yours with a winter three hundred days long. I looked up at two suns, not one. Two moons lit our night skies. And that is true!"

"Ahh. . . ." She could see his eyes glittering as he looked up at the moon then down at her again. "How old are you, Lahela? In our years."

"Twenty-four. A double dozen. You see I'm an old lady compared to you."

"Tchah! Six years! A mouse's sneeze." He put tentative fingers on her shoulder and walked them down in sly spider pats to touch her breast.

"Loahn." She caught his hand and held it away from her. "When I took you to serve me, I did *NOT* mean in my bed. That place is already occupied."

"I have a sadness, Lahela." He sighed with exaggerated despair. "It's going to be a long service."

"And you're a graceless scamp. No, don't try me with that plaintive face." She sat up briskly, nearly knocking him over. "Sit down. Over there. Out of reach. Do you hear?"

"I hear, si'a gikena." His voice sounded reproachful, but she saw his grin shining in the moonlight.

"Somehow I seem to have lost my mystique." Aleytys brought her knees up and wrapped her arms around them. "Loahn?"

"Mmmm?"

"When we meet others, you'll be the respectful and awe-struck acolyte?"

"Of course. I'm not stupid."

"I never thought that, my friend." She sat staring blindly into the darkness. The trivial desultory conversation around the fire floated piecemeal to her ears as she tried to pull her emotions into some kind of order. Loahn's eyes slid around again and again to rest momentarily on her then flick away. She sighed. "I wonder what you really think of me. Behind that barrage of words."

"First," he said calmly, "I want to make love to you. I have food in my stomach, that arrow out of my back, and hope for the future for the first time in days. The most beautiful woman on Lamarchos sits beside me in the moonlight. How else should I feel?"

"You're direct."

Loahn chuckled. "I've never found that women are insulted by the asking, rather the reverse."

"So cynical at eighteen."

"Rather, intelligent." He reached out and wrapped long fingers around her ankle. "Lahela . . ."

"What?" She felt her heart speed up while a familiar ache spread through her body.

"Come for a walk with me." He moved his hand slowly a few inches up her calf, then slid it back to her ankle. "Away from the fire. And them."

She reached down and closed her hand over his. "I will not after tonight."

"Take the days as they come. Tomorrow—who knows what that brings?" He stood up, pulling her up with him. "Right now," he murmured. "Tonight, you're curious about me and I'm taking advantage of that curiosity. Pushing hard as I can."

As they stumbled down the swell to the thicker grass in the depression between the hills, she said dryly, "At least you're honest about it."

"You said it, Lahela gikena. Who can lie to you?"

Chapter V

"My father had a horse run by Lake Po. We never got along. I told you that. He had the sensitivity of a brick wall, and not a nerve in his body."

"I know the kind." Aleytys ran her fingers through her hair. "Damn these burrs."

"Let me." Loahn sat up and began picking the leaves and burrs out of her long, tangled hair.

"Go on."

"Mmmm . . . no, we never got on. I was a disappointment to him, a scrawny, screaming brat. Far back as I can remember I resented the way he treated my mother. Everything she did was wrong. In the first place, she was

fair-haired, daughter of a gypsy horse trader, not one of
the black-haired local beauties. He married her because
she was graceful and gentle and loving and then once they
were wed he resented all these things in her. He'd cut her
to pieces in front of anyone around to listen. He didn't
care how she suffered. I think he didn't even realize she
suffered. Sometimes he beat her. I remember once I heard
her crying late at night. My father was out with a foaling
mare. I tried to comfort her. She sent me away." He
stopped talking to ease a burr out of a complicated knot
of hair.

"Careful. That hurts."

"I'm trying not to pull." With a grunt of satisfaction
and a few tiny snapping sounds he worked the burr loose
and tossed it to one side.

"I never knew my mother." Aleytys spread her fingers
out and watched the moonlight shine off the nails.

"She died?"

"No. She went away. I'm on my way to find her."

"Your mother is Lamarchan?"

"No. This is . . . this is a waystop. It's a long and complicated story. Go-on."

His hands moved absently over her hair. " When I was
five, my mother died. She grew quieter and quieter. Simply faded away. She needed the open spaces and he . . .
he kept her in strictest purdah. He was a jealous man. He
kept closer ties on her than even the customs dictate,
locked her behind the walls of the house until a glimpse of
the sky tormented her." She felt his fingers moving with
careful gentleness over her back, brushing away the debris
that clung to her. "During that time and a few years after
I scuttled around full of hate and too stubborn to do anything my father told me without a tussle of wills. I always
lost, but we both ended up exhausted." He pulled her back
against him, cupping his hands over her breasts. "You're
getting cold."

"Never mind. Finish your story." She stretched and
yawned, gently freeing herself. "Are all the burrs out of
my hair?"

"Think so. But. . . ."

"I'm not too cold. Finish the tale."

"When the mourning time was over and my mother's
spirit safe on its trek to Ma-e-Uhane, my father married

again. This one was a strong, passionate woman. Jealous in her own way as my father was. She hated me. Why not? In three years she had three sons and none of them could take heir-right. Because of me. First wife's only son. She couldn't get around that. So of course she hated me."

"Hated." Aleytys touched his knee. "My dear."

"You needn't pity me. I returned the feeling full strength. Not the healthiest of atmospheres for a growing boy. She was jealous of my mother too. Sometimes when the moon was very bright and the air was still and clear, my father would go out of the house as if it burned him. He'd climb the promontory by the lake and sit there all night, I swear, remembering my mother. In the morning he'd ride off on the run and stay away for three or four days. My stepmother was a fury those times. I learned early that the best thing for me was to disappear."

"I know that jealousy," Aleytys said softly. "An aunt of mine. I kept out of her way soon as I could walk."

"Then you know. As my brothers and I grew older, she hated me even more. You see, none of my half-brothers could match me with the horses. My mother's blood showing in me. After a while my father noticed this and my life was both easier and harder."

"I see. What about your brothers?"

"Not so bad. I can't say they liked me much but they weren't malicious about it." He chuckled. "You need a few brains to be malicious."

"Meow. Pull the claws back, boy."

"Boy! Tchah!"

"Go on with the story." She held his hands away from her. "No distractions."

He shrugged. "So. My father began training me as heir. I was out of the house five days in six. A kind of unmentioned truce held between us. I even managed to feel a brief glow of pride when I heard him bragging about one of my exploits to some neighbors. I think eventually we might have come to a kind of peace. But he died. One minute he was roaring with rage at a failing of the men. The next he was falling, blood gushing from his nose and mouth."

"And your stepmother kicked you out."

"Of course not. She couldn't. I was heir. The pyre was raised on the promontory by the lake. My orders. She hated that because she knew why I did it, why I built his pyre where my mother's had been raised, where he used to go to dream of her. In the house my father lay on his bed wrapped in the grave windings waiting for sunrise and the torch."

"I don't understand. How . . . ?"

"At sunrise, when our neighbors were there with the kauna of elders from Wahi-Po, she came staggering out of the house, screaming, tearing at her hair, thighs covered with blood. She swore I had raped her. She swore I had laughed and spat on my father's corpse."

"And they believed her?"

"They believed her."

"But where were you? Didn't they listen to you at all?"

"I was lying in a drunken stupor on the floor of my father's bedroom."

"She drugged you."

"Right. I was a fool. They found me naked and snoring like a pig, my own thighs and groin covered with blood, deep scratches on my face and arms. She pointed them out triumphantly, as evidence of how she'd struggled against me."

"Not a fool. How could you expect such a thing?"

"I knew how she hated me. I should have been alert for some such action."

"And they all believed her."

He laughed, a mirthless bitter sound. "Why not. I'd been going over a lot of house walls into women's quarters for the past year, leaving angry and suspicious husbands scattered along my trail. To speak bluntly, my reputation stank."

"Stupid."

"How was I to know?" He protested mournfully. "My lady friends were very willing. No cries of rape followed me. But . . ." He sighed. "I admit all this lent color to her tale. And then there were the years when I made no secret of how I hated my father."

"I see." Aleytys stood up and fastened the batik around her. "Is there much more?"

"Not much." He jumped to his feet and stood pinning his borrowed batik around his skinny hips. "I can finish as we walk back to the wagons."

Aleytys nodded and started up the slope.

"The kauna pronounced me pariah. Then they took me out, threw me in a horsetrough to wake me, shaved me bald top and bottom, slapped me on the back of that ramshackle pensioner of a horse and drove me out, still dazed and not quite comprehending what had happened to me." He yawned. "And here I am."

"How'd you get the wound?"

"I needed water." He shrugged. "Took a while to learn how to sneak it. I got the wound first week. Had to live with it." His square teeth gleamed whitely as a grin nearly split his face in half. "Or die with it except for you happening along."

"I doubt there was much chance to our meeting." She stopped him, hand on his arm. "How far is Lake Po from here?"

"There's a crossroad ahead some hours. On that, a two, two and a half day trip north by caravan."

"You want your father's land back?"

"Damn right I do."

"And your half-brothers?"

"I've nothing against them. Remember, I'll be serving you for what time you choose, gikena. They can take care of the place for me." He glanced at the lowering moon. "The dew's coming down and it's cold out here."

"A minute more. Will my being gikena really be enough to get the curse lifted and put you back in your place?"

"Yes."

"And the kauna will listen to me?"

"Lahela, the gikena speaks for the Lakoe-heai. Would they want their mares to die in foaling, their crops to turn black dust in the earth, their water to go foul, their dreams be filled with horror, the very air they breathe turn poison in their lungs?"

"They believe that?"

Loahn grunted. "It happened once in another place. That's not a thing to be forgotten."

"Ahai!" Aleytys shivered. "I hadn't realized. Come on, I'll get you a quilt."

"A quilt?" Hairless eyeridges arched in unspoken question.

"My bed is taken," she said firmly.

They trudged to the top of the swell then began sliding

downslope to the dark, silent caravans. Aleytys jerked to a halt. "Loahn."

"Change your mind?"

"My god, is that all you ever think of?"

"Can you think of better?" He grinned. "What is it, then?"

"The other woman. Leyilli. She's a killer. And she doesn't like men. I'm going to have enough trouble convincing her to turn aside without your making it more difficult. Don't play your tricks with her."

"Jealous."

"Idiot! There's another thing you ought to know, my naive young native. Leyilli's the leader of this mismatched group of thieves."

"A woman?" He sounded skeptical.

"A woman. Don't underestimate her. Barehanded that dainty little creature could kill you so fast you wouldn't even know you were dead."

"Nice company. Thieves and killers."

"We're all here for our private reasons, Loahn." She shrugged and moved away from him. "Remember what I said."

"Si'a gikena. Tell me what you want and I'll do it."

"Then I say this. Treat Leyilli as if she's a cocked crossbow aimed at your heart."

"With respect and caution."

"Yes."

He nodded at the caravan looming black before them. Stavver sat on the back steps watching them pick their way downhill. "What are you going to tell him?"

"The truth." She bit her lip and frowned unhappily. "He'd not believe anything else. Why waste my time and his?"

"How'll he take it?"

"I don't know. I don't know yet how I take this."

He looked skeptical. "You're no innocent."

"But my experience has been limited. I've never had to face this kind of thing before. My lovers till now have been strictly sequential."

"You're a strange one."

"You ought to see me from the inside, you'd go dizzy trying to figure out the twists and turns." She sucked in a deep breath. "Hello, Keon. Can't sleep?"

He nodded briefly acknowledging the name change. "Good evening, Lahela. Did you enjoy your walk?" His voice changed on the last word, turning harsh.

"It was educational."

"Educational?" His eyebrows arched, tangling with the thatch of hair falling forward over his brow.

"Loahn told me the story of his life." She nodded at the caravan. "Would you get me one of the spare quilts for our new recruit?"

"Recruit?" As he stood, holding the curtains parted, he looked startled. "Have you talked to Leyilli about that?"

"In the morning."

He nodded and vanished inside.

Aleytys turned to Loahn. "I suggest you sleep under the other caravan. It'll keep the dew off you."

Stavver stepped out and handed the folded quilt down to Aleytys. "You sure you want it this way, Lahela?" He nodded at the other man. "Or should we change places?"

"Don't be silly. He knows better, so should you."

Loahn took the quilt and walked off, humming cheerfully, to the other caravan.

Chapter VI

"Well, Aleytys?" Stavver leaned back against the side wall, face somber, hands clasped behind his head.

"I should ask you that." Nervously she settled on the other bunk, careful not to disturb the baby. "I don't know." She tucked her legs into lotus position then rested trembling hands on her knees. "It's up to you how we go on from here."

"Me?"

"We're friends. At least, I thought we were." She tapped her fingers rapidly over the firm flesh of her thighs.

"So?"

"I like you, Miks."

"Thanks a lot."

"I mean it. You don't need to sound like that."

"So how should I sound?"

"You're not helping." She struggled to see his face in the gloom inside the caravan. "I never...."

He slid off the bunk and stood in the back doorway staring outside.

She rubbed her thumb across her palm, chewed on her lip. His face, silvered by the moonlight, was drawn and cruel. She felt anger and amusement in him. Amusement! Pulling wings off flies. An odd satisfaction in seeing her squirm. A tinge of self-disgust. A harsh desire to punish her, to flog her with his silence.

"We're loners, Miks. You and me," she said abruptly. "And I'm half Vryhh. Mother left me a letter, explaining—warning me—no lasting ties ... ever ... it's not in me to give that much." Her voice trailed off. She shook herself and straightened her back. After a difficult silence she began talking again, as much to herself as to his unresponsive back.

"My friend, we live together in an uneasy alliance, both aware of its impermanence. So anything that threatens it causes a disproportionate upheaval. I suppose I'd feel just as destructive if you went with another woman. I don't know. I really don't know."

He stirred, hands moving in an abortive gesture as if he reached for her then denied the impulse. "Fine philosophy."

"Ay-mi, Miks. You don't own me, but we are friends. I will not deny that or let you deny it. And I need you. The loyalty of need. Isn't that stronger than sex? I don't know your ... your bottom line beliefs, the ones that go below conscious thought. You never let me know you that deeply, did you." She slipped off the bunk and edged up to him reaching for his arm.

He jerked away and dropped down the steps.

With an impatient exclamation, Aleytys ran after him.

He swung around to face her. "Lee, leave me alone." He ran nervous, jerking hands through his hair, frowning at the growing anger in her face. "Words!"

"More than words." She flung her head back, the black mane rippling like a skein of silk.

"All right. Just let me alone. Give me time to think. Okay?" He wheeled and strode away, disappearing behind the other caravan.

She stood a while till her feet ached from the cold,

damp grass. Sighing, she trudged up the steps and dropped on the bed. Resting one ankle on her knee, she wiped the cold, gritty mud off with a piece of rag. When she finished the second foot, she sat lumpishly on the bed, staring into the dark.

The baby stirred in his blankets and gave a tentative whimper.

"Sharli-mi, Baby-mi," she crooned, bending over him. She lifted him to her breast and rocked him for a little while she scrubbed an edge of the blanket over her nipples. Then she let him suck.

"My son," she murmured, suddenly filled with a blissful contentment. "My little one. You're getting so big. So big and strong. You'll be a fine man one day, Sharl-mi. Without the twist your mother suffers from. A fine, strong man. Like your father. Ah god, baby, be like your father. . . ." She sighed and settled back, the baby warm across her body.

The hours passed. Somehow. Sharl went back in his bed, sleeping the deep, placid sleep of contentment and a full belly. Aleytys pulled the quilt around her and huddled unhappily, waiting for Stavver to return. If he chose to return.

The caravan creaked and swayed as he came up the stairs. He pulled the curtain aside, hesitated, then stepped into the caravan. "Leyta?"

"Here, Miks."

"Good." He dropped beside her shivering as much from over-stimulated nerves as from the night cold. "I'm a fool," he muttered.

"I think so too." She touched his cheek. "You're freezing. Come under the quilt with me."

He hesitated, passed shaking hands over his face.

"Isn't it time to stop acting like a boy? You're a man."

"What's a man?" With a deep groan, he stretched out beside her, letting the quilt fall over him. He pulled her into his arms. "I never thought maturity would be so complicated." Relaxing against her soft warm body, he let the dregs of resentment wash out of him.

Chapter VII

Aleytys stroked her hand over Olelo's soft, russet fur as he cuddled against her, watching Stavver smother the fire with a shovel full of sandy dirt. Behind her the orange sun was a fat pimple on the horizon, throwing extravagantly elongated shadows that flickered in a stilting dance behind Loahn and Kale as they buckled harnesses on side-stepping, restless horses and backed them over the wagon tongues.

Maissa came walking with short tense steps over the top of a knoll. Halfway down, a dozen paces away from the campsite, she stopped abruptly, her face crumpled in a bad-tempered scowl.

Aleytys sighed. The omens pointed to a bloody-minded confrontation when she informed Maissa that their plans had to be changed. She hesitated, reluctant to precipitate the conflict, then took a deep breath and called, "Leyilli."

Maissa whipped her head around, the scowl deepening as she focused on Aleytys. She jolted downhill, kicking viciously at the cold wet grass. When she reached the level ground of the campsite, she halted, shivering, arms crossed over her bare breasts. There was a drawn look to her face and her skin humped in blue-tinted gooseflesh. "What do you want?"

Aleytys glanced at Loahn then lowered her eyes, let her shoulders droop, minimizing her own personality to offer less abrasive challenge to Maissa's hypersensitivity. "The pariah boy," she said softly. "We have to take him back to his people."

Maissa hissed and took a short step backward, coming up on her toes like a snake poised to strike. "So?"

"He has to be put right with them."

"We stick our fingers in the fire for that?" Trembling from anger and cold she jerked a thumb at the watching boy.

"If you want peace and quiet, we take the boy back. Unless he's put right with them, we're all in trouble."

Maissa's nostrils flared. "Put a knife through his throat, put him under dirt, there's no more problem." She rubbed her hands up and down her arms. "This damn lump of shit." She was shivering more violently. "The sooner we get off . . ."

"You do it that way, you've got another problem." Aleytys' voice was cool and crisp, pulling Maissa back around in a wary hunter's crouch. She straightened and glared at Aleytys.

Stroking a gentle hand over the speaker's fluff, Aleytys nodded toward the boy. "Me. You'll have to do me too. I will not stand aside and watch that boy killed. I will not."

"You!" Lips curling in a contemptuous sneer that was part snarl, baring her small ivory teeth, she ran insolent eyes over Aleytys from head to feet then back up again. When she spoke, her voice was hoarse, the words came out in clear harsh syllables. "Filthy grubling. You will not? Phah!"

She wheeled and leaped at the boy who stood gaping at the fury plunging toward him. Face contorted with a hideous combination of rage and killer-lust, hands set for the killing blow, she was a screaming death missile. She bounced off Stavver as he leaped between her and her prey. Moving faster than Aleytys had ever seen him shift his long thin body, he whipped past her as she tottered off balance and wrapped wiry arms about her. "Leyta," he grunted out. "Get that damn magic of yours working."

The diadem sang, flowing in phantom splendor on the blue-black hair while in her head fragmented images of cool wary black eyes flickered hazily at the rim of mental vision, triggering confusion and a ravening curiosity in her. Her body moved, clumsily at first, then with a swift sureness that startled and delighted her. For the first time since the diadem had started taking her body she wasn't wholly pushed aside, a helpless prisoner in her own skull. She shared the grafted skill and the pleasure she found in it added to the confusion that wheeled in her head. Stavver's strained face, Maissa's hate-ugly one reflected the phantom sparks of flickering colors from the jeweled centers of the diadem flowers as they caught the light and reflected it back. "LET HER GO." Her voice sounded strange to her as if it struggled toward a resonant baritone an octave below her normal tones.

Stavver nodded. He released Maissa, shoving her roughly forward while he leaped backwards several paces.

With a shriek Maissa whipped a hand in a three-finger strike at Aleytys' throat, not bothering to cover out of her contempt for what confronted her. Aleytys swept the hand aside and struck hard, whipping her fist around so that two knuckles slammed into the juncture of jaw and neck, drawing a grunt of pain out of the smaller woman. Maissa fell back but hit the ground in a quick roll that brought her to her feet poised to attack.

As soon as the strike was completed Aleytys threw her suddenly skilled body back, ready to attack again if necessary.

Maissa circled warily probing for weaknesses in Aleytys' defense, eyes chilling into reluctant respect as she failed to find any opening. Finally, breathing a little too quickly, she moved out of reach and dropped her hands, staring fascinated at the glimmering diadem coiling regally above a stern, drawn face, set in strange lines, a shifting of features into a new conformation that altered Aleytys almost out of recognition. Made obscurely uneasy by this change, Maissa focused on the jeweled crown. Greed seeped in to replace the anger. "The diadem," she breathed. "The Rmoahl diadem. Stavver said you had it."

The black-eyed presence flowed imperceptibly from her nerve webbing as the chimes dimmed to taut silence. Aleytys shrugged. "As you see," she said, her throat tight, her voice shrill in reaction to its plummet into the lower tones. Olelo came scampering to her, small black hands out, begging to be taken up. Absently she settled the speaker on her shoulder. "Will you listen now?"

Anger clamped Maissa's full lips into a tight line. She nodded, head dipping in a taut small arc, body rigidly erect, muscles contracted for the attack that her cooling brain refused to initiate.

"If the boy stays alive, for our sake as well as his, I have to take the curse off his head. It won't add that much time to the length of our stay here . . ." She kicked at the clodded sandy earth, toes sending up a spray of coarse soil. "Four days . . . five . . . not more. But we'll roll into Karkys sunk layer on layer deep in the life of this world. The boy is bound to me body and spirit until I release him. I guarantee he'll prove no danger to us."

"Guarantee." The word reeked scorn but Maissa had herself firmly in hand. She watched Aleytys from unblinking eyes, cold as death.

"Yes." Aleytys tapped her temple so that the others staring fascinated at her heard the chimes.

Maissa turned her head without moving her body and glanced at Kale from the corner of her eye. "Kale."

"Yes."

"What she says."

Kale jerked his gaze away from the impudent grin on Loahn's narrow face. Reluctantly he nodded. "If we plan to continue, gikena's got to lift the curse."

Maissa's eyes flickered over Stavver, rested on him a minute while her fists closed and opened again, then faced Aleytys. Reluctantly she nodded. "We need you, woman. For the moment. Don't push your luck. And keep that brat out of my sight." She whipped around and scowled at Kale and Stavver. "What are you standing around for, fools? Do you want to waste more time?" She strode to her caravan, pulled herself tiger-fast and smooth onto the driver's seat. Taking the whip from its loops she sat caressing the smooth braided coils. "Well?"

As Aleytys walked to her caravan, she felt a sickness of the soul turn her knees weak and set a darkness behind her eyes as images of the battered horses Maissa had driven the first day on this world burned behind her eyelids. She stopped by Kale and laid a hand on his arm. "Let her alone," she murmured.

Kale looked startled.

"The horses won't suffer too long and she'll wear the rage out. It won't be pleasant, but. . . ." She shrugged. "When we stop for nooning, I'll heal them."

His dark eyes met hers a minute. Then he nodded.

"Good. Let her lead off. Tell her to take the first turning to the north. . . . a minute. Loahn."

He edged around the horse's head, curiosity vivid in his face.

"First turn to the north?"

He nodded. Clearing his throat, he said hesitantly. "Then just follow the main ruts. Lake Po's turn-off comes mid-morning the second day."

"Good. You understand, Kale?"

Flicking a two-fingered salute to mark his understanding, Kale padded to Maissa, sliding over the ground like the hunting cat inked on his skin.

Maissa lashed the whip across the flanks of the off-side horse, startling a pain-filled scream from the gelding. Her caravan rumbled past, swaying and rocking precariously. With an angry nausea turning her mouth sour, Aleytys swung up on the seat. "Drive, will you, Keon? Loahn, you'll keep out of sight. Ride inside or sit in the back door. As you please."

He grinned at her, some of his usual self-possession returning. Aleytys frowned awfully at him. "Move, imp. Even the dust cloud's disappearing." Stavver chuckled and slapped the reins on the horses' backs, starting them forward at a brisk trot. With a shout of laughter that was an affirmation of the soaring spirits in all three, Loahn raced around the caravan as it began to pick up speed and swung himself up into the interior.

Aleytys leaned back, feeling a sudden lightness, her spirit floating like a bubble. "Miks, did you see her face. Ahhh. . . ." She giggled and stretched, wriggling on the hard plank of the seat.

He reached out and flipped a stray curl off her face. "She never thought a barbarian land-grubber could handle her like that."

"Well, she was right, wasn't she." She wrinkled her nose at her hands. "I wasn't the one working these."

Miks sobered. "In a way it's too bad we couldn't keep that card stashed for the future. Maissa's a snake, Lee. She knows now she can't take you from the front. You watch your back."

"I don't understand." She scratched at her knee with a forefinger, worrying at a small flake of dead skin. "You keep telling me how evil and cruel she is. All right. So she mistreats animals. Loses her temper easy. Tried to kill Loahn. None of that's very sweet and gentle, but she hasn't really done anything to us."

"She needs us now."

Mid morning, they swung off the main track onto a narrower lane, as deeply rutted but not so bare. Spindly weeds, dry and dusty as little old men, hunched between the whitish wheel tracks. The wind had turned and came to them from the north instead of the west, lakeland's breath instead of the hot dry effluence from the stone-

lands. As they moved north the air grew progressively
more humid, the tough, thin-bladed grass giving way to
another species more succulent than herb, until the land
was covered by a crunchy green carpet a double-handspan
high. At intervals darker lines of green to the left or right
marked one of the hundred lakes that gave this section of
Lamarchos its name. Twice after they passed by branching
tracks she caught glimpses of slender crimson towers swelling at the top to tulip shaped bells that looked open to the
sky. She assumed that these marked towns or villages.

On either side of the road split rail fences, aged by time
and weather to a velvety grey, shut in pasture land, the
seried sections enclosing brood mares in one, then year-
lings, then pihayo, mares again, stallions and geldings,
pihayo, repeating the pattern over and over. A vine with
heart-shaped leaves and trumpet flowers wound around the
fence horizontals, cascades of leaves plunging in a ragged
green fall, while the nodding fist-sized blooms released a
flood of heavy sweet perfume. Hour on hour of vine.
Hour on hour of sickening sweet perfume mixed with air
that grew heavier and heavier with moisture so that the
dust kicked up by the horses' hooves and the iron-tired
wheels clung like itching powder to bare skin.

Occasionally a horse or two would come to the fence
and watch them pass, wide dark eyes bright with interest,
quivering nostrils snuffing and snorting in nervous excitement. Once something spooked a small herd of two-year-
olds, all sorrels with blazed faces, so that they wheeled,
galloping off, tails high, manes whipping the air. Aleytys
exclaimed with pleasure then met Stavver's laughing eyes,
feeling a warm complicity in their shared enjoyment.

Several times they saw distant riders, but none near
enough to show interest in the travellers.

Just before nooning they moved past a field with a herd
of grazing pihayo. This time the odd-looking creatures
were close enough to examine in some detail. They were
heavy animals with massive thighs and wide muscular
bodies, looking at first glance like dirty tan sheep grown
outsize. Instead of a sheep's close curled wool, their thick
hair was straight, long and shaggy, heavy with oil. Their
sharp rancid stench was strong enough to break through
even the overpowering perfume of the trumpet flowers.

Aleytys wrinkled her nose, slightly sick at the thought of eating meat that smelled so bad on the hoof.

When the sun's glow spot crossed zenith in the circustent sky, they came on Maissa's caravan pulled to one side in a lay-by, a circle of trees drooping over weathered tables, benches and a flat-roofed structure held up by a series of wide flat poles carved into stylized, simplified animal forms. Maissa sat on the edge of a stone-lined well, her back to the road, staring out across the rolling swells of the grassland. As Aleytys watched, she flipped a small yellow capsule into her mouth. Immediately Aleytys could sense the drug slipping into the woman's veins, feel it with sudden acuity, feel it so strongly it dizzied her until she could jerk herself free.

Wiping her hands fastidiously together figuratively cleansing herself of the slime bubbling out of the depths of Maissa's soul, Aleytys went quietly to the horses standing head down, skin twitching, too beaten down to move from the spot. She put her hands on them, taking away the pain, healing the torn bruised flesh, soothing the hurts in them as best she could. When she looked up, Kale was leaning against one of the pillars watching her.

Once again she brushed her hands together. "You think you could do the driving the rest of the day?" She examined her palms thoughtfully. "Without precipitating a crisis?"

"Not if you suggest it to her."

Aleytys laughed. "Right. I'll keep out of the way."

"The drug should help. She won't eat anything, probably sleep most of the time." He rubbed his hard back slowly against the post, glowering at her in a kind of irritated compassion. "Why?" he burst out. "Why let her control you?"

Aleytys spread her hands out, shrugged. "She has the ship."

"You cut loose from her, you could get passage on another ship. With your power. . . . And you wouldn't have to deal with her. Or you could stay here. I don't know why you're star-hopping, but. . . ."

Aleytys twitched her shoulders, brushed at the dust on her body. "Ay-mi, Kale, I dream of a bath. To soak my neck deep in warm soapy water. To wash my awful hair and spread it in warm sun to dry. Ah well, I'm hungry. Have you eaten?"

He watched her a minute, then nodded. "We got in about an hour before you."

Aleytys nodded and left him to rejoin Loahn and Stavver.

When they went on again Aleytys chased Loahn out of the back and settled herself on the mattress, lying out flat, letting her body adjust to the jerk and sway of the caravan. Out front Loahn and Stavver were talking quietly, their words mingling with the rumble of the wheels and the steady clop clop of the horses' hooves.

Sharl woke and announced discomfort with an angry imperative howl. Laughing, Aleytys sat up and swung her feet over the edge of the bunk. After pinning on a clean dry diaper she poured water into a bucket, added a pinch of soap powder, washed the soiled diaper, rinsed it in fresh water, then hung it out the back to bleach and dry in the sunlight. All the while Sharl babbled happily, kicking his feet vigorously, clutching at any hold that offered itself to groping hands, not caring whether it was a portion of his own anatomy or something extraneous.

Aleytys wiped her hands and picked the baby up. She rocked him a few minutes then put him down on the mattress. Kneeling beside the bunk she played with him until he was worn out with laughing. Then she fluffed the blankets in the drawer and laid him down to sleep.

She watched him a few moments then climbed back on the mattress and stretched out, staring blindly at the swaying ceiling.

All right, she thought. You in my head. I'm not a terrified ignorant child now. She chuckled. At least, not so ignorant as I was. First time I thought I was dreaming you. Not now. I saw your eyes opening. . . amber. . . black. . . . you should make up your mind. . . . god, it makes me feel dizzy. . . . are you. . . . what are you? She closed her eyes and waited. The caravan rumbled along the road swaying and jerking over the ruts. Once more she became aware of Stavver and Loahn talking casually, intermittently, words lost in the steady plodding beat of the hooves, punctuated by an occasional shrill bugle from a stallion running along the fence issuing his challenge to a placid and uncomprehending world.

The muscles in her shoulders began to ache from the tension that rapidly tightened around her. "Ahai," she muttered, "It's been a long time . . . too long." Forcing her mind back to the valley of the Raqsidan, she painstakingly recreated the mind and body relaxers Vajd had taught her so long . . . she thought suddenly . . . not so long, only a year and a standard year at that . . . I can't believe it . . . no . . . that's not true. It's a different kind of time that's passed for me. Not simple seconds minutes hours, but time measured by the changes . . . big and little changes . . . in me . . . by that measure, the span of time since I left the Raqsidan is a hundred times my whole lifetime in the valley. Raqsidan . . . she smiled remembering the clean cold water of the mountain river, crystal clear sliding green on green. . . . dancing water white on the rapids and rainbowed in the mist of the two-meter waterfall below the bridge . . . abruptly she was wretchedly miserably homesick. . . .

She wrenched her mind from its destructive cycle and disciplined herself into the first and simplest of the exercises . . . watching the breath flow in and out counting exhalation one through ten one through ten. . . . The grim determination with which she began, a self-defeating tension itself, slowly . . . too slowly . . . evaporated and her mind grew calm. She lay, heartbeat slow and powerful like a long distance runner's, mind detached and serene, body attuned to its surroundings so thoroughly it adjusted itself to the bumps and shudders without intruding more than minimally on her thoughts. . . .

I open myself to you . . . come . . . we share my body . . . once I was angry and disturbed by you—I am no longer. I accept you . . . I must . . . knowing I can do nothing else . . . you hear me. . . .

Tension jarred the placid surface of her mind, then died away. She lay close to coma, life a faint glow somewhere far off. Amber and black flickered like witchfire across the back of her eyelids then died away . . . she breathed slow, slow. . . . The witchfire flared again. Dimly she felt . . . something . . . something struggling toward her, but as in a nightmare the struggle went on and on endlessly and fruitlessly. . . . The thing that struggled cried out in frustration a soundless echo that throbbed across her brain and . . . retreated . . . leaving that feeling behind, frustration carried to the point of exhaustion. . . .

She closed her hand into a fist, the small movement started her blood flowing faster, her breath deepening and quickening. Sighing, she opened her eyes, pushed her tired body up so that she could swing her feet over the edge of the bunk. Her head throbbed with a pulsing ache that blurred eyesight and hampered thought. She rubbed her temples and winced at the answering chimes.

Sharl whimpered in his sleep. Aleytys straightened him out and smoothed the blankets around him. "Not so long ago, baby, I thought having this thing riding me was the end of living. Funny what one can get used to. . . ." She rubbed the back of her head where her skull joined her spine, then massaged her temples with the heels of her hands, ignoring the slight sounds this produced. "Now that I know it hears me," she went on slowly, fluffing his curls with a forefinger, "it's not so bad. Makes me not quite so much a slave, baby. I know one thing from this. I'd hate being somebody's slave." She yawned. "Ahhhhgh, I need some fresh air." Fingers cupping to touch his small warm body, she murmured, "We've got some interesting times ahead of us, baby."

She thrust her head out between Stavver and Loahn. Shadows were rapidly lengthening and merging as the sun squashed down past the western horizon. Overhead, clouds were blowing together into a purple-pink mass. Above and around the true clouds the aerial bacteria were clotting into their nightly clumps. "Will it rain?" She raised her voice so that Loahn could hear her over the rumble of the wheels and the howl of the rising wind that blew scraps of debris around them.

"Sometime tonight."

"Then you better come in with us." She touched Stavver's shoulder. "That all right?"

His mouth twitched down, then he shrugged. "Why not."

She tightened her fingers briefly in appreciation, then was intensely aware of the texture of the flesh under her hands, sorry immediately that she had succumbed to pity.

Stavver tilted his head back so he could see her face. He grinned sardonically at her, appreciating her sudden flash of regret. He stood up, motioning Aleytys back inside the

caravan. Then he handed the reins to Loahn. "Take care
of things."

The boy flashed an impudent grin at him. Gathering the
reins into one hand, he closed the other into a fist, thumb
projecting upward. "Hard and long," he said cheerfully.

Stavver threw back his head and laughed. "Keep your
mind on your job, boy, and let a man do a man's
business." He ducked his head and vanished inside the
caravan.

Loahn snorted and gave the two inside a rough several
minutes as he slapped the horses into a trot, sending them
slaloming back and forth across the ruts. Then he let them
slow until the caravan rolled placidly along in the darkening twilight.

Chapter VIII

Grey and massive city walls rose ponderously from a low
cliff that overlooked Lake Po, but despite this evidence of
concern for defense the iron-bound double doors stood
wide open. She pulled the horses to a stop and eyed the
mosaic pavement that began at the outer edge of the walls.
"It looks like the inside of someone's house. You sure we
just drive in?"

Invisible inside the caravan, Loahn answered her impatiently. "Like I told you. Straight ahead to the square."

"Here we go." She slapped the reins on sweaty flanks,
starting the horses forward at a slow walk.

The wide avenue was paved with small black and white
tiles in a stylized pattern taken from the creepervine covering the fences that lined the road. On either side of the
wide street the houses were blank and enigmatic walls that
had no windows on the lower two floors, only a heavy,
iron-bound door. Like the city gates these doors stood
open to the vagrant breeze that stirred the hot humid
mid-afternoon air. As the horses clopped past, Aleytys
caught glimpses of green and lovely courtyards, sometimes
with a part of a fountain visible. People were strolling in
both directions, chatting leisurely, even those with definite

destinations or errands unhurried and ready to stand staring at the newcomers. By the time Aleytys drove into the central square a number of the curious were following, eyes fixed on the two caravans.

The black and white design split into two sections forming a wreath around a tall slender minaret rising nearly a hundred meters before it flared out into the tulipflower capital, reminding her of the crimson towers she had seen occasionally in the past days. Now that she was close to one of them she could see that the color wasn't solid, but resulted from thousands of square crimson tiles set in a white matrix. The tower rose like an exotic flower among the starker realities of the blunt-faced buildings and the black and white pavement. Winding in a spiral around the minaret a set of steps delicate as white lace climbed to the watch platform at the top. Just below that the tower was pierced by an oval hole. A large, bronze bell hung massively motionless in the opening.

From small open-faced shops and eating places scenting the air with the smell of meat and new-baked bread and this world's version of tea, people came out to view the arrival of the strangers. No one spoke directly to Aleytys or the others. They circled and speculated but waited for her to make the first move, to indicate who she was and what she wanted.

Aleytys stopped the horses by the minaret. She wound the reins around the cleat and turned to Stavver. "Time to ring the bell. You ready?"

He nodded then swung down from the seat. Hitching up the sagging batik he strode briskly to the tower, pulled the bell rope free and tugged vigorously on it.

The deep musical note sang out over the startled faces of the townspeople. He counted five, then pulled the rope again. Counted five and pulled the rope again. Three strokes . . . the summoning of the Kauna. He wound the rope around the cleat and returned to the wagon.

The square stilled to a thick hush. Aleytys sat deliberately motionless, her face a calm smiling mask, projecting a confidence she was far from feeling. Stavver lounged against the seat back, a grin on his face, thumbs hooked behind the worn leather belt.

The silent staring crowd moved aside for a procession of six men and one woman, all frowning, all pompously without humor in their faces. Each wore the ubiquitous batik wrapped around their prosperous paunches, but added to this short, feather cloaks glowing with a gold-orange sheen, locked with gold chain around their pudgy shoulders. Each carried a staff in the shape of a long handled canoe paddle, intricately carved over the whole surface.

The leader stopped beside her. "Why do you summon the Kauna, strangers?"

Aleytys looked at him a minute in silence watching as he grew slightly uneasy under her frowning regard. She stood so that he had to tilt his head back if he wanted to look above her knees. "Olelo."

The speaker dived through the curtains, balanced a moment on the seat back then scrambled up her arm to stand erect on her shoulder, bright, black eyes flickering over the stunned faces of the elders.

"I am Lahela gikena."

Murmurs of surprise fled around the square. The watchers pressed closer.

"I have come to accuse Wahi-Po of injustice, of condemning the innocent."

The Firstman of the Kauna bowed his head politely then turned shrewd sorrel eyes on her, uncomfortable at having to bend his neck to look up at such an angle. "You are welcome, gikena. But we don't understand. What do you accuse us of?"

Olelo tittered suddenly, the small sound shattering the dignity the Firstman sought to project. "Oh elder," he shrilled. "I see your eyes looking at me. Wide open eyes." He tittered again. "Three months gone, you kept them shut so you would not see."

Firstman blinked and shifted his feet uneasily on the black and white tiles. Behind him the others, necks sore from the bending, looked down at their pudgy toes, but then they felt even more uneasy, being looked on when they were not looking, so they kinked their necks again to see her face.

Unsmiling still, Aleytys nodded. "The Lakoe-heai sent me here. What was done must be undone. Loahn."

The elders gasped as the boy stepped through the curtains and stood behind the seat. A murmur of surprise with anger in it this time ran quickly around the crowd.

The Kauna moved closer to one another, seeking the comfort of numbers, eyes slipping unhappily over the thin form of the pariah.

"Bring me the woman Riyda and the sons of Arahn."

Firstman frowned. "I've never seen you, woman. You call yourself gikena. How do I know your true chosen?"

"I don't have to prove anything, old man. I came here to give you a chance to make good the wrong you did to one who was innocent. You know I need not have come. The boy could serve me the time I set him and come back here with no one to deny his right. If he wanted to come back to a desert. You understand that, Pukili, elder of Wahi-Po? I do not threaten you, I merely explain. If I turn from this place it is cursed."

Firstman turned ashy pale. "No, si'a gikena." He turned to the others crowding close behind him. "Mele, Lukia. Take wardens and bring the woman. Bring as many of the boys as you can find." He dipped his head obsequiously to Aleytys. "One or more of the sons of Arahn may be out on the run."

"That is acceptable. Though whichever of the sons is not here will have to be fetched to me eventually."

The elder glanced at Loahn, the dislike he couldn't hide drawing his stringy face into sour lines. "You say that one is innocent?"

Aleytys raised an eyebrow. "You tread on my heels, old one. Are the Wahi-Po without courtesy? Hold your patience till the woman comes."

"Then may I offer you the hospitality of my house? Water, shade, perhaps some meat or tea?"

"I will not step under roof in this place until the evil is cleansed, the wrong is undone. Nor shall I eat or drink here until what I came to do is done."

The people in the square shifted uneasily, families and friends shrinking closer together to gain strength from the feel of flesh against flesh.

"Loahn, get inside. I don't want her to see you." Aleytys spoke softly so that the others couldn't near.

Time passed slowly, marked only by the sun shifting a degree of arc in its afternoon slide toward the western horizon. Aleytys stood immobile, fighting a need to scratch that grew to ridiculous proportions. She wondered how Maissa and Kale were taking the tedious waiting, hoped

Maissa was dreaming the time away with the help of her
drug.

Finally she heard a growing disturbance, a woman's
shrill voice soaring in a screaming descant over the sullen
muttering of the crowd. The woman Mele and the man
Lukia marched past the caravan in a stone-faced silence.
Behind them two Kauna wardens had hold of a woman's
arms, a dark woman, attractive even in her anger, her lush
body writhing against their grasp. She vibrated with a vi-
tality that made the elders look dull and old, that leached
the personality even from the tough stolid men who forced
her around so she faced Aleytys.

Firstman bowed his head. "This is Riyda wife and
widow of Arahn."

"And the sons of Arahn?"

"As you see. The three of them." He pointed at the
stocky scowling youths standing behind the wardens.

"Olelo?"

The speaker stroked his paws over the fall of white fur
covering neck and belly. "He speaks truth, gikena sister."

"What's all this about?" Warily Riyda examined
Aleytys. Then she turned on the Kauna. "I'm an honest
woman. A widow with the soul of my man in care. What
of my rights, si'a Pukili? You tear me from my house like
some sideroad whore!" Her eyes flashed righteous indigna-
tion. Around her the people of Wahi-Po muttered more
loudly, casting unfriendly eyes at the stranger who had
come among them to attack one of their own. "You know
my father. My brother stands there. You, Mele. You're
my mother's sister." She jerked her arms free from the
loosened grasp of the wardens. "Why have you done this?"

Aleytys could feel the crowd responding to Riyda. The
stench of the anger in the square pinched her nostrils. She
shivered. This had to go right. Damn but the woman was
a fighter. She reached up and touched the speaker. As he
wrapped a small black hand around her finger, warmth
and confidence flowed back into her. She smiled. "You ask
why, woman?"

Riyda swung around and glared at her.

"You ask why? You? If the punishment of the Lakoe-
heai comes upon Wahi-Po, you, Riyda by name, are the
cause."

"Punishment?" Anger faltered in Riyda a minute but

she could not afford to admit weakness. Her face softened, took on an expression of amazement. "Me? I don't understand. I've done the proper rites, I've been true to my man. No other man can say I've willingly lain with him. I've honored the dead and gone dutifully about serving the living. I'm a poor helpless defenseless woman, my only protector finding his way to Ma-e-Uhane to await his rebirth. What could I have done?"

"I am gikena, woman. Play your games with those who cannot see through them. You have dishonored your man. You have cheated his first born out of birthright. You have lied, woman."

Riyda was frightened. Like a cornered animal she reared back her head and prepared to fight. "Why do you do this to me?" she cried. Turning to face the crowd, she held out trembling hands to them. "Help me. Help me, my friends, my blood kin, my people, blood of my blood. This woman lies. How can she be true gikena if she lies like this to you, lies about me? I am innocent, I did nothing."

An ugly murmur swept through the crowd. Ignoring the angry scowls, Aleytys stood unconcernedly erect, apparently untouched by the danger. Inside she was terrified. Olelo patted her cheek then leaped to the roof of the caravan.

"Wahi-Po," he cried, his small voice suddenly having the force of the thunder that rumbled threateningly from the multi-colored cloudless sky. "Gikena my sister speaks truth! The woman lies, she seeks to have you turn on one sent by Lakoe-heai who speak to you now through this small one. Before you let body rule mind, remember what happened to Wahi-Aliki." Again thunder rumbled. Hairline cracks opened in the mosaic pavement as the earth shifted underfoot, momentarily as unstable as water. The minaret swayed and groaned. Then Olelo scampered down and perched himself on Aleytys' shoulder.

Swallowing hastily she pointed an accusing finger at Riyda. "Speak truth, woman. You drugged the boy."

"No . . . no . . ." Riyda wheeled to flee but the wardens caught hold of her and dragged her back. She turned and twisted, trying to pull free.

Aleytys snapped her fingers impatiently. "Still you will not tell the truth." She swung down from the caravan. "Lie with my touch on you. If you can."

Riyda screamed as Aleytys reached toward her, screamed again from terror and pain as fire seared through her writhing body. Overhead the sky took on an ominous coppery color, the pastel sworls of pink and blue and lavender and apple green and yellow drew away to a narrow ribbon circling the horizon. A hot dry wind rose to a mournful wailing as it blew over the city. The crowd, once hostile and threatening, disintegrated to individuals shuddering in superstitious fear shrinking back from the terrible scene by the tower. Riyda felt the difference in them through the haze of pain and sobbed wordlessly.

"You drugged the boy," Aleytys repeated sternly. Her fingers rested lightly on the woman's temples and she looked down into the sweating face with little pity in her.

"I—I drugged the boy," Riyda whispered.

"Louder, woman. So everyone can hear."

"I drugged the boy."

"You smeared an animal's blood on yourself."

"No . . . ahhhh . . ." Pain coursed through her, fire burning her alive, eating her. "Yes, yes," she shrieked. "I killed a water bird and smeared its blood on my thighs."

"You lied when you said Loahn raped you."

"I lied. I lied. I lied."

"You lied when you said he spat on his father's corpse."

"Yes, yes." Her body was shuddering with hard deep sobs. "I lied. I lied about it all. Take your hand away, gikena, take your hand away; please . . . please . . . it hurts . . . I lied, yes I lied. I hated him. He was no good. If it wasn't for him my sons would have birthright. My sons, not hers. He never forgot her, he married me, I was better for him, but he never forgot her. Witch. She sorcelled him, bound his soul to hers." Her head fell forward and she hung limply in the arms of the wardens.

Aleytys stepped back and climbed once more into the caravan. Her face composed in a forbidding mask, one hand touching the speaker the other hanging free at her side, she swept the stunned and silent crowd with cold blue-green eyes. "You have wronged the innocent, people of Wahi-Po. Those of you who had reason to resent the boy let your prejudice blind you and the rest are no better, following blindly the lead of their fellows. And you, elders of the Kauna, you didn't stay to hear the boy, but condemned him to a lingering death and went placidly back to your wallows. Loahn. Join me here."

Loahn stepped through the curtains and stood behind her, facing the chastened Kauna.

"You owe him reparation, elders of Wahi-Po. First, you will return to him his birthright, his place in the community of Wahi-Po and his father's holdings. Yes?"

Firstman Pukili tightened his fingers around the staff until the bones of his hands stood out in high relief. Reluctantly he bowed his head, then straightened. "Mele. Sound the summoning."

The big woman dipped her head in curt response. Freeing the rope from the cleat she hauled powerfully on it. Once-twice. Once-twice. Once-twice. The great bell rang out in the thrice repeated double note that summoned the people of Wahi-Po to meeting with the Kauna. After settling the feather cloak until it hung unruffled over her broad shoulders, Mele stepped back to her place behind Firstman.

"Be it heard." Firstman Pukili's voice rose in a high chant. He knocked the butt of the staff three times on the pavement. "Be it heard." With the others trailing wordlessly behind, their staffs hitting solidly on the pavement in unison with his, Firstman circled the two caravans, repeating again and again the formal call. Too frightened to indulge his curiosity about the others in this mis-mated group who had come to disturb his peace, he hurried with as much dignity as possible through the obligatory round and stopped when he faced Aleytys once more. A final time he beat his staff against the black and white tiles, waited while the others one by one signified their assent by echoing his action, then continued with his chant.

"Be it known. Loahn, son of Arahn father clan Hawk son of Selura mother clan Moon, wrongfully accused and cast out from home and birthright, we call you home to your people. We say to you we are under the frown of Lakoe-heai. We plead with you to forgive us, to take the cloud from us. Son of Arahn, stand in the clan hall of your father's house, master of men and beasts, master of the land in your father's holding." Pukili licked his lips eyes fixed on Loahn's expressionless face.

"That is not enough." Aleytys spoke softly, her words bringing a sickly smile to Pukili's face. "For one month,

Loahn son of Arahn hungered with none to give him food or warmth. He thirsted but could only steal a mouthful of water deep in the protection of night. When I came upon him, led to him by the will of the Lakoe-heai, he was bones wrapped in sunburnt skin, dying from a festering wound, the stump of a broken arrow protruding from his back. Elders of the Kauna, I hold you at cost for these things. One month it was. Times Three. Three stallions of the finest. Three brood mares in foal. Three times three pieces of gold." She stroked the soft fur of the speaker. "You who sent me to the boy, is that sufficient?"

The small one rubbed himself blissfully against her hand. Opening translucent eyelids, he swung eyes filled with a malicious glee over the people. "Barely, sister. Barely. And the giving better be free-handed and ungrudging. We hate a cheerless giver." He snuggled back against her head and closed his eyes.

Aleytys nodded to the Kauna. "You hear?"

Pukili lowered his eyes. "We hear, si'a gikena."

"It will be done?"

"It will be done." He banged his staff in official assent and reluctantly the others of the Kauna followed his example.

"Good."

"The woman Riyda. What do we do with her?" Pukili jabbed his staff in her ribs as she crouched in a miserable heap at his feet.

Aleytys frowned, aware that whatever she did or said, she had already destroyed a person. Now that it was too late, the result of her interference gave her a sick, dirty feeling. Somehow there must have been a better way to do this, a way of healing . . . healing. . . .

She wheeled and caught hold of Loahn's arm. "You're the injured here, it's for you to say. Do you want her cast out as you were?"

The boy watched the shaking huddled form, eyes implacable. Then he shrugged. "I serve you, si'a gikena. But I don't want that one making more trouble for me."

"I cured your body, Loahn. If I can purge her soul, will you accept her into your house?"

"She was my father's wife. What th' hell, she's only a woman. Do what you want, si'a gikena." Looking past his stepmother, he grinned at his half-brothers standing beside the Kauna, fifteen-year-old Keoki hiding his fear and un-certainty behind a scowl, Pima who was fourteen strug-gling to imitate him, Moke the youngest smiling shyly at him.

Loahn jumped down and faced Pukili. "My brothers had nothing to do with this lie," he told the Firstman. "They are welcome in my house if they wish to return." Ignoring Riyda he smiled at the boys. "Keoki, I need you, brother. Will you come?" He held out his hands. "We were never bad friends."

Ignoring his mother as Loahn had, Keoki stepped up to his brother, hesitated a minute, then thrust his hands out with a wide grin that transformed his heavy sullen face. They grasped forearms, then hugged, laughing with a touch of hysteria. Pima and Moke ran to them and joined the happy wrestling match that ensued.

Keoki broke away and quieted his brothers. He knelt before Loahn and held out his hands palms pressed to-gether. "I give you service, Elder brother."

Pima and Moke knelt in their turn, performing the same simple ritual.

"Loahn." He walked to the caravan and looked up at her, wondering what she wanted. "Take your brothers home, my friend. Leyilli can drive you."

"I understand, si'a gikena. We will set aside rooms for you there."

"You know our requirements." She hesitated. "Loahn, I may be bringing Riyda back with me. I'm not sure, but make arrangements in case." She swung down beside him, touched his arm affectionately, then walked back to the other caravan taking short nervous steps, reluctant to face Maissa. For the first time she really understood what Stav-ver had meant when he said he didn't trust Maissa. Damn this walking on eggs, she thought. She stopped and smiled pleasantly up at the unreadable mask turned to her. "Leyilli, I would be pleased if you would take the brothers to their home."

Malice glinting in her eyes, Maissa smiled back at her, enjoying her discomfort. "Of course, si'a gikena." Her hands tightened on the reins and Aleytys winced. Maissa chuckled. She handed the reins to Kale. "My house is theirs," she said demurely.

Aleytys watched as Kale turned the horses and drove

away, two young faces lively with curiosity peering at her through the back curtain. When they disappeared out the gate, she moved silently to Riyda and knelt beside her.

The dark woman lifted a haggard face. "Even my own sons."

"You drove them away. The hate in you has soured things for you. If you change that, the rest will change." Aleytys felt the curious crowd pushing in around her, staring down at the broken woman with the cruel enjoyment of that multi-segmented creature called Mob. "Send these away," she snapped to the Kauna. "You stay as witnesses." Cold blue-green eyes swept the dark avid faces. "Clear the square."

The Kauna elders pressed the onlookers back until they were a thick sludge around the edges of the square where they squatted patiently, eyes on the little group by the tower. Aleytys nodded her satisfaction with the efforts of the elders then focused her attention once more on Riyda.

"Help me to help you, Riyda," she murmured. She reached out to touch the woman.

Riyda jerked her head away. "Help you. . . ." Anger fought with fear. "Help you? When you've stolen everything from me?"

"You know that's not true." Aleytys reached toward her again but Riyda knocked the hand away. "Do you really want to be outcast?"

"I want nothing from you."

Pukili ground the end of his staff in Riyda's ribs, drawing a grunt of pain from her. "Ungrateful bitch. You waste your time on her, si'a gikena."

"Get back," Aleytys exploded. "Fool! This is none of your concern. Back off and let me do what I must."

Offended and a little frightened, Pukili retreated and stood frowning sourly at the two women.

Aleytys ignored him and spoke softly, soothingly to Riyda. "I am healer, woman. Hate is a sickness in you that is destroying you. Let me give you peace, Riyda." She reached out again.

"Don't be afraid, Riyda. Let me help you. Look at me. Look into my face. See me, my poor wounded one. . . ." She crooned the words over and over until Riydal was staring dazedly at her. Slowly, carefully, she extended her hands until she touched the woman on the temples. Sliding her fingers around she pressed the palms of her hands on the woman's sweaty forehead.

She closed her eyes and let the black water flow through her fingers to wash over Riyda's sick and aching brain. Not knowing what to do, where to guide the flow she let it splash at random until the current began to race in a roaring torrent around a glowing thing like a hard cancerous knot. Around and around the black water rushed, eating away at the knot, eating and eating until at last the knot was gone. The torrent slowed to a trickle.

Aleytys opened her eyes feeling her heart thudding, her body shaking with exhaustion. Riyda lay flat on the pavement writhing slowly in small animal twitches, the intelligence drained from her face leaving it ugly, shapeless, inhuman. Sighing, weary to the marrow of her bones, Aleytys rocked up onto her knees and touched Riyda's shoulder. "Little one, it's a new world for you. Open your eyes and look at it."

Riyda moaned as she opened her eyes. Stiffly she pushed herself onto her knees until she could straighten her back and face Aleytys. After a minute, she spread her open hand over her heart. A timid tentative smile twitched at her full lips. "It's gone," she murmured.

Aleytys stumbled to her feet and held out her hands. Catching hold of Riyda's she pulled her erect.

Riyda looked around. When she saw the avid greedy eyes of her friends and relatives, dark blood flooded her face. She pressed her hands against her face. "I'm so ashamed. Ay-gikena, I'm so ashamed."

"No need, little one." Aleytys put her arm around Riyda's trembling shoulders. "That was the hate. Don't worry, you've got a home still. Loahn wants you to hold house for him while he serves me. You don't need to fear him either, I'll take care of that."

"How can I look at him after what I did? And them. . . ." She waved a frantic hand at the people in the square. "They all know."

"Think this: Any one of them might have done the same. Koen, help me with her." Aleytys tugged at Riyda, pulling her toward the caravan. Stavver slid down and together they got the stumbling weeping woman up the back stairs into the caravan and laid her down on the mattress.

For a minute Aleytys leaned back against Stavver, his

hard healthy flesh a healing anodyne for her tattered spirit. He wrapped his arms around her and held her with quiet affection. "All right now, Leyta?"

"Life keeps getting more complicated," she sighed. "Well, let's get back to those idiots outside."

"Think about this, love. When we get to Loahn's place you can have your bath."

Chapter IX

On the way to the house Olelo murmured in her ear, "The first task is done, sister."

"Oh, is it then?" She eyed the bouncing rumps of the trotting horses. "So. What's the second?"

"A little thing."

Aleytys snorted skeptically. "And what is that little thing?"

"You are to curse the city Karkys and drive the Karkiskya off Lamarchos."

PART II

Chapter I

Karkys rode the ridge, a heavy, basalt lump dark and massive against the whorls and streaks of pastel tints that made the sky a delicate wonder. Behind the city the ridge flattened into tableland where a number of slender needles were partially visible. Star ships. Beyond this the western horizon broke into gradually increasing waves of land until a wall of mountains melted dim and blue into the multicolored sky streaked with the hordes of aerial bacteria until it resembled a circus tent. As they came closer the clouds of dust from the unpaved road swirled up from beneath the hooves and wheels and feet to throw a softening veil over the harsh contours of the city.

Aleytys wiped the rag across her face, scrubbing away briefly the mixture of sweat and dust that prickled like nettles against her skin. "What a mess."

"Soon over." Stavver brushed fastidiously at his arms and frowned at the mob of humanity surrounding them. "We could do with a bit fewer bodies."

Aleytys laughed, then regretted it as the clogging dust swelled into her mouth. She spat, then spat again. "Phahh! I get your point. But we'll be lost among them."

"I'd settle for a thinner cover." He sneaked the rag off her lap and scrubbed at his face. "I haven't seen Loahn for a while. You send him off somewhere?"

"You were sleeping. He went ahead when we were way back down there. To get us a good place to camp. I sent Olelo with him to keep him out of trouble. With that stubble on his head someone'd probably try to kill him as outcast."

"Mmmmm."

A man on horseback trotted past, glanced curiously at them then vanished in the dust pall. Slowly, in a painfully drawn-out creeping forward, the line of wagons and complaining herds and plodding packtrains wound up the hillside. The noise was appalling.

The massive walls loomed higher and higher as they crept near.

"Formidable." Aleytys raised her brows. "The four of us are supposed to get around that?"

Stavver shook his head. "That pile of stone isn't where the difficulty lies." He leaned forward peering through the eddying dust. "The pinch is in the electronic gear concealed in those walls. The scanners by the gate will be taking apart everything that passes them. That's why my tools sit in Maissa's Vryhh-box. One smell of them. . . ." He laughed then spat in his turn, grunting in disgust.

Aleytys stared fascinated at the looming gate. Then she shook her head. "Anything more complicated than a crossbow makes my head ache."

"Leave it to me, mountain girl. That's my business. Why I'm here." He yawned, shielding his mouth with a hand, then stretched and groaned. "Another hour of this at least."

"Ahai, Miks, seems like a year to go."

He glanced at the sun's glow spot. "Since we started the climb at sunup, that's not so long."

"It's just seeing the thing so close and not being about to get there." She frowned and jerked her head toward the caravan behind. "Maissa. How's she taking the crawl?"

"She's a cat in her fastidiousness but she can take anything she has to when it helps her get what she wants. Her temper won't be at its best." He chuckled. "Not that it's ever much to depend on."

Aleytys frowned at the bobbing tails of the horses. "I understand now, Miks, what you meant about not knowing what she'd do next. She's crazy."

"No."

"Huh?"

"She functions. Her values are skewed at a wide angle

from ours. In some societies that's the definition of insanity. But . . ."

"I should think so."

Stavver shook his head. "On Immat'kri the children kill their elders when the old ones reach a certain age and eat them with tenderness and love."

"Tenderness!"

His eyes were narrowed on her, his spine curved in an indolent arc as he leaned against the seat back. "It's their way. If you judged sanity by social norms, would you be the sane one there?" He nodded at the dusty anonymous forms crowding in around them. "Even here. If you weren't gikena, you'd be crazy to expect a man to take notice of what you thought. Maissa functions with a measure of success causing minimal damage in the society she chooses. What more do you want?"

"Ahai, Miks, it makes me dizzy."

He smiled. "You'll get used to it, Lee. Besides it's not too likely you'll have to spend much time on any one world. But when you set foot off Star Street, you play by groundlings' rules if you're smart. Otherwise you'll be dead. Fast."

Aleytys sighed. "Complicated."

He wrapped long fingers around her hands, the warmth of his flesh comforting on hers. An angry wail came from behind the curtains. Stavver took the reins from her. "Your master calls."

She stood and stretched, keeping her balance with the ease two weeks of riding had developed in her. Then she slipped around the seat and through the curtain.

A fine layer of dust lay over every flat surface. Aleytys pulled a clean rag from a drawer and dabbed at her breasts with it. Dropping the rag over her shoulder she picked up the baby and settled cross-legged on the bunk, back against the wall.

"Dirty face," she murmured affectionately. She wiped the red and angry face with firm fingers. "Hungry, Sharli, Sharl-mi? One minute, one minute. Don't rush me, dirty face. There. That's better." She lifted him to her breast, smiling dreamily as he began a vigorous sucking, hands and feet kneading at her body. She ran caressing fingers over the small head regretting briefly the shimmering coppery red of his natural hair, chuckling softly at his intense concentration on filling his belly. "You're going to be a survivor too, tough guy. Like your mother. Only better, you won't have the kinks in your soul."

"You finished in there?" Stavver's muffled voice interrupted her musing. "We're getting to the gate."

Aleytys slid off the mattress and removed her breast from Sharl. Holding his protesting squirming body against her shoulder, she worked her way around to the driving seat. When she was settled, she scrubbed her other breast and put him to suck. "That was fast."

"Faster than I expected."

Presenting this calm domestic image the caravan rolled unhurriedly past the hidden scanners. They were in Karkys. Minutes later Miassa's caravan rumbled onto the pavement inside the gates. Aleytys sighed. "So we made it. It's a little hard to believe."

"My admiration for the Vrya grows every day. I wonder what Maissa peddled for those favors."

"Why not ask her? I wonder where my eager acolyte got to. We need to know where to go."

Stavver pointed with the whip. "I think we'll find out in a minute."

The boy rode toward them, picking his way cautiously through the noisy miscellany flooding into the city. He maneuvered his excited mount around until he was riding beside Aleytys.

"You're looking cheerful," she shrieked at him, the incredible clamor trapped between the walls making normal conversation unworkable. "Did you find a good spot?"

He nodded. "Next to the wall where the stream goes under. Water for the horses. Makes it cool too. Trees for shade. The family Peleku clan Fox hold it for us honored to have gikena as neighbor."

Stavver lifted an eyebrow. "Where's the speaker?"

"I left it with Puki. A girl. She's keeping ground clear for us."

Stavver grinned at him, one man to another. "Where to?"

"Straight ahead. I found a short cut. Turn right two streets on. Watch where I go." He kneed the horse to a faster walk.

Stavver slapped the reins on the horses' backs, urging them out of their tired amble, edging them out of the main stream of traffic toward the right side of the wide street.

Aleytys settled the baby in her lap then passed the rag over her face and breasts. "Ayee, Miks," she screamed. "At least the dust is behind us. But the noise!"

Stavver didn't try to answer, just nodded. The iron-rimmed wheels rumbled over the neat stone pavement. Horses tramped, whinnied, squealed. Excited adolescents shrilled banalities. Adults called greetings to acquaintances and clansmen. A small herd of pihayo bellowed their resentment at the prods of the drovers that forced them over the sterile stone in spite of their thirst and hunger. The whole kaleidoscope of sound was sucked in and amplified by the blank-faced buildings, the interminable walls rising twenty meters sheer and unornamented, acting as reflectors for the melange of noise bombarding them.

Holding Sharl against her, protecting his ears with her hand, Aleytys leaned over to Stavver. "What's in the houses? I thought the Karkiskya stuck to their own quarter."

"Visitors. Off-world traders from other Companies."

The second street opened out. The tail of Loahn's roan vanished around the corner. When Stavver followed him, the noise began rapidly abating. Aleytys looked curiously around. The walls rising on either side of this narrow alley were lower, with thick greenery visible, a hint of trees growing in hidden gardens.

"Why aren't others coming this way?" Aleytys glanced over her shoulder but Maissa's was the only caravan rumbling behind them.

"Loahn said it was a shortcut. Probably they don't know about it."

Loahn rode placidly ahead, his horse's tail switching like a metronome. He didn't bother to look back to see if they were following but sat relaxed and indolent in the saddle, whistling some lilting song with a strong beat to it. After winding around a few shallow curves, the street opened out into a wide campground already teeming with people who bustled about like ants from a spilled anthill.

Loahn threaded his way through the laughing chattering crowd, still whistling nonchalantly. Where the wall loomed over a scrabbly bunch of trees, he pulled his horse to a stop and slid off. A slender girl, Olelo cradled in her arms, moved out of the shadows and smiled up at him. Line patterns of dancing foxes pranced in twin ranks from her breasts to her shoulders and twin fox masks, delicate tracery in blue, lifted and fell coquettishly with her smile. The speaker curled happily on her breast, eyes half-closed in bliss as her small fingers searched through his fur.

"Did you have any trouble holding for us?" He started walking to the water with the girl, the horse pacing beside him.

She laughed, a joy-filled carefree sound that sent quivers through him and made him smile in response. "Two came." Her small straight nose wrinkled in disgust. "One was really dreadful. I'm glad he won't be next to us. He wasn't going to leave even when I told him gikena had claimed. He just laughed. But Olelo, he stood up and told the creep to move off before his horse fell dead under him. He turned the color of lye-ash and went off so fast he nearly ran into the wall there." She looked back, eyes fixed on Aleytys. "Is she the gikena, the one with the baby?"

Loahn nodded. "Lakoe-heai call her sister."

"Ah." The girl's eyes opened wide.

Stavver pulled the caravan around and backed it under the trees, slanting it at an angle. Kale did likewise so that the two wagons enclosed a triangular space of ground giving the campers a measure of privacy. While the two men began to unharness the teams, Aleytys settled the baby back into his sleeping drawer after shaking the dusty blankets out the back door. Grimly silent, Maissa took a bucket to one of the crude taps to fetch water for washing. Aleytys came out and stood on the back steps.

"Si'a gikena . . ."

Aleytys ran her hand through her filthy hair and smiled at Loahn. "It's a good place. Thanks, Loahn." She nodded to the girl. "Is this the one who held the place for us?"

"Yes, si'a gikena." His voice was respectful, but there was an impudent twinkle in his eyes.

Olelo chattered excitedly and began kneading Puki's arm with nervous pricking feet. She sighed and reluctantly lifted the small animal out from her body. "The speaker was much help."

Aleytys laughed as she took Olelo back. He scrambled up her arm and settled contentedly beside her ear. She touched him lightly and smiled at the pretty girl. "What's your name, my dear?"

"Pukipala Peleku's daughter clan Fox, si'a gikena." She dipped her head in a shy but graceful bow.

"And I am Lahela gikena, Puki. No doubt this one's named himself." She jerked a thumb at the grinning Loahn. "But may I present to you Loahn Arahn's son, clan Hawk holder of clan Poaku, owner of a hundred horses, a thousand pihayo now serving gikena by his own will until she sends him home to his people."

Puki opened her dark eyes wide and dipped into a bow of exaggerated reverence while Loahn shouted with laughter. "My father bid me say you will be welcome at our fire, gikena Lahela," she said when she got her composure back.

"Give him my thanks, Puki, but not tonight. I'm tired and dirty and certainly not fit for company." She glanced over her shoulder at the other three puttering about setting up camp. "Loahn, is there a bathhouse around?" She shuddered. "I stink."

He shook his head. When Puki tugged at his arm, he turned with an impatient frown. "I know where it is," she said quickly. "I have to get leave from my father first, but then I'll show you."

Aleytys sighed with pleasure. "Another thing I have to thank you for, young Puki. Loahn, would you arrange for me? The baby too. And the others if you can get room." She stretched and yawned almost dislodging the speaker. "To be clean again after that dust!"

Puki ran off. They could see her talking excitedly with a stocky grey-haired man standing beside a small fire. After a minute he nodded and she came flying back. "My father says yes but will you be sure nobody bothers me, Loahn, he doesn't trust anybody here but a gikena is different."

Loahn chuckled. "Catch your breath, Puki. If I were your father I'd be as suspicious as a lakelander running before the horde."

The girl blushed a dusky rose. Suppressing a smile Aleytys said, "Take Olelo with you while you're arranging for my bath. He'll keep the pair of you out of trouble." She watched the two of them walk off together, Loahn striding importantly while Puki's slender legs took two steps to his one.

"The playboy's found himself a new interest."

Aleytys chuckled and leaned back against the arm circling her shoulders. "Miks, our playboy friend's feeling all tender and protective for the first time in a misspent life. Miks . . . no, I have to get used to calling you Keon. Will I ever manage?"

"We're Lamarchan for the next few days." He pulled her around, cupping his hand around her head. "You had the worry out there on the trail," he murmured. "This is my time, gikena Lahela."

"Mmmm." She laughed happily, feeling her breath vibrate against his skin. "Set Loahn dusting the caravan while I get my bath. Flying dust makes me sneeze."

"And you think we're going to make the dust fly?" She could feel the rhythm of his heart beats quicken under her cheek.

"Mmmmmmmm."

"Before that, we take a stroll through the city by the trade house. We didn't come here to play."

"Business. Phah!"

"What's that?" Maissa bowed her head in outward respect. Her eyes slid over Stavver and darkened with the compulsive anger he roused in her. "Shouldn't you be getting your readings? We haven't come here for playing."

Aleytys giggled in spite of her firm resolution to avoid irritating Maissa. When the hot black eyes swung back to her, she said hastily, "Keon was just telling me the same thing."

"I've got my mind on business all the time." There was a mocking glint in Stavver's dark-dyed eyes that Maissa chose to ignore. "We walk the city tonight to get a look at the layout."

Maissa nodded briskly, changing in the blink of an eye to a clear-headed business woman. "Kale saw a man he knew some years back before he left this godawful ball of mud. The man gave no sign of recognizing him but he wants to take no chances. He'll be keeping close to camp, watching the stock. I suppose the gikena sets up shop tomorrow."

"Yes. I'll spread the leather after breakfast."

"Good. Kale will be mending harness under the trees. The boy can take care of the animals and I'll regulate the people coming to you. Think you can handle the fortunes part of this?"

Aleytys shrugged. "I'm no seer, but I've had my palm read. The trick is to be vague enough and exciting enough that the mark fills in the blanks without realizing it. The old witches in the caravans on Jaydugar were masters of this nonsense. I can remember the patter. It's not hard."

"Good. With that and the healing and the boy chatting up his girl friend, we should be good and tight in camouflage. Stavver."

"Keon, if you please."

"All right." She ran her tongue over small sharp teeth. "Keon. Any idea how long before you're ready to hit?"

"After I get a look at the place and my probes do a bit of careful snooping I'll be better able to say."

"You know where to look?"

"If Kale's sketch was accurate."

"Good. You better pick up the probes now so you'll be ready for your walk." An odd grimace stirred her soft flesh but she disciplined herself immediately. "The brat's coming back." Her restless eyes flicked to the lowering sun then swept over the camp ground. "Not much light left. You sure you don't want to start now?"

Aleytys wrinkled her nose and ran her hands over her sweat-caked hair. "No. I'm too tired and I need a bath."

Stavver added smoothly, "And the Karkiskya discourage visitors during the day. We don't want to be conspicuous."

Maissa shrugged one shoulder, a brusque impatient movement that spoke more eloquently than words about what she thought of the two of them. She frowned angrily at Loahn who was leaving Puki at her father's fire. As he started toward them she walked quickly away.

Aleytys went to meet him. "My bath?"

"The attendant said you may have as long as you need, Lahela. He was mightily impressed by the small one here and wouldn't even take coin." He tossed the small moneybag up and down several times listening to the trade metal clink inside. "Probably plans to drain your bathwater and sell it to the gullible."

"Good god, whatever for? Why should anyone be so foolish as to buy dirty water?"

"Now, si'a gikena." The impudent grin sent the hawks fluttering on his cheeks. "Water that had touched that fount of power, a genuine gikena? He'll make himself a small fortune." Laughing, Loahn turned to the caravan. "After you're finished, the others can bathe. Also free of charge."

"And you, my young friend, are a rogue. Do you get a share of the profit?"

Loahn looked shocked. "No indeed, honored one. How could you think that of me?"

"I wonder just who thought up this little bathwater business?"

"You think a simple farm boy like me could be so devious?"

"Simple farm boy, my foot. Horse trader's more like it. With the morals of a slipworm."

"Ah, well, he'll spread word about you faster than fire gone wild."

Aleytys nodded. "Good. Let me get my things and tell the others. Then you can take me there. By the way, while I'm bathing, you can clean out the caravan, give the mattresses a beating. And do a good job of it or I'll give you a plague of boils where you sit."

"Of course, si'a gikena." He lowered dancing eyes in mock humility.

She shook her head. "Simple farm boy. Ha!"

Chapter II

The moon was a disc of dirty curded milk that swam with dizzying lightness through the starfield, a shark swallowing the stars while it lit the streets of Karkys with deceptive brilliance. In the farer's quarter the camps overflowed one into the other turning the pale peace of the hard-trodden ground into cheerful flamboyant uproar . . . shouts . . . laughter . . . snatches of song . . . crackle of fire . . . animal noises . . . improvised drums . . . wail of flute clashing viciously with tin whistle . . . shrieks and giggles from clumsy adolescents. . . .

In the inner city, the quarter of the Karkiskya, the holiday noise of the campground was muted by distance and the towering walls of the secretive houses. The broad stone-paved streets scrubbed clean even of dust were empty except for an occasional spectral figure . . . one of the long thin Karkiskya, body shape concealed in thick grey robes.

Aleytys shuddered and shrank against Stavver as the faceless darkness under the cowl swung toward them. "You sure it's all right for us to be here?" she muttered.

"You heard Kale. Calm down and look at me, love, like I'm the moon in your nights. Privacy's why a couple comes here."

She relaxed against him as they strolled on in the silent meticulously clean street. She tilted her head and examined the markings on the moonface. "There's a man on the moon, a drummer. Look." She pointed. "You can even see the pattern on the drum. I wonder what tales the old ones tell their children about him."

Stavver laughed, the sound incongruous in the somber streets, an intrusion of life into the curious precise deadness around them. The Karkiskya dealt in the art of an entire world but apparently had not the slightest spark of inborn appreciation of any aspect of what they sold except the money value. Stavver's laughter made the harsh blocky buildings even uglier than before. His fingers began moving gently among the instruments hidden in her hair, tiny thumbnail-sized chips of metal.

Aleytys glanced at the building rising several stories above the cloaking curtain wall. "That's the worst one yet."

"A bank vault doesn't have to be pretty." He backed her against the wall and began kissing her, lightly and repeatedly, their forms sinking into the stark shadow like ghosts. After a minute he stepped back, took her arm, and strolled on.

"What now?" Aleytys rubbed her cheek against his hand feeling softly happy and, at the same time, disturbed. The kisses were simply part of their cover.

"Around the block to get readings on all four sides. Stopping now and then, of course." He chuckled. "To work the moonlight out of ourselves."

Aleytys pulled away. "I don't like. . . ." She scrubbed at her mouth. "Business! I don't like being used."

"Hush. Let it ride, Leyta. We have to do this."

"I don't understand any of it."

"Let your instincts take over. The Vrya are notorious for their genius at instrumentation."

"Ha! You know better about me. Instrumentation. I used to get confused over a wind-up clock." Stavver turned her around the corner. "Does thieving always take such tedious preparation?"

"When you go for big things."

"And this is big?" She glanced again at the blackish ugly building.

They walked in silence, feet grating with faint small sounds on the meticulously roughened stone. "Lamarchan stones have a very nice market." He leaned against the wall and pulled her into his arms. Face nuzzling close to her ear, he murmured, "Not worth a planetary income like some things, but nice. The really old ones are rare enough and beautiful enough they'll bring the price of a small starship. And this is a Company world." He pushed away from the wall.

As they turned the last corner, Aleytys said hesitantly, "Company world?"

He glanced frequently at the dark building as he spoke. "Karkesh Company. They enforce trade monopoly in this sector of space. Some Companies run everything on the worlds they own, but the Karkiskya keep to their fortified cities."

"Own? A whole world?" Incredulous, she let her voice rise until he hushed her impatiently. He pulled her with him into the middle of the street. "Let's go take a look at the landing field out back. "I'll show you Star Street maybe."

"Maybe?"

"We can't go through the gate with those probes in your hair. If no Karkiskya are around we can ditch them and stroll through get something to drink, just take a look at what's happening."

"Maybe find a friend? Or a way off Lamarchos and let Maissa do her own scavenging?"

He grinned at her but didn't answer.

They strolled casually through the wall shadow toward the back of the city. Aleytys scratched an itch behind her ear where one of the probes was rubbing against her skin.

"Jaydugar wasn't a company world, was it?" She shook her head. "No. I won't believe that."

"No, Leyta. I think you can be sure no Company has tamed that damn mantrap world."

"Mmm. What gives a Company the right to claim a world?" She scowled at the wall that blocked the street ahead of them. "People. . . . People, Miks! Haven't the Lamarchans anything to say about who runs them. What gives the Karkiskya the right to say you trade with us and no one else?"

"Power, Leyta. Money. Ships. Weapons. It adds up to power."

They turned a corner and walked in the shadow of the towering wall. Ahead light fanned out in a yellow patch on the stone pavement and faint sounds of laughter, shouting, music, drifted through the gate. Aleytys felt excitement growing in her so that she actually was trembling as she heard the noise strengthen into a solid reality breathing stirring promises of new things. She wanted to see. She wanted to feel. She wanted to taste everything on the other side of the wall, the hunger in her a force as strong as the water of her black river.

Stavver laughed at her, but she felt something of the same excitement in him. His steps quickened. His hands began hunting in her hair for the probes.

"Go back." The grey-robed figure stepped out of shadow and blocked further progress.

"My apologies, sho Karsk." Stavver tightened his hand on her arm, swung her around, and pulled her after him as he strode back down the street his long legs reaching out in quick nervous steps that ate space like a rock cat consumed prey. Aleytys was forced to run. The painful grip on her arm threatened to jerk her off her feet.

"Miks!"

"Shut up."

He dragged her around the corner, then slowed, stopped. Leaned against the wall his face turned away from her.

"Miks?"

"Shut up, Lee. Just don't say anything for a minute."

She rubbed at her arm, oppressed by the silence in the dead street.

Stavver came away from the wall, dropped an arm

around her shoulders and pushed her ahead of him along the street.

"Tell me about Star Street. What is it anyway?"

He blinked and then laughed, jarred out of his brooding silence. "Hmm. Groundlings and starmen don't mix well." His tone was gently amused and he radiated a strong feeling of relief as if retreating into the world of concept enabled him to forget his impotence in the world of action. "And groundlings have the edge. There's a hell of a lot more of them in any one place than there are starmen. So they set up a ghetto for them that the starmen call Star Street. Whatever world they're on. Star Street. Lively place." He grinned at Aleytys.

The street turned through a narrow pointed arch. In the campgrounds beyond the arch the fires were dying to beds of glowing coals with one or two ruminative figures sitting beside them, faces painted red and black by the firelight. Stavver and Aleytys walked a wandering path, picking their way between the camps until they passed Loahn and Puki sitting beside her father's fire talking quietly while Peleku lounged on the unfolded back steps of the caravan puffing tranquilly on his pipe. He raised a hand, nodded his head in greeting, but didn't bother to shift out of his placid contemplation of the drifting tobacco smoke.

Stavver's fingers wandered through her heavy hair touching the instruments hidden at the nape of her neck, touching the skin, tickling through the short new hairs until she sighed with pleasure. He turned her so she was looking at Peleku. "There's a man who knows a good thing when he has it."

"Not like us. She sighed and yawned, then moved away from him and climbed the steps into her caravan. Kale looked up as she stepped through the curtains. The baby snuffled as the caravan shifted, then murmured his way back into sleep. "Thanks for watching him," she said softly. Kale nodded and left. With a tremble of love Aleytys straightened the blanket and tucked it around the baby again.

Stavver came up the steps and stood behind her. One hand curved around her head and smoothed down over her neck onto her shoulder, holding her against him. "He's the center of your universe, isn't he."

Aleytys sighed. "What can I say. I swore a promise to

him and to me, Miks, that he'd know love. Always. That I'd never, never leave him like my mother did me."

Stavver stepped back to the other bunk taking her with him. He made her sit and after she was comfortable, he dropped beside her. "Do you really need to go to your mother?"

She stared in surprise at his night-obscured face. "I thought you wanted to find Vrithian."

"Little chance of that." She could feel him shrug, his body shifting against hers. "They're arrogant bastards. Male and female both. Lee, I don't think you'll like Vrithian. Or the Vrya."

"You forget I'm half Vryhh?" She bit her lip and stared blankly at the dusk in the wagon. "I want a place to belong to. People I belong with."

"There's too much caring inside you, Lee." After a moment's strained silence, his arm tightened around her. "Stay with me, Lee. You and the baby."

Aleytys laced her fingers together. "Miks, I . . . damn. I like you . . . more and more. . . . I don't know . . . I think too much to . . . to stay with you."

"You're not exactly flattering." She felt a small hurt grow in him; it had cost him to make the offer, cost perhaps even more than he knew.

"Miks . . . oh god, whatever I say is wrong. I'm going to Vrithian to find my own. A place to belong." She moved away from him, sliding around to face him, taking his face between her hands. "I've been a stranger since I was born. Don't tell me I won't fit there either."

He pulled her hands down, his face set in a cruel mask. "Forget it. Turn around so I can get the probes out of your hair." There was no quick caressing touches this time. His hands worked efficiently, slipping the tiny instruments free. "Go to bed. I'll be working on these a couple of hours at least."

A cold knot in her stomach, Aleytys slid off the bunk. He was punishing her. That sensitive streak in him was wincing with the hurt she'd inflicted on him. Though he knew clearly and coldly that he didn't really want to take on the responsibility of a woman and a baby, a baby not even his own, the rejection had him bleeding internally. Until he slept it off she would be left alone in a kind of coventry.

Silently she unpinned the batik and shook it out.
Silently she folded the cloth and put it in a drawer with
the others. She lay down, pulled the light quilt over her,
and lay watching him trip the circuits, the marching numbers sending flecks of light flickering over his intent face.
Worn out by the flood of events in the day, she yawned
and tore her eyes away. In minutes she was deep asleep.

Chapter III

"Si'a gikena."

Aleytys looked up from the square piece of leather she
was spreading beside the back steps of the caravan. Puki's
anxious face hovered over her, full mouth pinched in, a
faint line of worry between her winging eyebrows.

"Hand me that pillow, will you please?" Aleytys tossed
the crimson velvet pillow onto the leather and turned to
face the girl "What's the trouble, Puki?"

The girl dropped to her knees and pressed her palms together before her face. "Si'a gikena, come you to Karkys
as gikena?"

Silently Aleytys sank down onto the pillow. "I sit on
leather, waiting."

A bright triangular smile lit the small face as Puki
dropped her hands on her knees. "The sister of the wife of
my father's brother came to Karkys in hopes that the
Karkiskya would heal her with their magic. A thing grows
in her belly that gives her pain and will not let her eat.
She brought a poaku to buy service but the pain has made
her so weak she cannot go to them and they will not come
here."

"And?"

"Will it please you to heal her, gikena Lahela?" She
held out a hand, a deep green stone cupped in her palm.
"The one of whom I speak bade me give you this."

Aleytys took the poaku from her. Turning it over and
over she marvelled at the sheer sensuous pleasure she
derived from running her fingers over the pseudo-soft
silken surface of the heavy, tough green stone. It was

carved in low relief into a severely spare nearly abstract representation of two horses' heads, necks merging just above the shoulders, manes flying in a suggested breeze, a creation of line and hollow to enchant the eyes as thoroughly as the feel of the surface bewitched the fingertips. Aleytys continued to run her fingers over the stone as she gazed thoughtfully toward the stark towers of the Karkiskya quarter, wanting the stone until her heart ached with the pain of her desire, unwilling to let it out of her caressing fingers.

Olelo came scampering down the steps and sat himself next to her legs, his whole weight resting on her, a small soft spot of warmth, his head tipped back so that brilliant eyes, so black they looked all pupil, fixed on her face with a hint of amused wariness.

Reluctantly Aleytys gave the poaku back to the girl. "No need for this," she said slowly. "The poaku is one with your kin. No need to sacrifice so much for one small moment of my time. I'll come with you now." She glanced over her shoulder but relaxed when she saw no sign of Maissa. "When I have done, then is the time for gifting."

Glancing repeatedly over her shoulder to see if Aleytys was actually following, Puki darted around her father's caravan and stopped beside a somber black and green wagon parked with its front wheels chocked at the very edge of the stream. As soon as Aleytys reached her, Puki smiled nervously and knocked on the wall beside the heavy black curtains. "Makua Hekili, may we come? It is keikeia Pukipala and Lahela gikena."

"Be welcome." The voice coming from behind the curtains was forceful despite the evident physical weakness.

Puki pulled the curtains apart, holding them aside for Aleytys, then followed her inside. The woman lay on the leftside bunk, her head propped up on a pillow, her skeletal body stretched out under a light quilt that was appliqued with a fox pattern which echoed the hunting foxes on her face and arms. She smiled at them, dark eyes huge and lively in her drawn face. "And doubly welcome, gikena." Her bony hands moved slightly on the quilt. With a grave formality she said, "It has been years since a gikena has come to us."

Aleytys smiled at her, responding intensely to the vital

personality of the sick woman. "Si'a Hekili, you will permit me to touch your person?"

Hekili chuckled. "Lahela gikena, my body may be feeble but not my mind. Do what you will with me."

Aleytys knelt beside her. "Relax as much as you can. This may hurt." She laid her hands on the bulging knot swelling out from the center of the emaciated body. Breathing slowly she reached out for the black river of power that raced in vast and irresistible currents around the stars of her birth heaven swamping planets that bobbed like wood chips on the glassy surface. The waters roared through her hands cleansing the body that writhed and screamed under her fingers.

Puki watched fascinated and repelled. The air around the gikena shook with the power in the strange woman. Hekili's groans disturbed her until she closed her hands into fists, bearing down so that her fingernails cut moon arcs in her palms. The gikena's face was strained, eyes, blue-shadowed patches on a face pulled in tension so that muscles stood out like ropes. Puki heard startled exclamations outside and heavy footsteps coming fast toward the caravan. She ran her tongue over her lips, glanced at the two linked women, fidgeted from foot to foot, then thrust herself through the black curtains in time to face her father.

"Puki?" His eyebrows arched up, giving his round face a startled clown's look. "What's going on in there?"

"Gikena heals, father."

A long shuddering groan floated past Puki's shoulder.

"Healing? Move out of the way."

She thrust her hands at him, palm out, fingers trembling. "Makuakane Peleku, give the honored one time to complete the healing."

The groan came again, softer and weaker. Peleku shoved his daughter aside and slapped the curtains back. Inside, he clutched at Aleytys' shoulder then grunted and wrenched his hands away as the power that twisted the air around her seared along his arms.

Aleytys let the water image collapse. Weary almost to exhaustion, she rested her head a moment on the quilt, her hands sliding limply down to hang by her side. After a minute she blinked her eyes open and forced herself back on her feet. Ignoring the intruders she bent over Hekili, smiling into the huge weary eyes. Touching the older woman's cheek with a gentle exploring finger, she murmured, "How are you?"

"No more pain." The words were a strengthless sigh but the lined face was filled with a new peace. "I think I'll sleep."

Aleytys patted her cheek then turned to face Peleku. "Si'a Hekili will live." She nodded her head at the place where the quilt lay over the center of the older woman's body. "The growth is absorbed and won't trouble her any more."

He stared down at Hekili, cousin and sister-in-law. Her face was waxy pale, her mouth hung slightly open as she drew in the deep steady breaths of profound sleep. With a quick neat movement that sat oddly on his bulky body, he caught hold of her wrist and laid his fingers on her pulse. The slow strong beat brought the sweat of relief popping out over his body. Then he let a hand float gently down over the wrinkled quilt. "It is gone."

Aleytys ran her hands nervously through her hair, her strength beginning to flow back. "Yes. Of course." As he backed away, licking at trembling lips, her mouth twitched into a gently amused smile. "Hekili will need rest and nourishing food. This has been a great strain on her."

Breathing raggedly, Peleku rubbed his hands together, muttering, "Pardon, gikena, pardon my clumsy doubts."

She touched his arm, feeling him flinch involuntarily at her touch. He reddened with embarrassment. Aleytys turned her head. "Puki."

"Si'a gikena?"

"Lend me your shoulder back to my camp." She stretched and sighed. "I'm a bit tired."

Aleytys settled onto the pillows with a sigh of relief. Behind her in the caravan she heard Stavver stirring, the floor creaking under his shifting weight as he moved about. Kale sat half-obscured under the trees, pulling a harness through his hands looking for places that needed repair. He nodded when he saw her looking at him. Maissa sat on the bottom step, dark eyes glittering. Aleytys winced away from the emotional mix she projected, glanced around for Loahn.

Puki came back. "Is there anything I can do for you, si'a gikena?"

Aleytys smiled at her. "Yes, indeed. There is. Make me
some tea, will you? I'd like that."

Eyes sparking with her eagerness to be of service, Puki
trotted away toward her camp's morning fire.

"So. Lovely thing, compassion. And what do we get for
this little bit of gratuitous good-heartedness?" Maissa
swung onto her feet. "A cup of tea. A cup of lousy tea."

Aleytys shrugged. "How do you price friendship?" She
smoothed her hands over her thighs, running her thumbs
across the pleats in the batik cloth. "What's a woman's life
worth? A cup of tea? Why not. If something's beyond
price, any price is right."

"Fine philosophy. Lady goody-good. Phah!"

Aleytys stretched then chuckled, suddenly too content to
bother with Maissa. She spread her hands out, the laughter
diminishing to a bubble in her blood. "When you think of
why we're here, isn't it silly to bother about a few cop-
pers?" She flicked a hand at the growing numbers of Lamarchans circling at a respectful distance. "If you're
worried about collecting my fees, go line them up and
guide them gently to the magic circle. Cross my palm with
silver and gold. A dark stranger will come into your life.
Beware the man with the cast in his eye. Be generous, fine
lady, and all your dreams will come true." Laughter kept
bubbling up. "Bring on the marks, Leyilli, sweet gentle
Leyilli."

Maissa's eyes flashed as her face paled, then she smiled
and the laughter died in Aleytys. The small dark woman
firmed her full lips, stepped past Aleytys and bowed to the
east, north, south, west. "Farers in Karkys," she called, her
hoarse voice breaking occasionally. "Farers in Karkys,"
she repeated. "Gikena heals. Gikena reads the signs of
what will be. Touch her with silver. Touch her with gold.
Who will come? Who will be first?"

The rest of the morning passed swiftly as Aleytys healed
small difficulties, a wart here, defective eyes there, read
happiness and sorrow in a dozen different palms. At noon
Puki came hesitantly over to her.

Aleytys waved away the anxious-eyed woman standing
before her. "Come back another time," she said smiling.
"No matter what you think of my skills, I do not live on
air. The sun's at zenith and my stomach cries out." The
woman's face wrinkled into an unhappy frown, but she

moved reluctantly away. Aleytys reached out for Puki, letting the girl help her up as her cramped legs protested. "You wanted something?"

The girl ducked her head shyly. "My father said you've been so busy this morning you must be tired and no time to fix food and why should you have to tire yourself more, so will you join our fire for nooning?" She enclosed the whole camp with a graceful gesture of a friendly hand. "All of you."

A quick smile curling her lips, Aleytys glanced at Maissa. "Perhaps your father is more generous than he knows. I could eat a horse and a half. But we accept with gratitude." She turned to the woman who stood like a cold shadow behind her. "Leyilli, take care of the leathers, will you?" She flicked a careless hand at the pile of coins. "That too. Then join us with the others, please?"

Maissa nodded with carefully measured respect, eyes modestly lowered. "As you say, gikena Lahela," she murmured.

A while later Peleku handed his eating dish to Puki so she could ladle more of the spicy stew into it. To Aleytys he said, "There is more meat, si'a gikena. Don't be shy about filling your bellies."

"None for me." She raised her eyebrows in interrogation. "Nor for my people, thank you."

Peleku looked ponderously around the circle calmly contented as his eyes passed over the faces of his family. Then he smiled. "Si'a gikena, you've been introduced to my daughter, but you have yet to meet the reason we're in Karkys this particular year."

The boy across the fire jumped up, grinning broadly. He was a skinny imp with lively dancing eyes, not too impressed by the mystique of the gikena. Not that interested in her either, a mere woman who was fathoms beneath any special attention by a soon-to-be-blooded male. "He gets his Karkiskya blade tomorrow and his blooding when we get back home." Hakea grinned even wider so that his face was all mouth, nose a mere bump, eyes disappearing into black-fringed slits. At a nod from his father he ran off, loping around the end of the caravan like a spirited colt suddenly on the loose.

"Si'a gikena."

"Si'a Peleku?"

"If I might speak to you a moment?"

Aleytys nodded. Frowning, annoyed, Maissa got to her feet and followed the others back to their camp. Peleku glared at his own people. Hastily the women collected the dishes and scuttled away.

Peleku sat back, hands flat on his knees, fingers tapping slowly on the thick muscles. "I wish to speak to you about the boy Loahn."

"Ah." Aleytys smiled. "An interesting young man."

"As you have seen, my daughter finds in herself a growing tendency to seek his company. His head was shaved recently."

"Yes. He was declared outcast. The Kauna of Wahi-Po named him pariah."

"Pariah." He frowned heavily. "I will not tolerate such a connection. Pariah!"

"Not by his fault. He was falsely accused. The Lakoe-heai have taken an interest in him. Why, I don't know. They sent me to him. Before coming here I stopped by Wahi-Po. The error has been corrected, the Kauna pays reparation, and Loahn is restored to honor among his people."

"Ah."

"As to his background . . . mmm . . . his father was Arahn of Wahi-Po. At his death, with the slight hiatus of his time as outcast, Loahn became a man of wealth and substance, owning a horse run with, I understand, quite a good reputation for its stock."

Peleku nodded briskly. "I've bought horses from Arahn. A good holding." Pursing his lips, he contemplated his knees. "Why was he declared outcast?"

Aleytys drew up her knees and rested her chin on them, staring into the red heart of the fire. "A jealous woman is a bottomless well. There is no satisfying her."

Peleku ran the tip of his tongue over his upper teeth. "So?"

"Arahn's first wife died leaving one son. He married again."

"And his second wife had sons." He grunted. "She couldn't get rid of firstwife's ghost either I suppose."

Aleytys smiled into the shrewd twinkling eyes. "Right. When Arahn died, she accused Loahn of raping her."

"And he didn't."

"No. She drugged him. The Kauna listened to her. She had an aunt among them. Riyda confessed her lie when I brought the boy back to his people. The Kauna thus had to reinstate him in the community and pay him reparation."

"Ah." Curiosity glinted in his eyes. "Why does he serve you instead of managing his holding?" His eyes moved over her as his face took on a grim look. "If you don't mind my asking, does he serve your bed?"

"No." She was startled. "Why?"

Peleku sighed. "I'm glad to hear that, si'a Lahela. Lakoe-heai know I'm fond of Puki, but beside you she's like a day-lily on the day before. I wouldn't want her playing second to any woman."

"Don't worry about that. Serving me earns him esteem at home. He's far from stupid, Peleku. Also . . ." She chuckled. "You know what a young man is. He's getting the itch out of his soul wandering around with me."

"Mmmmph." Peleku pushed up onto his feet. "Then he is free of my camp. If he wishes to speak to me, I will hear him." He chuckled. "Ah, to be young again. . . ."

Jumping up with a laugh, Aleytys tapped his arm with dancing fingers. "Si'a Peleku, you'll be young when your ashes float from the pyre."

He shook his head, a rueful grimace pulling his heavy features together. "The flesh. Ah, the flesh, si'a Lahela. The day comes when the body pants along far behind the spirit." He stood up. "Will you wait here a minute, please?" He swung into the caravan and seconds later came out again, a bag made of green-dyed suede dangling from his hand.

"Hoakne Hekili ate today. She doesn't hurt any more. There's no real way we can pay for your gift, so I don't try, but we of clan Fox will be honored if you accept this poaku."

"I am the one honored." She took the bag. Nodding gravely she left without another word, respecting his dignity by giving him her most formal courtesy.

The afternoon crept slowly past as the endless line of the curious came to her for a reading or healing. She promised more exciting futures, removed more warts and moles, straightened a crooked nose that had secretly tormented a girl, cured rickets in a badly fed baby, grew enamel over cavities, straightened crooked bones, did a hundred different minor magics that sent her clients off in a haze of joyful awe.

After supper, Maissa stood up with a sudden jerking motion that focused all eyes on her. "We talk." She frowned at Loahn. "Not you. The four of us will be there." She nodded at her caravan. "You stand watch out here. Ears shut and eyes open."

Loahn's nostrils twitched. He turned deliberately to Aleytys. "Is that your wish, gikena Lahela?"

"Don't be stupid," Aleytys snapped. "You know who gives orders here. Do it."

He bowed with exaggerated respect. "As you say, si'a gikena."

Aleytys threw up her hands.

In the caravan Maissa stood at the front, eyes on the others. Aleytys sat on the bunk at the left, Kale on the right. Stavver leaned a hip on the bunk behind Aleytys, arms folded across his narrow chest. He carefully avoided touching Aleytys and she knew she was still unforgiven. She felt unhappy amusement as she looked around at the four separate islands of humanity. "We band of brothers," she muttered.

"What?" Maissa pounced on the murmur. "If you've something to say, let us hear it."

"Nothing. It's nothing." She folded her hands, resting them on her thighs.

"Stavver." Maissa's fingernails clicked like hail on the hard wood. "You got all you need? When do you hit?"

He lounged against the back wall, thumbs now thrust behind the worn leather belt. Under his weight the back wall creaked and creaked again as he shifted several times. "The wards and locks are no problem. These Karkiskya depend too much on their orbiting sensor probes. I can walk through their security down here like a ghost. No problem there. But."

"But?"

"I have to get inside, take a look around." He shrugged and the wood creaked again. "I think I know where they keep the stones, Kale's report was clear enough and fit with the readings, but putting an eye on them would be better."

"And how do you plan to do that?"

Kale lifted his head. "No problem." Stavver and Maissa both turned on him at once, surprise loosening the muscles of their faces so that mouths dropped slightly open, eyes rounded. Aleytys leaned back watching with secret appreciation while the man Maissa treated with contempt both as man and groundling took control of the talk.

"A poaku will get you in." He spread out his hands. "How do you think they do their trading. They damn well don't come out here. Just walk up to the gate and wave a stone under their cowls and you're escorted inside. All the way to the buying room. Right through the showroom where they keep their store of stones. And . . ." He transferred his grin to Aleytys. "You've got a stone right to hand."

Their heads swung to her. She grinned. "My pay, Maissa. Peleku gave it to me after lunch."

Stavver straightened, hair brushing against the lintel. "Then, barring accident, I go in late tomorrow night."

Chapter IV

Sharl kicked his feet and burbled happily in the improvised sling, a strip of batik tied in a knot over Aleytys' left shoulder, crossing her body so that the baby lay snuggled around her right hip. In the glow from the orange sun swimming low in the polychromatic sky, the stark drab buildings looked uglier than ever. She glanced up at Stavver walking coldly silent beside her, his only concession to her presence the curtailment of his long stride to match the scissoring of her shorter legs. "Still mad at me. . . ." she muttered.

Around them the street was beginning to fill with farers, all male. She was the only woman. Stavver speeded up a little and the others politely moved aside to let them pass, eyes flickering between disapproval and respect. Disapproval for a woman invading a male preserve and respect for her status as gikena. She fought off a nervous uneasiness and looked around for Peleku but couldn't find him in the laughing chatting groups of men that formed and reformed as they strolled toward the central building the tallest in the Karkesh quarter.

"Why the hurry?" She put her hand on Stavver's arm, mouth curling up as she felt his muscles twitching in rejection. "I thought we were supposed to lose ourselves in the crowd."

"Don't talk about it now."

"Why? Who could hear?"

"Shut up."

"But . . ."

He glared at her. "Later!"

Aleytys subsided, sighing. She worked her hand into the sling and let Sharl play with her fingers, losing the jar to her self-esteem in the flow of warm tenderness she felt whenever she touched her son.

Stavver stopped before the gate, frowning again as the Lamarchans already in line stepped aside to let the gikena go first. She could feel the suppressed anger in him and saw the muscles in his throat work as he swallowed his annoyance. Then his sense of humor defused the situation. He smiled down at her. "Not much use trying to be inconspicuous, is it?"

She trembled with relief and dredged up a feeble chuckle. "Not much."

Two grey figures swung back the steel grid then stood blocking the way to the roofed passage leading into the building.

Stavver cleared his throat. "I come to trade stone for steel."

"You have poaku?" The figure on the left was the one speaking, his voice a startling basso coming from under the cowl.

"Poaku." Stavver held up the leather bag. "To buy Karkesh blade for my son." He nodded casually toward Aleytys.

"That is woman."

Aleytys sensed the surge of laughter which Stavver instantly suppressed. Face a grave mask, he said, "Your eyes are sharp, sho Karsk."

Resisting an impulse to jab her elbow in Stavver's ribs, Aleytys lifted Sharl from the sling. "His son," she said briefly. The Karsk nodded, the edges of his cowl flapping around the inky darkness that obscured whatever he had for a face. When she settled the baby back into the sling, he pressed a button and stepped aside. A third billowing grey figure slid through an opening in the wall and beckoned to them. As she followed Stavver into the building she heard a male voice say behind them, "I come to trade stone for steel."

Their guide rested a gloved thumb on a button. The heavy door blocking the way slid silently back into a wall at least a meter thick. Stavver smiled down at her worried face and shook his head.

The corridor narrowed so that there was room—barely room—for one. Stavver's none too broad shoulders nearly brushed both sides. Aleytys trotted along behind him feeling like a parasite in some great stone animal's intestine. She hugged the sling in front of her, afraid that Sharl's head would knock against the wall. There was no visible lighting but on the other hand no lack of light. Aleytys dismissed the phenomenon with a shrug and wrinkled her nose at the hideous muddy brown color of the walls.

Without any warning Stavver came to a stop. Aleytys stumbled into him, waking Sharl who whimpered then yelled out his fear and annoyance. As she lifted him to her shoulder and tried to quiet him, the Karsk touched the back of a heavy glove to a touchplate. He stepped through the sudden opening with Stavver close behind him. Humming gently to the subsiding baby, Aleytys was in the room before she noticed the change in the space around her. The echoing boom of her feet startled her, brought her eyes swinging up.

The room leaped to a vaulted ceiling so high it was lost in the curious weaving of light and shadow that struck her suddenly as a deliberately structured thing, an unexpected form of art from creatures ostentatiously lacking in aesthetics. Set in niches and on pedestals, numberless poakus glimmered like stone silk: Topaz and vermilion . . . turquoise . . . ebony . . . viridian . . . umber . . . forms a delight to the eye, seductively alluring to the touch.

Aleytys glanced at the leather sack swinging from Stavver's left hand and suddenly felt an intense possessiveness about her poaku. She wanted to snatch the stone and run from the building, run, escape, clutch the poaku to her breast and run.

Sternly repressing this insanity she followed Stavver, holding Sharl tight against her breasts instead.

Through an arched opening in the far side of the echoing room, the silent procession stepped into another rounded ugly corridor. A few paces on the Karsk stopped again and keyed open a door. He stepped back. "Enter, please."

Stavver frowned. "What waits?"

Patiently the Karsk repeated his words. "Enter please. The buyer waits."

Ignoring Aleytys with proper male pride, Stavver strode into the small room, one hand on his own knife hilt. Aleytys stepped through behind him, head held high in consciousness of her dignity as gikena. After Stavver was settled in the seller's chair, she seated herself on a shelf jutting out from a side wall. She settled Sharl comfortably on her lap, moved the batik off his face, and swung her eyes from face to cowl as the bargaining began.

The Karsk sat silent, waiting, gloved hands tucked into the wide sleeves of his robe.

"I come to trade stone for steel." Stavver sat on the edge of the chair, spine very straight, eyes boring into the darkness under the droopy cowl. The bag with the poaku he held on his lap, one long fingered hand cupped protectively around it.

The Karsk bowed his head. Pushing his chair back, he pulled a leather box from somewhere behind the desk and settled it gently and precisely on the flat surface in front of him. Fingers moving surely in spite of the muffling thickness of the gloves, he flipped the catches open and swung the lid up. As he slid the box around a light bloomed overhead, caressing the polished blades snugged in neat rows in the lid and base. Stavver leaned forward, sucking in his breath, then he relaxed in the chair.

Aleytys struggled to maintain her gravity as she watched Stavver operate, appreciating the gently underplayed portrayal of a shrewd but nervous native. Sharl's small body lay across her knees sending a warmth into her that disarmed her own wariness, distracted her so that she gave less than full attention to the scene before her. She bent over him. He was going to wake soon. Hungry. She sighed and hoped he'd wait until they were back in camp.

Stavver set the bag with the poaku on the desk and

reached into the box, pulling free the blades one by one. He turned each over in his hands, testing feel and balance until he set all but three aside. Then he thrust his hand into the pouch and slid the poaku out. Hands moving as precisely as the Karsk's, he set the green stone on the desk, the carved side toward the buyer. "Stone for steel," he said brusquely.

"As custom." The answer was short and sharp. "One stone, one blade."

Stavver nodded briefly. He swept up the three blades and was on his feet with sufficient suddenness to startle the Karsk into jerking back. Ignoring this he ceremoniously presented the knives to the baby, holding them above him one by one. Sharl slept peacefully. "Wake the boy," he said coolly, his mouth tucked in to keep in laughter, his eyes twinkling at her.

Aleytys fried him with a glance but after a minute shook Sharl gently awake. The baby blinked up at the shining things, his long curling lashes moving slowly up and down over wide green-grey eyes. Aleytys shivered but kept her face blank as he chewed on his fist, ignoring the first two of the knives Stavver held over his head. When the third knife appeared over him, Sharl kicked against Aleytys' ribs and reached for the shining thing.

Aleytys gasped and pulled him away from the blade, shutting her lips firmly over the river of things she wanted to say to Stavver.

The thief grunted with satisfaction. The first two knives he pushed away. The chosen he set gently in the center of the desk beside the poaku, hilt toward the Karsk. "Stone for steel, sho Karsk."

The grey figure ran gloved thumbs over the carving. "It's a new stone." The tone was gently disparaging as if the buyer refrained from sneering only under the urging of courtesy.

Stavver bowed, grave-faced. He turned the knife so that the point faced the Karsk and gently removed the stone from his fingers. "My regrets, sho Karsk, for wasting your time."

"Man of the falcons."

"Yes?" Stavver half turned, standing poised in the doorway. "My eyes grow old. Perhaps . . ." The narrow, subtly-wrong hand reached smoothly out, waiting.

Stavver hesitated. "If the stone is not worthy . . ."

"You have an extraordinary son to be so young a judge of a fine blade."

"Perhaps if the light were stronger. . . ." Stavver walked back to the desk and placed the stone in the reaching hand. But he did not sit down.

"Although it is new stone, the design is quite attractive. The work is skilled." The gloved fingers slid facilely over the polished contours. "Steel for stone?"

"As you say." Stavver picked up the knife. "There is wrapping?"

"As you say." The Karsk dipped a hand beneath the desk top and pulled a square of fine soft leather from a hidden niche.

Silently Stavver wrapped the knife in the leather, then thrust the bundle under his belt. Once again he inclined his head. "That bargain is best when both are pleased."

"As you say." The Karsk closed the box and replaced it out of sight. In the process he must have pressed a summoning button because another silent grey figure appeared in the open archway. Folding his hands on the bare surface of the desk, the buyer said, "May you be blessed with many sons."

Stavver drew himself stiffly to his full height. "May your children be as leaves on a tree." He beckoned to Aleytys and stalked from the room.

In the street outside they walked past the ragged line of Lamarchan farers waiting to trade for their Karkesh blades. Halfway back to the camping ground a familiar imp face grinned at them.

"Hakea." Aleytys stopped beside him. "Going for your blade this morning?"

"Yes." He darted a grin around and pranced excitedly on the spot, too full of bubbles to stand still.

"The morning has been good to you, si'a gikena?" Peleku smiled at her, then frowned down at his son. "Your manners, young huale."

"Very good, my friend." She glanced at Stavver strolling on toward the camp. Patting the sling, she said, "My son, young as he is, now has his own blade to be put aside for the time of his blooding. Thanks to you."

"Isn't it a bit early. He should make his own choice."

"He has made it. My son's no ordinary baby. Besides, I

don't know when I'll be back this side of the world.
Lakoe-heai often take my feet in strange paths." She
glanced after Stavver again. "I'd better get on my way.
Good bargaining, my friend."

She caught up with Stavver as he sauntered through the
archway into the campground. "Did you see enough?"

"No."

"No?"

"It'll do." He chuckled and ruffled his hand through her
hair. "There's never enough to make a strike foolproof."

"Greedy." She shifted Sharl to her other side and took
his arm. "Then it's tonight."

"Talk about something else."

"Well . . . why do those eerie characters creep around
through . . . through wormholes like that?" She shivered.

"Apparently they're innate agoraphobes."

"Huh?"

"Afraid of open spaces." He freed his arm and dropped
it around her shoulders, pulling her against him as they
walked together toward the caravan. "In a way, that's a
blessing for this world. Keeps the scaly foot off the Lamarchan neck."

"Hm. What are you going to do the rest of the day?"

"Sleep."

"Just sleep?"

He chuckled and held her against him. She could feel
his ribs shifting. "Well, maybe not all afternoon."

Chapter V

"Ah." Aleytys touched the palm with the tips of her fingers. "I see a time of change coming for you. A time
when you stand ready to make a choice."

The girl bounced excitedly on her knees as she bent her
dark head over her palm. "Makaoi. You see him? Will he
ask my father . . . ?"

Aleytys slanted a glance at her suppressing a smile. "It
may be so. However the scales balance very evenly here.
See this line. It branches here going both right and left. A

change comes in your life soon, a point where you balance between joy and sorrow. And see here, the promise of sons." Once again Aleytys tapped the palm, fingers pattering lightly across the plump flesh. "There is another thing."

The girl sucked in her breath. "Ay, gikena, what is it? What is it?"

"See the jag in the line here. A sorrow comes. For a little while there will be a strong unhappiness. But it will end and your life runs smoothly thereafter. As all things pass, so will this time of pain." Gravely she closed the small hand into a fist. "That is all." She pulled her hands away and rested them on her knees, eyes lowered in dismissal.

After bowing so deeply her head nearly touched her knees the girl jumped to her feet and ran away, staring intently at her hand.

Aleytys granced briefly at the patient figures sitting cross-legged waiting their turn with the placidity of a people who regulated their time by the changing of the seasons rather than the petulant ticking of clocks. She sighed. "Leyilli?"

"Si'a gikena?" Maissa bent over her solicitously, her pointed face smoothed into a bland courtesy.

"I'm tired of this stupidity."

Maissa bent lower until her breath brushed against Aleytys' hair. "Don't be foolish. Don't change the pattern this day of all days."

Aleytys' hands clenched briefly into fists then opened. She smoothed them down over the batik, then slapped them onto her knees. Without a further word she surged onto her feet and walked without haste toward her caravan. Maissa swallowed her anger but her throat was too constricted for speech so she snatched up the leather with the pillow caught in the folds and followed Aleytys into the caravan.

Stavver lay stretched on the bunk, deeply asleep, his body relaxed as a cat's. On the other side of the narrow space, Sharl snuffled peacefully in his morning nap. Aleytys touched the curls on her baby's neck, then stepped a single step away and looked fondly at the other sleeper. His black hair still confused her image of him though she was gradually getting used to it. She let her fingers flicker

over his head barely disturbing the fine hair, then stroked
the wispy curls beside his ears feeling a gentle tenderness
suffuse her and she wondered what it would be like just to
stay with him, to forget about. . . .

Maissa slapped the curtains aside and hurled the leather
to the floor. When Aleytys turned a startled face to her,
she hissed, "What do you think you're doing? You want to
ruin everything? Get back out there."

Stavver stirred restlessly but didn't wake. Aleytys settled
onto the bunk beside him, her hip fitting into the curve
under his ribs. "If you wake him up, he won't like it."

Maissa coiled her small hands into claws. "Ignorant
ground-walking shit. Don't you know anything? I can't believe you'd break pattern the day he goes in? Begging for
those fucking snakes to spot the anomaly and rope us in?"

"Pooh!"

Maissa gaped, unable to believe what she heard.

"Nonsense." Aleytys chuckled. "Relax. Pattern? Tchah.
These people know I'm gikena. Whatever I do, that's my
pattern. Ahai, Maissa, relax before it's you who blows the
cover."

Maissa glared at her, then stamped out of the caravan,
her nerves strung so taut that her body seemed to jerk
even when she stood still. Aleytys slid off the bunk and
leaned out the back watching her go. Then she sighed and
slid the heavy curtains shut. As the rings clattered along
the rod Stavver grunted in his sleep, shifted position
slightly, bringing Aleytys to hover over him. But his
breathing steadied. She sighed, ruffled Sharl's hair. He
murmured in his sleep, then his breathing was soft and
slow again. "What stimulating company you are, my
loves."

She stretched out on the mattress so that she lay staring
up at the painted ceiling, her hands clasped behind her
head. Working through the exercises that relaxed her body
and mind, she sank into the deep semi-trance that let her
touch the creeping tendrils of the diadem's influence. The
hazy uncertain presence grew aware of her.

"I greet you, rider in my head." She let the words flow
slowly smoothly across the tranquil surface in her mind,
surface like a deep black pool, cool and placid, unchanging and remote. Shimmering in the water ghost images of
amber eyes opened, then faded, opened again and faded

once more. Frustration tingled through her. The black water surface shattered. Tension hardened the muscles in her neck. Carefully she quieted her pulses, letting the black pool form again.

"Don't do that." She let little trills of laughter like pink and curling ribbons frame the creeping words. "I need your help." The words flowed off leaving the water tranquil again. Amber light flared and vanished. "Good." For a hundred slow heartbeats she rested silent, holding her body rhythms slow and deep until the air, the earth, the whole Lamarchos throbbed in union with her.

"I need you." On the mirror surface of the black water pool the words drifted momentarily then dissipated. The amber light came back. With it, on the edge of her consciousness, came the dim perception of a feeling of curiosity. "Stavver goes into danger tonight. I feel that if it weren't for me he'd have got himself out of this mess long ago." She rested again, lying on the swelling breast of the world. "I want to go in with him, but only if I can be of help. That thing you do when you stop the world . . . if we get into a mess could you do that for us? Both of us?"

She waited. After a time while she listened with all her being, the amber light flared briefly and she felt a distant sense of acquiescence, like a yes whispered into the face of a storm. "Madar bless, Rider. There's another thought I had." Again she gave the words time to sink. A ripple of curiosity flittered around the corners of her mind. "Yes. I know so little about you. Could you warn us if one of the Karkiskya is coming? Or if we were heading into some kind of trouble?" She hesitated, coming up a little out of the trance state as she struggled to phrase the query so that she could wring some kind of meaningful answer out of the fragmentary impressions that constituted the only means of contact she had with the diadem. "Could you warn me—somehow—if someone was coming?"

As she lay holding her senses open to the faintest of twinges, feeling the slow thud of the muscle clenching and unclenching in her chest grow even slower . . . she felt the pulses, counted them, one hundred . . . two hundred . . . a shock of fear jolted her body upright until she was standing beside the bed trembling and disoriented. "Ahai Madar!" she gasped.

Sharl lay on his back playing happily with his toes totally entertained by the feel of his own fascinating self. She looked across at Stavver. He was flaccid with sleep, the discipline of his craft strong enough to overcome all the disturbances around him. He slept each time before he worked the night. He slept, allowing nothing without or within to interrupt this time of blankness that honed body and mind for the intense effort ahead when his senses would be stretched to their widest outreach. She sighed and lay back on the mattress. When her body had slowed to trance she murmured into the silence of her head, "You really pulled strings that time, Rider. I take it you can warn me if some inconvenient insomniac wandering around is liable to stumble over us."

Feeling of amusement and agreement.

"Good. And . . . um . . . a small twinge, please. The halls in that place don't have room for more. I'd bust my head."

A brief flash of humor pricked like insect feet across her brain.

"I suppose I'd better leave it at that. If you'll stay ready to pull us out of swampy spots."

Feeling of acquiescence.

"And warn me if guards or other night ramblers are coming up on us."

Flash of amber. Acquiescence.

"Funny. It's easier to talk with you this time, Rider. Maybe, given a little more time and practice. . . ." She sighed. "Never mind. Leave that till later. Ah. . . ." She sucked in a deep breath, then pushed herself up until she was leaning against the wall. Her head ached until she sent the pain away. She closed her eyes and built a mandala in her head.

For the next hour she sat in meditation, passing slowly through the mandalas Vajd had given her. Slowly, slowly, the great circles revolved before her, bringing comfort and tranquility into her uncertainty.

A hand touched her shoulder. She looked up, moving her head with slow reluctance, to see Stavver's anxious face swimming over her. Her mouth stretched into a smile, then drooped as she forgot to hold the corners up. His voice sounded harsh against her ears. Distant. As if he spoke through wads of cotton. "Wake up, Leyta. Time to eat."

Aleytys rocked gently from side to side, breaking herself out of the stillness. "I think I went too deep."

Stavver shook his head. "It's beyond me." He stretched and yawned. "Fix me some tea, will you? I need to wash the fog out."

"Yes, master, certainly, master, anything at all, master." Her grin faded. "Miks." He was at the door, his hand on the curtain. "Wait a minute before you go out."

He leaned against the back wall, smiling sleepily at her. "What is it?"

"Sit down. Please." She waited until he dropped onto the bunk, his face twisting into an amused somewhat impatient scowl. "I'm going with you tonight."

"No."

"Miks, I'd keep out if I didn't think I could help. No. Hear me out. I've got in touch—in a way—with the diadem. Look. You say you're the best. Maissa says you're the best and she doesn't like you. But any thief can find himself in a tight place even if he is the best. You've seen what the diadem can do. There's more. It warns. You're going in late when all sensible beings are asleep, but how can you control the actions of the Karkiskya. Or there might be guards in the halls. I don't know, you may have instruments that could do the same for you, Miks, but should you reject this extra edge? You told me always learn as much as you can even if you don't need the knowledge. Isn't this the same thing?" She dropped her hands in her lap and waited for his response.

Stavver sat frowning, eyes focused somewhere beyond her. After a minute he blinked. "You feel a strong need to go?"

"Yes."

He straightened the curve in his spine, rubbed the tip of his long nose. "You haven't shown any sign of clairvoyance before."

"What's that?"

"Never mind." He pushed off the bunk and stood looming over her, staring intently into her face. "Do you ever find yourself developing new talents?"

"I don't know." She ran her hands through her hair, then reached out and took hold of his arms. "What's it matter now? I haven't thought about it. Do I go with you, Miks?"

"You come. Keep your mouth shut and don't do anything unless I tell you to."

"I won't mess things up, Miks."

He ruffled her hair, grinning affectionately at her. "Good. Now, woman, remember your promise. Fix your master some tea."

She bowed until her hair tickled her knees. "Yes, wise and honored master, full of . . . um . . . extraordinariness beyond description."

Chapter VI

A fugitive breeze fluttered the worm-eaten leaves sending a rain of powdery dust over Aleytys. She sneezed and wrinkled her nose then followed sounds of laughter down slope to the stream.

Loahn and Puki stood talking animatedly beside two strings of horses obviously having timed their arrivals so they would meet. While the horses sucked greedily at the sluggishly flowing water the two young Lamarchans stood very close but not touching. Aleytys scratched Olelo's stomach. Looks like he's serious about this one. She smiled, feeling a gentle surge of affection for the boy. Then he turned and saw her.

"Si'a gikena?"

"Good evening, Loahn, Puki." She glanced up at the darkening sky and shivered, nerves tightening as she remembered what was to come. "Loahn, leave the horses with Puki. I have to talk with you." She set Olelo on the ground and pushed him toward the girl. "Keep watch for us, little one."

The speaker sat up on his haunches and regarded her with a suspicious gleam in his black eyes. Then he flipped onto all fours and trotted briskly to Puki.

With a quick nod, Loahn tossed the lead rope to the girl. "They've had about all they need. Take the team to Kale when they're done."

She ducked her head and watched unhappily, radiating

a confusing queasy blend of fear and jealousy, as Loahn walked apart with Aleytys.

Breaking through the flimsy line of spindly low-growing brush, Aleytys came to a backless wooden bench. She turned and waited for Loahn.

"What is it, Lahela?" She could hear the concern in his voice. He wasn't worried yet, simply disturbed that she should call him apart this way. She brushed at the dust and leafy debris on the heavy plank seat, then dropped down facing him.

Rubbing at her forehead, she stared past him at the muddy water. "Poor Puki, she didn't like your going off with me."

"You didn't call me to talk about the demoiselle." The archaic term of respect for an unmarried girl was a deliberately unemphatic refusal to discuss his relationship with Puki. "What do you want?"

"Sit down." When he was sitting stiffly beside her, she went on. "You know why we're here. We hit tonight. I want you to stay with the baby. I don't trust Maissa with him and I can't leave him alone that long. Kale . . ." She shrugged. "He'll be at watch."

His head jerked up. "You?"

She laughed, the brief low sound almost lost in the increasing rustle of the leaves overhead. "I'm a thief as much as any of the others, Loahn. I can't let him go in alone." The silence between them thickened. Aleytys rubbed her thumbs over the folds of the cloth where it bent with her body, feeling through her preoccupation the smooth movement of the coarse weave over the skin of her thighs. Abruptly she broke the silence. "I saw your face when Firstman gave you back that knife." She bent forward and flicked the hilt with her forefinger, feeling him shudder with a kind of dread.

"Without it I'm not a man," he said simply.

"That I can't believe. You were very much man with me the night after we found you on trail."

"The blade was mine again as soon as you lifted curse; there only remained the actual body return." He shrugged, stroked the smooth worn hilt with loving fingers, touching it with the familiar affection and ease of a long accustomed lover. "The Karkesh blade cut my foreskin at my blooding, drank the dark blood that ran warm from the center of my being."

"Ummmm. What if a man has sons but nothing to buy the steel?"

Loahn shuddered again. "Never. Don't say such a thing." He stared at his toes as they dug into the dampish earth and flung tiny clods into brief flight. "Why do you ask such things?"

"What if Karkys vanished?"

"You?"

"I don't know?"

"Why?" His thumb caressed the colored stones set into the hilt moving up and down over the smooth surfaces.

"Lakoe-heai set me four things to do. The second was to curse Karkys and drive the off-worlders away." She pinched her lips together and clasped her arms over her breasts, running shaking hands over her biceps, fumbling toward the only certainty she knew, the solid reassuring feel of her own flesh. "Ahai, Loahn, I don't pretend to know the rights and wrongs of this. It seems to me the Karkiskya do no real harm here. You've made them part of your lives, an important part. This is your world. Tell me what to do."

"Me!" The boy looked shattered.

Overhead the sky darkened, the ever-present sworls of color tightening against the approach of night into amorphous lumps that drifted above the earth like thunderheads. Hidden by the thin screen of brush they heard Puki urge the two teams out of the water and lead them away. Loahn rubbed a hand over his inch long stubble. "No Karkys. . . ." He muttered. "Why?"

Aleytys wrapped her fingers about his leg just above the knee, feeling the tension that hardened his muscles. "Could be the Lakoe-heai are jealous. The Karkiskya don't recognize them. It sounds foolish . . . to destroy so much for an itch in the vanity. I don't know. The Karkiskya are cheating you, do you know that?"

"Cheating us?" He swung around to face her. "How?"

"Keon says the poaku you trade for your blades bring many many times the worth of a knife off-world."

His mouth twisted into a one-sided smile. "And how would we get the poaku off-world? Why should we try? A bargain is a good one if both parties are satisfied. If you drive the Karkiskya off, how will boys know they're men?" His head moved slowly away from her toward the ugly towers that rose above the tree tops. "They've been here a long time . . . a long time. No one remembers when there was no Karkys." The lines deepened in his thin face, aging him suddenly beyond his twenty years. "If the Lakoe-heai demand it. . . ."

"I don't have to do it."

"They'll make you." He licked his lips. "They're a nasty lot to tangle with."

"I could talk with them. If they realized they were wrecking their own people. . . ."

"Their own people! You don't think they really give a damn about us, do you?" He spread out his hands. "I know it sounds funny for me to say that after what they did for me. It's caprice, Lahela. Why they do things is beyond . . ." He tapped his forehead with his forefinger. "Beyond the working of our minds." He jumped up and prowled back and forth in front of her. "That's how we live, Lahela, waiting for the dice to roll. Most of the time, though they leave us alone. For which we give thanks."

Aleytys stood. "I can't do it, Loahn." She walked around the bench and stopped with her hand on the dusty bark of the tree's trunk. "The Karkiskya, this city. They're both important to people. If I curse the city who would come here?"

"No one." He glanced up again at the towers. "Gikena says, we do."

"Dammit, I won't be driven. No." She kicked at the dirt and flung her head back defiantly. "I won't do it."

He caught her hand and held it against his face, saying nothing.

"Loahn. Tonight. Come in the caravan with us; it'll be well into the night before we leave and I don't want to have to hunt you in the dark."

He nodded. "Lahela?"

"What is it?" She rested the fingers of her free hand against the trunk, once again reaching out for security to solid physical things.

"You're totally committed to that man?"

She felt a lurch in the beat of her heart, a knotting around her stomach. "Totally? Why?"

"Puki."

She freed herself and moved away from him. "Yes," she said quietly. "I'm committed to him." Then she smiled and shook her head. "I'd never make it as a woman on this world, Loahn. You'd be wanting to strangle me before the leaves turned."

His cool skeptical eyes went flickering over her slender body. Then he shrugged. "Maybe so."

Chapter VII

Stavver thumbed a stud on his belt, waking a circle of light that spread out under his feet. In the chameleon web he was a faint flicker in the deep shadow under the wall, hands and face floating in mid-air, the mooncream absorbing light until even these were reduced to vague blurs. A hand blur gestured impatiently.

With considerable trepidation Aleytys stepped onto the light circle. It shuddered under her bare feet like something alive, sending tremors of distaste shivering up her legs. She clasped her arms around him and pressed herself against him. Under her entwined fingers she felt silent laughter vibrating in his chest.

Riding the pale circle they drifted up over the wall then skimmed along the facade of the building. Stavver stopped the ascent beside a narrow window sealed with a thick block of clear material that somehow didn't look like glass to Aleytys. Didn't feel like glass either when she reached out an exploratory finger. She withdrew her hand and clung to him as he ran the softly buzzing tool in quick swooping sweeps back and forth across the plug. The clear material glowed sickly yellow then began to flow sluggishly in a messy dribble down the stone.

When the embrasure was clear Stavver moved the circle of light up until his feet were on a level with the sill. Then he maneuvered them inside. They floated near the floor with a tidy economy of motion. A hand's breadth above the dull rubber matting he tapped the stud on his belt. They fell the short distance to the floor, Stavver sagging slightly, Aleytys stumbling, falling to her knees.

The corridor outside the room was barely wide enough to accommodate Stavver's body, waking a claustrophobic shudder in Aleytys. The thief turned to the left and moved swiftly, intently along, ignoring her.

. . . . Tread the obscenely warm . . . obscenely soft . . . rubberoid flooring . . . like walking the intestines of a worm . . . coil round and round in a downward spiraling helix . . . terror . . . growing slowly, slowly more intense . . . her breathing quickened, sweat blurred her eyes, there was a tight constricted feeling around her chest. . . .

At each branching of the worm hole, Stavver hesitated, glanced at the dial face nestled in his palm, then moved forward, following the pointer.

. . . . Down and down . . . an eternity . . . boring . . . boring . . . boring. . . nausea surged sourly into her mouth as fear churned the juices of her stomach . . . better, a thousand times better, to walk the fields in the sunlight doing the hard unending labor of a farmer . . . what am I doing this for? Why am I here? Mother . . . phah . . . Shareem of Vrithian. . . . Madar, what made me think that stupid capricious female would find a place for me . . . Loahn wants me . . . no. . . .

No, another voice whispered to her, he wants your power. He's greedy for the respect of his own, having suffered their spite so many years. Do you really think you could spend the rest of your life . . . the rest of my life . . . how long will that be . . . how long. . . . The Vrya live long long . . . how long could Loahn tolerate an unaging wife . . . what would he do when he doddered about a white bearded elder with a wife who looked like his grandchild . . . could any man endure that . . . maybe that's why she said we never have complete relationships . . . maybe . . . grandchild. . . . do I want more children. . . . I love Sharl . . . god, he's the one thing I can love . . . I don't want another baby . . . how many years until he's old enough to be on his own. . . .

Amber light flared behind her eyes triggering a spurt of fear. She jerked to a halt. Ahead the corridor split into three branches . . . a brief image like a figure illumined by lightning . . . a hooded Karsk coming swiftly down the righthand passage. She blinked, startled, then touched

Stavver's arm, feeling him flinch from her touch. He's forgotten I'm here, she thought.

His eyes were hard and impatient.

"One comes. There." She flicked a finger at the passage.

Moving tautly, Stavver slid into the side passage. He
pushed her behind him then crouched against the wall,
facing the main corridor and nearly invisible in the web
suiting. The hooded Karsk glided bonelessly past, radiating
a calm heedless security, totally unaware of the intruders
in his territory. When the sliding slap slap of the narrow
feet died away, Stavver twisted his torso around to face
her, eyebrow raised in interrogation.

Aleytys nodded. "Not the slightest notion," she whispered.

Once again they wound downward through the too-con-
stricting passages until Aleytys wanted to scream and claw
her way out of the entrails of the beast building. Then,
where the corridor stretched empty and straight, the amber
light flared again. She swung her head searching for a corner to conceal them but there was nothing, not even a
doorway. The walls were pinkish grey and rubbery and
terrifyingly unbroken. She touched Stavver again. "One
comes."

"How close?" Stavver slipped a short black rod from a
pocket in his belt. Aleytys sensed it was a weapon and
shuddered at the thought of seeing a being killed. She
closed her eyes. "There. Where the corridor turns. About a
half-minute beyond."

Swiftly, silently, Stavver ran over the matting then
crouched at the point where the curve turned most tightly.
Aleytys fingered the rubbery walls drowning her fear in an
active resentment of this coiling curving wormhole without
any straight lines—even the place where the flooring met
the walls was a gentle curve. She raised both hands and
touched her temples. In flashing disturbing vignettes she
saw the Karsk come closer and closer. Sick and shaking
with the emotions clawing at her, she clutched at her head.
She heard the soft shuffle of the alien feet then a tingling
chill shuddered through her drowning out the fear. The diadem chimed softly. "Miks."

"Shut up," he hissed.

She ignored that. "Be ready to move."

The sliding footsteps were nearer. They heard a senile

muttering. Then the diadem chimed a second time and the
sound plunged down to a subsonic itch. Aleytys shoved at
Stavver, pushing him ahead of her. He was pliable enough
but seemed to have lost any spark of intelligent control
over his body. Struggling with the awkward flesh puppet
she maneuvered him around the curve past the bent frozen
shape of the old Karsk. The air was thick, gelatinous. It
was hard to breathe, hard to think, but she fought down
the new burden, an unwanted addition to the fear and
claustrophobia she already suffered.

Breath sobbing painfully in her ears, she pushed and
tugged Stavver's shambling body past the bent, grey
ghost-figure. Then she turned to see if the old one was balanced properly. If he fell when the spell lifted. . . .
Whimpering and miserable, she fought around the second
curve then propped Stavver against the wall while she
tried to catch her breath and listened to the diadem sing
time back to reality.

Stavver stepped away from the wall, shaking his head,
still dazed from his plunge into stasis. Then, abruptly, he
was the predator again. He slid to the curve and peered
around to see the slobbering old Karsk go muttering
unconcernedly off, having noticed nothing at all. He
turned, touched Aleytys on the arm and pointed on down
the corridor. "What's ahead?" He whispered the words as
he slid past her.

"The way's open ahead."

On the ground floor Stavver knelt before the massive
door leading to the showroom. Unclipping the compact
bundle from his belt, he unrolled the tool kit, spreading
the soft black material like a splash of ink on the floor, the
bright metallic surface of the tools shimmering amid the
darkness.

As Aleytys watched, calmer now, his fingers played over
the pockets, plucking things from their places with a swift
efficiency that obscurely pleased her. She leaned against
the wall while he constructed a spindly thing whose working was incomprehensible to her but whose purpose became immediately apparent as the door slid silently open.
Resenting her ignorance, she transferred that resentment
momentarily to the thief calmly getting on with his
business. Then her sense of the ridiculous reasserted itself
and she stifled a giggle.

Folding the instrument roll into a tight bundle, Stavver hitched it to his belt again. For the first time in minutes he acknowledged her presence, jerking his head toward the opening. Disgust etched lines in his face. He murmured. "Not even a soundplate inside there. A baby could crawl in and take what it pleased."

"Not worthy of you, Miks?"

He tugged at a lock of her hair, grinning at her. "Come on." He reached inside the web suit and pulled out a pair of thin elastic bags, then packs of spongy tissues. "Be sure you wrap each stone before you bag it. A chip would cut the value in half."

After a while Aleytys hefted the bag. "Miks."

"What?"

"One more rock and I can't lift this." She hauled at the bulging sack. "Can that gadget of yours handle the extra weight?"

He nodded, a brief angular movement of his head. "Rest a minute, Leyta. You're feeling better about all this, aren't you."

Startled at his perception, she let the bag sink onto the floor and followed it down to sit with her arms wrapped about her legs, watching him as he stripped the shelves. After the wash of emotions that had scoured across her psyche she felt an overwhelming desire to sleep.

"Leyta. On your feet. Time to get out of here."

"Back the way we came?"

"Right."

Sighing, she pushed herself onto her knees then onto her feet. With a groan of distaste she eased the strap of her bag onto her shoulder and straightened her back. "All the way up there?"

"Unless you want to wait for the Karkiskya to open up in the morning."

"Huh!"

Chapter VIII

Aleytys settled the bottom of the sack on the bunk, sliding the strap off her shoulder with a sigh of relief. Rubbing gently at the red pressure mark it left in her skin she backed away and watched Maissa dig greedily into the opening, pulling out one poaku after another. Stavver set his sack beside the first then settled beside Aleytys on the end of the opposite bunk, a hard, sardonic smile tightening the muscles of his narrow face.

Cooing over the carved stones, most of them little larger than the palm of her hand, Maissa inspected them then passed them on to Kale who rewrapped them and stowed them neatly away in the Vryhh box concealed beneath the driver's seat.

After a minute Stavver stirred, his body brushing against Aleytys. "We've paid passage."

Maissa looked up, fingers still moving over a pale green poaku. She pulled her shoulders down in a noncommittal shrug, eyes glinting with a harsh scornful light. "All right. You have."

"More than paid. Agreed?"

She frowned. "What's this?"

"I want to have it clear. Your word, Maissa. You know I'm a hard man to keep bound so that's something you won't break. I want your word you'll take us to I!kwasset."

"Or—" She pulled herself up onto the bunk beside the bag.

"No threats. Either way." Stavver tapped long fingers lightly on his knee. Her eyes flicked to the movement then away, a tic jerking beside her mouth as her precariously controlled nerves screamed in protest. She swung around and hunched over, burying her face in her hands. Aleytys saw her shoulders shake, heard her ragged breathing, then Maissa swung around to face them again, smiling, eyes brilliant, mocking.

Stavver watched, his own face bland and noncommittal.

"No passage, no stones. Is that it, Stavver?"

"That's about it."

She looked down, saw the sea-green poaku she'd dropped glowing softly in the point lamps tacked above the bunk. Her fingers closed protectively about the stone. "All right. My word. If you're at the ship when I'm ready to leave, I take you to Ilkwasset. See you keep up with me on our way out."

Aleytys felt a falseness in her; she bit her lip and glanced up at Stavver. He nodded shortly, unwilling to press further and push the unstable woman into a screaming tantrum. "We'll be there, captain. Believe me."

Maissa shrugged and passed the poaku to Kale.

Kale sat on the floor at the front of the caravan almost lost in the shadows. Aleytys watched him, disturbed by the way he handled the poaku, touching them with a jealous possessiveness. After a minute she shook off the chill. Trust Maissa to keep her greedy fingers on her prize. A soft exclamation swung her eyes back to the slight figure sitting on one foot.

Maissa held up one of the larger poaku. It's warm amber-veined russet gleamed with a silken glow in the harsh illumination. The deep relief was a hawk in mid-swoop, carved with such skill it took advantage of the shading in the stone to suggest the varying coloration of the hawk feathers. The lines of the figure were simple, the simplicity of great genius, each curve eloquent of life, the whole breathing its age, breathing its ancient magic into the air around it. Maissa's face flushed dusky red, her tongue licked daintily around her lips as if she was about to eat the stone in the excess of her greed. Reluctantly she handed it to Kale and reached in the sack for the next.

Aleytys sighed with relief. It seemed a sacrilege that Maissa's bloodstained hands should caress such beauty. Then she remembered the age and lure of the stone. Such things swim in blood through the ages coveted by greedy men willing to do anything to possess them. She glanced at Kale, wondering how he'd feel about this one.

He was running trembling fingers over the hawk's tense body, breath sobbing in his excitement. The stone meant something special to him, something more than all the others . . . talk of being willing to kill for. . . . She shifted against Stavver, the feel of him against her bringing a

measure of comfort. He smiled down at her, rested his
hand on her shoulder, making a pool of warmth against
her neck.

As Kale rewrapped the poaku and thrust it in the box
with sweaty face and trembling hands, Stavver slid off the
bunk and began stripping away his working outfit, tools
and web suit. Taking his batik and belt from the drawer
beneath the bunk, he dressed himself back into the role of
Keon. Then he tucked the web inside the tool pack and
tied the roll shut. "Kale."

The Lamarchan jerked nervously, nearly dropping the
poaku he was pushing into the box. "What?"

"Shove this in there before some nervous Karsk picks it
up on his screen."

Without a word Kale caught the bundle. A sheen of
sweat glowed over his skin and his eye-whites glistened intermittently in the light as his eyes jerked nervously
around.

Maissa went rapidly through the rest of the stones, none
of them as fine as the hawk. By the time they were all
packed away she was breathing as hoarsely as Kale, hair
gone stringy from the sweat rolling off her scalp. Her body
jerked, then her breathing steadied and she relaxed. With
the first uncontrived smile Aleytys had ever seen on her,
she nodded at Stavver. "Good work thief. Hah. I need
some tea."

She pulled open the drawer beside her dangling legs. Inside was a small tea set with an automatic heater. "Have a
cup with me?"

Stavver shrugged. Kale straightened painfully, grunting
as his stiffened joints protested. "Good," he muttered.
"There's a chill in the air tonight."

Maissa dipped into the tea cannister and dropped a generous pinch of leaves in each cup. Then she poured the
boiling water over them and handed the steaming cups to
the others, saving the last for herself. With a quick laugh
she raised her cup. "To the Karkiskya who give so nobly."

Kale sniggered, then gulped at his tea. "To the Karkiskya," he muttered.

Aleytys felt an overwhelming tiredness. She sipped
silently at the tea, appreciating the warmth it spread
through her. She leaned against Stavver, feeling her
muscles grow flaccid and trembling with her weariness.

Stavver's face looked more fine-honed than usual, the lines cutting deeper, dragging downwards. "What time is it?"

Maissa's cup clattered as she set it down. She looked at Kale. "Well?"

"Maybe two hours till dawn." He handed his cup to Maissa and yawned. "You going to stay up or try for some sleep?"

"Me, I'm for sleeping if someone'll carry me to my bed." Aleytys set her cup down, feeling a ripple of silliness flutter through her as it tipped on its side, spreading a five-fingered stain on the mattress. She clutched at Stavver. "Thanks for the tea, Maissa."

In their own caravan she sank on the bunk, giggling in small squeaky bursts while she watched Stavver shake Loahn awake.

"How'd it go?" The boy stretched and yawned. "What's wrong with her?"

"She's just tired out, reacting to the strain. Wake us up in a couple of hours."

Loahn frowned. "You sure?"

"Have to be. Look, you can sleep here the rest of the night. Whatever you want." He rested a hip on Aleytys' bunk. "God, I'm tired. Lee, stretch out." He pushed her down and spread the quilt over her. "You'll feel better after a little sleep."

She reached up and pulled him down beside her. "Stay with me, Miks."

"Lee, I'm too tired. And you're nearly unconscious."

"Just stay with me." The last word trailed off into an indistinct mutter as she sank into sleep. Stavver lay beside her and was immediately deep, deep asleep.

Loahn sighed. He worked the quilt from under the long man and spread it over the two of them. The quality of their sleep made him a bit uneasy, then he shrugged and returned to the other bunk.

For a time he lay awake, his brain circling around and around the problem of Aleytys. He looked across the caravan where her face was a pale blur beside the thief's. "La-hela," he muttered. "It's not your name." He shut his eyes, huddled further under the quilt, disturbed about the sight of her curved against that man. Abruptly he turned to face the wall, hugging the quilt about him. After a while he slept.

Chapter IX

A sharp jab of intense pain stabbed through her head. Another followed blasting along the path of the first. Aleytys stirred, dimly aware of a disturbance in her body overlaid by a foreboding that strained the hot sunny day dark with gloom. Clutching at her head, a head throbbing in a hangover worse than the time she'd got into the Azdar's stock of hullu-wine and drunk herself silly at reaping festival one pre-puberty fall, Aleytys sucked in a lungful of air, then regretted it immediately. After a minute she opened her eyes.

Stavver was snoring next to her ear, his face slack in drugged sleep. There was a sourness around him that woke her stomach to nausea again. She plucked at her wrinkled batik, rubbed the red spot where the brooch pin had marked her, brushed at flies crawling over her stomach ... flies ... too many flies ... and the smell. ...

She swung her legs over the edge of the bunk, keeping her eyes shut to minimize the vertigo, then she looked down.

"Ay mi sa Madar!" She fell off the bunk thudding onto her knees.

Sharl was gone. Oh god, thank god, Madar. Help me. Sharl. . . . She brushed the flies off Olelo's body, feeling his fur stiff under her fingers from the gout of blood that had spurted from his savagely torn throat. Oh god, Sharl. . . . Maissa!

She leaped to her feet, clutched at the bunk until the world steadied, then thrust her head out the back curtains. The brilliant daylight hit her like a blow in the face. She leaned against the sidewall until her eyes cleared then looked again. The other caravan was gone.

Clinging to the wall, she turned back inside. Shutting her eyes she fumbled for the black river and sent the power splashing over her body until she could think coherently again. She opened her eyes. "Miks . . ."

Sinking fingers into Stavver's sinewy shoulders, she

shook him. He muttered vaguely. She buried her hands in his mop of hair and rattled his head against the mattress. "Stavver, wake up . . . is he dead, dying . . . ?" Amber light flashed around her and she flushed angrily, this time at her own stupidity. With the healing power she flushed the drug from his body, then shook him awake, muttering swift thanks to the diadem for its timely jab.

Stavver sat up, blinking at the light. "It's late." He glanced at the other bunk. "Where'd he get to?"

"I don't know," Aleytys said impatiently. "Forget him. Look at this."

"The speaker. Maissa!" He slid off the bunk but she stopped him before he got to the back of the caravan.

"She's gone."

"I should have expected that," he muttered. "If we're not at the ship, she'll leave us." He dropped an arm around Aleytys' shoulders. "Damn. That tea."

"I suppose so." She began to tremble. "Miks . . . Sharl, she took Sharl, came in here and took my baby. Why?"

He held her against him. "He'll be all right. Face it, Lee. She could have killed him here, like she did the speaker. Since she didn't. . . ."

"Oh god, Miks—"

"He'll be all right."

"He's too young, he can't live away from me, how'll he eat . . . how will. . . ." Her voice grew shriller and shriller as terror flooded her. She shoved at Stavver, struggling to get past him, to get out and. . . . An empty, aching horror grew in her, an eating out of her center until a bleeding shell was all that was left, a raging fury and pain that filled the emptiness with hate.

Stavver slapped her, shocking her from the surges of rage and loss that rattled her mind out of any chance of coherent thought. She gasped and collapsed against him sobbing painfully.

He stroked a hand over her hair, across her shaking shoulders, following the path over and over until the storm of emotion blew itself out and she rested against him, weary, ragged breaths creating a damp warm spot on his chest. "He'll be all right, Lee. He's your son, a survivor like you. Maissa will take care of him."

"Maissa . . ." The word was a sorry wail muffled against his chest.

"I know," He murmured. "I know, Lee. We'll catch up to her if you pull yourself together."

Aleytys drew in a deep shuddering breath and leaned back against his arms. "Thanks, Miks." She stepped away, rubbing her red, aching eyes. "I suppose you'd better see to the horses. If Maissa left us a team. I . . . I've got to get Olelo back to the earth."

He nodded, smoothing out the wrinkles in his batik. "If she didn't, I'm sure we can promote something from this crowd." He ducked through the curtains and clattered down the back steps.

"Yeah. Promote." She sighed, ran her hand through her tangled hair. Flies were crawling noisily over the stiff body of the speaker sending a shiver of disgust through her. Then she shrugged off the oppressive distaste, recognizing in the ugly swarm the natural and necessary process of decay and rebirth. She closed her eyes. Rider, she thought, help me.

As calm grew within her she noted something else. It was too quiet outside. The cheerful clamor of the close-packed campground was stilled for some reason. Hastily she wrapped the bloodstained flannel around Olelo's body and carried him out through the back curtains.

Silent frowning Lamarchans stood in shifting groups, each family or sept group drawn apart from the others, all watching intently three grey cloaked figures as they stalked from camp to camp, searching the caravans, speaking briefly to the people, then moving on, winding a complex path through the camps. By the time Aleytys stepped down onto the ground, they had worked with formidable frightening patience half way through the throng. She bit her lip, looked down at the bloody bundle in her arms, then back at the approaching Karkiskya.

Stavver came up leading a pair of horses. "Puki had them by the stream. Doesn't look like we're going anywhere, though." He wound the lead-rein around the spokes of a wheel. "Keep your cool, Lee."

"You think they're looking for the poaku?"

"Probably." He nodded at Olelo's body. "I don't think it would be a good idea to bury anything right now."

"What?" She glanced down, vaguely startled. "Oh." She placed the bloody bundle on the steps then stood beside Stavver. "Well, they won't find poaku here." She swung around, her shoulder knocking into him. "Maissa wouldn't. . . ."

"Not a chance. She's not stupid."

Aleytys sighed and relaxed against him. "I don't know, Miks. She hates both of us."

"But she wouldn't leave a clue like that behind, Leyta," he said patiently. "It wouldn't take them an hour to run her down if they had reason to suspect her."

"Oh. What do you think happens when they finish searching?"

He shrugged. "They question us, I suppose."

"Miks?"

"What?"

"You. Even with that dye-job you don't look much like a Lamarchan."

He smiled down at her. "Every soma-group has its extremes. Besides, Lee, the more you keep their eyes on you, the less they'll look at me."

"I can do that all right." She spread out her fingers, contemplating the backs of her hands. "Yes."

"Don't do anything silly, Lee." Stepping back so that he could see her face, he frowned uneasily. "You'll be doing the talking." He pulled a finger down her cheek. "Keep your head. What're you going to say if they ask you about Maissa?"

She closed her eyes, her loss suddenly piercing through the insulation she'd wrapped about her nerves. Trembling all over she fought for control.

"Lee—"

"No. No . . ." She opened her eyes, willing the tears back. "I'm all right. Never mind, Miks. I know what to tell them."

"He'll make it, Lee."

"I now." She sighed and brushed the back of her hand across her aching eyes. "We'll find them. The diadem will help."

"Think about this too. We need Maissa."

"To get us off this world." She leaned against him once again, watching the three Karkiskya working closer to them. "But there's something you should know, Miks."

Exasperation sharpened his voice. "What now?"

"I'm about to defy the Lakoe-heai. I'm supposed to curse the city, drive the Karkiskya off Lamarchos."

"What?"

"I'm not going to do it, Miks. I can't. From what you told me, from what I've seen myself, the Karkiskya aren't bad for this world. And what would take their place?"

He frowned and pushed her around so he could see her face.

"You think I've cracked." She rested her hands on his arms. "Poor Miks Stavver. Only comfortable with the things he can see and hold." She ran her hands up his arms then clasped them behind his back, leaning her cheek against his chest. "In a way, I envy you." She tightened her grasp holding herself tight against him. "I'm glad you're here, Miks. God, I'm glad you're here."

He stroked her hair, moving his hands over the curve of her skull and neck. Then his hands stilled. "Lahela, some-one wants to talk to you."

Aleytys moved away from him, rubbed her hands once again across her eyes, then turned to see Puki biting her lip and fidgeting from foot to foot.

"Puki?"

"Si'a gikena, Loahn asked me to tell you."

"Tell me what?"

"That he couldn't wake you, that he kept the woman Leyilli from taking both teams, that she only gave in be-cause she didn't want a lot of noise over here, that he let her go because he didn't think you'd want a fuss either, that he's going to follow her to see where she goes and will come back and tell you as soon as he finds out."

Involuntarily Aleytys chuckled, smiling down into the breathless excited face of the girl. "You're wondering why I let this happen to me, aren't you. I can't explain, Puki." She looked up. The three grey figures were approaching Peleku's camp. "Quickly. Get back to your father. What you've just told me is nobody's business but mine, though you can tell your father if you need to. Do you under-stand?"

With a frightened nod, Puki wheeled and ran back to her family.

"Well." Aleytys sat down on the step beside the speaker's body. "That tells us what happened to Loahn."

Stavver laughed, a short barking sound. "The fatal spell."

"What?" She tilted her head to see his face. "What are you talking about?"

"Your lovers come to sticky ends. I wonder what's in store for me."

"Don't talk nonsense. I thought you didn't believe in spells."

"I'm learning."

"No!" She jerked her head away and stared at the ground. With a sudden swift movment she kicked the sand beneath her feet into an explosion of small particles. "Haven't I got enough on my head without that, Miks? You're wrong anyway. He's bound to Puki and you know it. Me, I was just pleasure taken on the wing." She kicked the sand up again and listened to it sing as it struck the earth. "He knows this world. He knows how to go."

Stavver grunted. She felt his disbelief and turned her back on him angrily.

The long grey figures stopped in front of them. One spoke. "You are?"

Aleytys straightened her back proudly. "I am Lahela gikena and Keon serves me." She used the polite forms indicating converse between equals.

"What is the bundle? There is blood there."

"The body of an animal." She unwrapped the speaker far enough so they could see the matted fur.

"Why is it dead?"

"By the will of Lakoe-heai."

"Why did you come to Karkys?"

"By the will of Lakoe-heai."

"There were three others in your party. Where are they?"

"I don't know."

"When did they leave?"

"Early this morning."

"Why did they leave?"

"By the will of Lakoe-heai."

"A gikena is said to be a healer."

"I have healed."

"Heal this then." He took a black rod from somewhere inside his robes and touched a stud. The flesh charred along Stavver's arm. The thief gasped with pain and fell beside the steps, writhing on the dusty earth.

Angry and frightened Aleytys knelt beside him. His

pain distracted her from her fury. She reached out,
dipped fingers into the black water, felt it surge through
her focussing body and splash out from her onto the
charred wound. Stavver screamed with pain as she touched
the raw flesh.

The Karsk radiated surprise and even awe as he
watched the destroyed flesh flake away and the new flesh
spread until it filled the wound with pinkly-pale growth.
She pulled her hands away and jumped to her feet, her
body between him and Stavver. "Keon," she said sharply.
"Get up. Go inside."

Head down, eyes averted, the healed arm pressed
against his side to hide the streak of too-pale flesh, Stavver
stumbled up the stairs and disappeared through the curtains.

The dominant member of the Karkesh trio turned to the
others. "Any reading?"

Aleytys heard the alien words, not understanding what
was said, then the automatic translator in her head crashed
open with a thunderous ache that threatened to blow her
head apart. When the pain cleared she understood but
took care to keep her face blank so she wouldn't betray
that understanding.

The second Karsk said calmly, "No, maistre. The caravan is clean."

The first turned back so that the darkness under the
cowl faced Aleytys. "There is no need to search your
wagon, si'a gikena. In one hour line up with the others by
the gateway there. You will be questioned by the searcher
of souls."

Aleytys nodded briefly and watched as they moved off
along the wall repeating the questions and the search with
each caravan they came to. Then she went aside.

"A thorough bastard." Stavver grinned at her, exhibiting
his arm with its wide streak of milky white flesh. "Wonder
what the searcher of souls will make of this?"

"Too much. Don't you have some stain or something
you can put on it?"

"Sure. Sitting in the Vryhh box in Maissa's caravan."

"Damn."

"Agreed."

"Might as well confess now as go in like that." She
touched his arm lightly, thoughtfully. "Maybe. . . ."

"Try. I couldn't be worse off."

That startled a burst of laughter out of her but she sobered quickly. "Don't say that, Miks. Don't tempt them."

"Hah!"

She closed her eyes and concentrated. Change a fine layer of the surface, she thought, brown, brown, red-brown, like the rest on the outside. She felt the power flow through her. Then she opened her eyes.

"You're a useful thing to have around." His arm was uniformly dark.

"Thing!" It was a relief to laugh.

"Person?" He ruffled her hair. "Lady person."

Chapter X

"This one is what they call gikena."

The narrow form behind the desk tapped thickly gloved fingers on the polished wood. "What's that?" He flattened his hands out and gazed somberly at them. "This isn't supposed to be a complex world."

"It has its quirks. When you've been here a little longer. . . . A gikena is a shaman-type, combination of healer and seeress. The natives hold her in exalted reverence. I've questioned the ones we've seen so far about her and they have no doubt she's genuine. I thought you ought to see her."

"That's her, then?" He turned his cowled face toward Aleytys who was sitting quietly in the low leather chair on the other side of the long narrow room. He shivered. "They are so . . . so uncovered. What do you think, is she genuine?"

"About the seeress part, I can't say. Maistre Echon tested the healing. He lasered the arm of her servant creating a deep burn, searing to the bone an area about six inches long. Took the woman less than a minute to repair the wound. I examined his arm myself. Not even a scar."

"Hunh. These blasted native religions."

"None the less, exaggerate the respect, honored one, or

you could be sticking your hand among a fleydik's tentacles."

"What's her psi-reading?"

"Needle jumped off scale."

"Hunh. Any chance she was involved in the raid?"

"I doubt it. However there are one or two odd things. I haven't questioned her about them yet."

"Odd?"

"Her baby's missing."

"Baby? What's that to do with anything?"

"Don't know. It's odd, that's all."

"What else?"

"She had another caravan travelling with her. Two people in it. And another servant. A boy." He fussed with the folds of thick grey cloth. "The couple took off this morning. Early. I checked the tape. The baby went out with them. A little later the boy rode out alone."

"They were scanned?"

"Down to the corns on their toes. Clean. Not a flicker on any probe or a small of anything that shouldn't be there. But why did they take the baby?"

The Karsk behind the desk turned his cowled head and scanned Aleytys, curiosity radiating strongly from him, evident to the psychologist by the poise of his neck, the slight clawing of his hands. "I suppose I'd better ask her about those things. But you're right about one thing. No pre-technological psi-freak broke in here last night."

"If I were a thief, honored one, I'd come in as a native."

"Be glad you're not. You'd be sitting downstairs contemplating the irons on your wrists. There's no way past the scanners."

"Nonetheless, someone got in here last night with tools sophisticated enough to bypass the alarm fields and melt the charka out of the window."

"Granted. But I think we're wasting time with these primitives. For that very reason."

"I suppose so. But Star Street and the merchants can wait a while. No one's going to leave until the auction's over. In any case Maistre Reikle is ferreting around the merchants and Maistre Friz is going through Star Street."

Aleytys listened to this exchange, struggling to maintain a smiling mask even when they mentioned her baby, confirming that Maissa had him. Fortunately the conversation went on long enough after that for her to steady herself and long enough for her basic curiosity to reassert itself. Then the Karsk switched languages and spoke to her.

"You are?"

"Lahela gikena."

"Why did the woman take your child away this morning? It was your child?"

"My son. The Lakoe-heai punish me."

"Lakoe-heai?"

"They who are the spirit and soul of Lamarchos."

"Ah. Your gods."

"No. Not gods."

"I don't understand."

"They ARE. That is their characteristic."

The Karsk dropped the unprofitable exploration and took up the other arm of her statement. "They punish you?"

"Were you told of the dead beast?"

"What beast?" He tapped impatiently on the desk, turning his cowl to the psychologist.

"There was an animal body wrapped in flannel on the gikena's caravan steps."

Aleytys nodded. "The one who died was a speaker, the beast Lakoe-heai use to communicate with gikena. The woman Leyilli killed it to warn me I must do what I was told to do."

"And what is that?"

"I was to curse the city Karkys, curse it body and bones so that no man of Lamarchos would dare enter the gates again."

"What!"

"The Karkiskya do no honor to Lakoe-heai and so they are angry. They are jealous of their honor." She spread her fingers out, resting one hand on each leg, then stared down at them. "You are skeptical. Let me tell you this. If I put curse on Karkys, you would not see a Lamarchan within twenty kilometers of it. Never. To come onto this piece of earth would make any one of them pariah, stripped of home, hearth, and clan, cast out of the community of man. And this is the least of it. Lakoe-heai would send flies to torment his flesh, nightmares for his mind, until reality melted around the edges for him. You also would feel their hand. Even though you don't believe, my curse would open beneath the city, swallowing whole buildings, the flies would come and other predators until your lives became a misery to you. As long as I waited out there." She flipped a hand to the south. "Out there beyond the gates, I would be the burning glass through which they funnelled their power." She was silent a minute. "I tell you this knowing you could kill me here, seeking to avoid this doom. But I warn you, this would not serve."

"You refused. Why?"

"Because we need you. Because I am healer, I am breaker of curses. What boy is ever a man without a Karkesh blade to drink the blood on the day of his blooding? I suspect you are equally satisfied with the stones you get in exchange." She shrugged. "Never mind. I didn't refuse from any love of you."

"Interesting." The Karsk shifted impatiently, tapped the tips of his fingers on the desk top. He turned his head to the psychologist, switching languages in the sure knowledge that no native could understand him. "Doctor, what's she read? Do I have to sit through much more of this nonsense?"

"She believes every word she says." He glanced down at the box resting on his lap, frowning. "Some odd anomalies, but nothing inconsistent with the truth. From the way the others spoke of her, I'd say she's right about the effect of her curse. So I'd be very, very polite and listen to her with respect."

The cowl swung back to Aleytys. "You know what we are?"

"I know this. Your kind had its beginnings under another sun. I've seen sky ships flying over my homelands, I saw the star fliers behind the wall there." She nodded to the north. "May I tell you a story I heard from my grandmother?"

The Karsk snorted impatiently but waved off a warning hand from the psychologist. "My time is limited, si'a gikena."

She inclined her head. "I'll keep it short, sho Karsk. One day the frogs that inhabited a pond, a place of beauty where the blue waters shone like sapphire under the many colored sky, these frogs decided they wanted a king to make them feel important." She smiled slightly as the

Karsk radiated impatience. "They named a log to be their king as it was the largest and strongest thing in their region. But they grew dissatisfied when their king just lay around and did nothing. So they determined they would find another. A stork came by impressing them with his grace and beauty. This king was indeed more active. By the end of the week he had eaten them all, for frogs are a major item in the diet of storks." She smiled again. "That is my story, sho Karsk. This is my reason for refusing to curse you off Lamarchos."

"Hm." He tented his narrow hands, placing fingertip precisely against fingertip. "Admirable logic, madam. If you can see so clearly, why are your patrons so obtuse? Can't they think of such things by themselves?"

"Who says they think?" She shrugged. "They ARE. They ACT. They SPEAK to me. Who knows how their thoughts walk, or even if they have thoughts?"

The Karsk shook his head impatiently. "And you refuse to do what they demand."

"As I have said." She shifted restlessly in the chair. "I must go after my son. Let me leave, please."

"If your patrons are punishing you, you said it for yourself, how do you expect to get him back?"

"I serve them, but I'm no slave. I have power of my own. I WILL have my son back."

The Karsk tapped fingertip against fingertip. Once again he turned to the psychologist, switching languages. "What do you think?"

"She believes everything she says."

"That doesn't make it true."

"I didn't mean that. However, if you really want my opinion, the faster you get her out of the city, the better."

Aleytys leaned forward, catching the interrogator's attention. He faced her, fingers tapping impatiently on the polished surface of the desk. "What is it?"

"A suggestion. You need to make your peace with the Lakoe-heai. I shall be burying the body of the speaker beside the wall where the stream goes under. Build a small shrine over the spot and out of each year's take of poaku, give one in honor of the Lakoe-heai. By paying them honor you may appease their anger. I don't know. Get a builder of Lamarchos to plan the shrine." She chuckled.

"You Karkiskya build the ugliest structures I've ever seen."

"We will consider it."

"So. Let me go. And my servant with me."

"Your servant?"

"Outside. Keon."

"Take this." He pulled a sheet of leathery paper from a niche by his knee and scrawled a series of ideographs over the face of it. "It's a permit to leave. The guards will let you through the lines if you show them this."

She took the paper. "I'll mark the place where the speaker is buried. Let me give you one last bit of advice. Start construction of the shrine as soon as possible. It's a small enough price to pay for survival."

PART III

Chapter 1

Flies crawled over her breasts, swarmed around her head. Buzzing. A persistent irritating intrusion. She wanted to scream. She couldn't scream. The flies would crawl into her mouth and down her throat.

They bit. They crawled over her breasts and her face and they bit.

She brushed and brushed at herself, skimming handfuls of crawling wriggling blackness, shuddering at the sticky prickly rustle of their legs, the unending unendurable tickle moving erratically over bare skin.

Stavver pulled on the reins, kicked the brake in, stopping the caravan. "Leyta. You can't—" Beating at her with a tattered rag, he drove the flies off for a moment then looked helplessly down at her blotched contorted face. "What's happening to you?"

She huddled on the seat, arms locked over her breasts while she stared blankly at the placid horses. Their tail-twitching, hip-shot lack of progress struck through the haze around her brain. She jerked her head up. "Why are we stopped?" She brushed at the flies. "Get going. Maissa. We've got to catch her."

"Aleytys!" He shook her, flushing with anger, then let his hands fall helplessly, unable to talk past the half-mad glare in her bloodshot eyes. "At least you can be a little more protected," he muttered. He moved around the end of the driver's bench and stepped over the threshold into the caravan. The drawer where Sharl had slept still hung open, piles of dust collecting among the folds of flannel.

With a muttered oath, he slammed the drawer shut and picked up a quilt.

Avoiding the glare in her eyes, he dropped the quilt over her shoulders. "Wrap this around you. It might help a little."

She nodded dully. "Miks—"

"Patience, shrew." He slipped the latch on the friction brake and slapped the reins down on the horses' backs. Moving with clumsy slowness Aleytys huddled the quilt around her then sat wiping at the nonexistent flies as she stared with desperate anguish at the road ahead.

"Lee!" Stavver's demand brought her eyes slowly around to him. "I thought you could control this sort of thing."

She turned away.

"Aleytys." He glanced irritably at the plodding horses, then turned back to her. "You want your son back?"

She gasped and huddled smaller beneath the quilt.

"If you crack up, woman," he went on, his voice edged with cruelty. "If you crack up, you'll never get him back. You think I'd waste my time chasing a kid that's not my own?" He tucked the reins under his leg and caught hold of her chin, forcing her head around. Speaking with exaggerated clarity, he said, "It's up to you, Aleytys. You."

She sighed and seemed to collapse in on herself. "I. . . ." Blinking and shivering, head bowed, she sighed again. "Please, Miks, let me alone. I'm hanging . . . hanging on with my fingernails."

He settled back on the seat, rescuing the reins from under his leg. "I never expected to see my witch as rattled as this."

"Was I so arrogant?" She made a small unhappy sound in her throat. The wind blew through her hair and seemed to blow some of the fog out of her head. "I remember bragging about what marvels of endurance I've accomplished." She leaned back, able to relax a little as the team moved steadily ahead, stride on stride putting the kilometers behind them. "Did I tell you? I was supposed to curse Karkys."

"That you told me." He grunted disgust.

"I told you . . . no, that Karsk. . . ." She shook her head. "Ahai, I'm falling apart like wet paper."

"I still don't see why you're making so much out of a

stupidity like that. Why don't you just curse the place. You don't really think that's anything but superstitious nonsense?" He fingered the reins idly, glanced up at the spectacular sky. "Even if it wasn't, these aren't your people."

She wrenched her eyes from the road long enough to scan his cool cynical face, a needle pain pricking her heart. "They're people, Miks. People. I've made friends."

"Worth this agony?"

She heard the harshness in his voice and shivered. It was a side of Stavver she preferred not to see. "Yes," she said quietly. "I think it's worth this bad time." With a shaking hand she rubbed at her face. "There don't seem to be so many flies around."

"Maybe those fucking elementals got bored," he burst out viciously, the emotion in his voice startling both of them.

She chuckled suddenly, a note of genuine mirth in the sound.

"What's so funny?"

"Your choice of words. I doubt if they have the equipment."

"Hunh!" He smiled tightly, reluctantly. "Good!"

"Good?"

"Think about it."

Aleytys laughed but let the sound trail away uncertainly. She looked around at the desolate stonelands where dust devils wheeled around wind-tortured stone carved into needle chimneys or chunkier buttes. "It took us half a day to cross this coming in." A hoarse wail floated downwind, followed by another. She shivered. "Rock cat."

"Some distance off yet. You think they're coming this way?" Stavver wound the reins around his hands, holding the nervously sidling horses on the rutted road.

"I don't know. Anywhere we can hear them is too close." She shut her eyes and reached into the skittish horses, calming them so Stavver could straighten them out and keep them to a steady trot, quelling an urge to send them racing down trail and out of the stonelands as fast as possible. Killing them in the process.

One brow flicking up and down again in sardonic appreciation, Stavver relaxed enough to take his eyes off the team. "Back to normal?"

"No." She closed her eyes, covered them with her hands, pressing the heels of her palms down until red light flickered across the inside of her eyelids.

The rock cat howled again. "Think you could handle a pack of them?"

"I don't know." She pulled her hands down over her sore swollen face. "Thanks."

"For what?" The horses were twitching, ears flickering in an uneasy rhythm, tails jerking, gait uneven, mouths pulling irregularly at the bits. "Settle them down again, will you?"

Aleytys nodded. When the team was once more moving easily, she said, "For breaking me out of the mind trap. They set it up and I tumbled right in." She sighed, brushed a few wandering flies from her face and watched them zip off into the dust blowing up and around the creaking rumbling caravan. After a minute she went on. "I let them use my fears and physical misery to beat me flat. Miks—"

His eyes were warily flickering over the convoluted rock which provided enough possibilities for ambush to keep him uneasily alert. He glanced briefly at her. "What is it?"

"You wondered if my involvement with these Lamarchans was worth this misery. What about you?" She let the quilt slide down and flattened her hands on her thighs. "If you kicked me off the wagon, you'd lose a lot of trouble."

"Don't tempt me." Then he laughed, an odd bitter sound that startled her into staring at him wide-eyed. "If it was that easy . . . " With quick nervous fingers he picked up the rag and wiped the dirt and sweat off his face, then tucked the rag back beneath his leg. "Aleytys." His voice lingered over her name. "Aleytys. You wouldn't let me go."

"Me?" She frowned. "You've muttered things like that at me before."

"No doubt."

"I'm so fascinating? Hah! I'm not stupid, Miks."

He was silent a while, brooding over the bobbing rumps of the horses, forgetting his nervous attention to the landscape, until a rock cat wailed again and whimpering answers came pulsating around the rock chimneys. He jerked upright. "They're getting closer. No question now."

Aleytys pulled at a piece of her hair and stared uneasily

around at the dust-hazed rock. "Lakoe-heai," she whispered. She brushed at her face.

"Well?"

"I don't know. Maybe they'll jump us in the stonelands, maybe wait till we camp. What did you mean, I won't let you go?"

"You don't know you're doing it." A hot blast of gritty air shot around the side of a butte and scoured over them. Stavver spat and rubbed the rag over his face. "Another talent, woman. When you need a man, you reach out and bind him to you."

Aleytys shivered. "I hope not."

"Hope." He shrugged, his mouth curving down in an ugly sneer.

"I don't believe you."

"So? That change anything? I'm stuck with you, Leyta. Until you stop needing me."

"I won't believe you. You're just digging up excuses."

He turned his shoulder on her. "For what? What do I get out of this?"

"Not me. I'm not worth . . . I'm a sometimes pleasant convenience. The poaku. And Maissa. That's it, isn't it."

"You want to believe that." He shrugged and wouldn't say anything more no matter how insistently she probed.

The road wound interminably through the desolate dry stone, the dust haunting them. Hovering around them as if they travelled in the center of a vortex that kept the powdered stone whirling around them. The flies came back, riding the dust storm, landing, feet pricking in a maddening dance over her dirty sweaty skin. Absently, automatically, she brushed them off her face, while she huddled miserably into the quilt. The heat, the monotonous creaking of the caravan, the steady thud of the hooves combined with recurring sick anxiety about her baby to weaken her defenses until she sank once again into a lethargy where hope was a distant concept cold as a winter sun.

"Leyta!" Dull and distant Stavver's voice came through the haze.

She looked over at him, still brushing, brushing at the flies crawling around her eyes and mouth. "What?"

"Get in back. Get some sleep."

"I can't."

"You're half asleep now."

"No!"

"Aleytys!"

"I don't dare. I'll dream. . . ."

He pulled the horses to a stop, kicking in the brake to keep the caravan from rolling on down the slight slope. "Get in back. When you're tucked in, I'll go on."

"No. . . ."

Overhead, thunder rumbled in mocking laughter from a cloudless sky where the streaks of pastel color visible through the swirling dust twisted themselves into slowly changing knots. Aleytys shivered.

"Leyta." He paused to wind the reins around a cleat, his eyes continually scanning the layered ledges of stone hanging over the rutted track. He stood up. "Lee, you look terrible. Those damn flies. I tell you, woman, if you don't move, I'll carry you."

"I don't dare sleep."

"The rock cats are keeping away. I'll wake you if they get too close."

"Not that." She touched her face with trembling fingers. "You're right. I must look disgusting."

"Never that, love."

"It's the nightmares, Miks. I'm afraid. I've hurt too many people. The faces of the dead . . . too many dead . . . because of me . . . because of me. . . ."

"Aleytys!" He pulled her onto her feet, the lines cut deep in his face drawn into a web of disgust. "Maudlin nonsense. Healer, heal yourself. What are you trying to do, punish yourself for some imaginary guilt?"

She tried to jerk away from his hold. "Damn you."

His hand slapped across her face, stinging painfully. "Stop it, Lee." His voice was cold and demanding, hammering at her. "Damn masochistic baby. Because of you? What makes you so damn egotistical! So damn selfish! Let us have our manhood. We're not figments of your sick imagination. We have a right to make mistakes, to make decisions. What right have you to take this away from us? Guilt? Phah!"

She collapsed against him sobbing weakly. He lifted her and swung her over the back of the seat. "Pull yourself together, Aleytys. Hand me out a quilt. This damn sandstorm is stripping my skin off."

The inside of the caravan was stifling, the hot air drained and lifeless. Aleytys groped to a bunk and leaned against it. Her body ached and her mind sank slowly through sloshing waves of fatigue. It would be so good to lie down . . . lie down and sleep . . . sleep . . . She splayed her fingers out over the hard surface and leaned on her arm, her dirty sweaty hair falling forward over her face Sleep . . . and dream . . . no . . . why can't I let them be . . . because of that thing in me, Miks said. The faces paraded through her mind. Vajd . . . eyes torn from his head, exiled . . . Zavar, little one, exiled . . . Tarnsian . . . dead . . . Raqat . . . dead . . . the nine nomads, dead. . . . NO! She straightened and pushed her hair back. "No! Miks is right. It's stupid to punish myself." She snatched a quilt from the bunk and climbed back onto the bench seat.

"I thought you were going to sleep."

"Later, Miks. Please?" She held up her hand palm out. "I couldn't sleep. Really. I know you're right about my stupidity."

"That's something. Here." He handed the reins to her and wrapped the quilt around his upper body. "That's better. Give those back, Lee, and heal your face." He chuckled. "I prefer to look at your face without a decoration of fly bites."

A while later Aleytys glanced uneasily at the sky. The glow spot of the sun was directly behind, throwing diffused shadows out before them like black stains on the rock. The banded swarms of aerial bacteria were beginning to coagulate into the false thunderheads, baring narrow stretches of blue sky along the eastern horizon. "How much longer?"

"Another hour's driving." As the track ahead turned between two towering colossi of rust-streaked, bluish-grey stone, he straightened his back and began scanning the ledges spiralling up their precipitous sides. "Haven't heard the rock cats in a while."

Aleytys closed her eyes and searched. Red thoughts of blood hunger prowled in shifting circling patterns. She sensed a waiting. "They aren't ready to strike yet."

"They'll follow us out of the stonelands?"

"Left to themselves, I doubt it. Predators have more sense than that."

"Then there's nothing to worry about once we're past those." He pointed to a pair of needle chimneys like dittos against the pale blue horizon line.

"No. They'll follow. Probably attack when it's dark."

"Lovely. Think you could control them?"

"I wouldn't count on it."

"Hm. I could hit something big as a horse if it was standing still. How about you? Know anything about those crossbows Kale stuck under the seat?"

"Man's work, Miks. With my people, anyway." She leaned back hugging the quilt around her. "Not so skewed against women as this world. Still. . . ."

"Poor planning, Leyta," He chuckled. "You should have learned to shoot."

"Hindsight."

"Then you better figure something else out, my love."

"Don't worry. I have."

"I don't relish the thought of providing exercise for a lot of teeth. It better be good."

"I suppose the diadem can handle a crossbow. It seems to be good at that kind of thing." She tapped her temple and pursed her lips into a pout as the faint chime answered her touch.

"If killing those four-legged appetites bothers you so much, why don't you just send them away?" He nodded at the horses. "I've seen what you can do with animals."

"Ordinarily. . . ." Aleytys shifted uneasily on the seat. "Miks . . ."

"What?"

"Maissa won't hurt Sharl, will she?"

"I don't know." He moved his shoulders impatiently, irritated by her constant preoccupation with the baby. "Drop it, will you?"

"Why'd she take him, Miks?"

"How the hell should I know. Look." He pointed to the east.

"Where?"

"There. See the green?"

"I remember now. We camped there. Are you going to stop?"

"We've got a little light still. No use wasting it."

As the caravan passed through the enormous pillars of

stone marking the boundary of the stonelands, they heard the rock cats howling behind.

"How many?"

Aleytys wiped the dust from her face. The flies were gone again as if the Lakoe-heai had recognized their use-lessness when she had repeatedly healed her face, the stim-ulus from the healing actually serving to pull her from each relapse into lethargy. "Five," she said slowly.

"All as big as that red horror we saw on the way in?"

"Hard to tell size. They're all hungry."

"Oh lovely."

The sparse grass thickened and deepened to a darker green while the air lost some of its leeching hunger for the water in their bodies. When the sun was an orange-copper point on the horizon Stavver pulled the caravan off the trail.

"This is as good a place as any. Water and wood. Stream down there."

She glanced at him. "You want to build fires."

He nodded. "How close are the cats?"

"About an hour behind. They don't like the grass."

"You sound sorry for them."

"They don't want to be here."

"Hah! Well, I don't want them to be here myself. Why don't they go home?" He slid off the seat and held up his hands to help her down.

"I told you to push me off the wagon." She swung down, steadied by his hands. "The light won't last long. We bet-ter get the wood."

"Wait a minute." He reached a long arm under the seat and pulled out a crossbow. "Maybe you'd better take this."

"What'd I do with it?" She walked away, shoulders slumped, feet stumbling because her legs were too tired to lift them over the clumps of grass. He tossed the bow on the seat and followed.

Aleytys dragged the heavy limb into the camp and dropped it beside the pile, then dusted her hands and straightened her aching back. "You think that's enough?"

He dumped his load beside her. "It better be."

"If you'll build the fires, I'll take the horses down to the stream. Deal?"

"Deal."

When she returned, he dropped the hatchet and rubbed his back. "How's the time?"

She closed her eyes. "They're circling out there."

"And . . . "

She shifted irritably. "How should I know? They still aren't ready to attack. That's all."

"Go sit on the seat up there while I light the fires."

"Fire won't stop them."

"They're not afraid of fire?"

"They're afraid. But it won't keep them off for long."

He looked up from the stacked wood. "Stop playing Cassandra, Leyta. Nothing's that bad."

She groaned and pulled herself slowly onto the driver's bench. "What's a Cassandra?"

"Don't ask me. Old word I picked up somewhere." He frowned at the stubborn wood. "Burn, dammit." He shaved off a few splinters with his knife and thrust the firelighter into them. "Means someone consistently pessimistic about the future."

"Dear, dear. A walking dictionary."

He looked up from his firemaking and grinned at her.

Aleytys bent over the back of the seat and fished under it for the second crossbow. She set it down leaning against the slatted back of the seat and watched the fires bloom in a circle around the caravan. One . . . two . . . three . . . four . . . five. . . .

Stavver climbed up beside her "Any quarrels for these?"

"Hunh?"

"Arrows, love. When you use them in engines like these, they're called quarrels. Or bolts."

"Dictionary."

He laughed. "Get up on the roof. I'll hand up the bows after I dig out some ammunition."

"Give me a push." Holding onto the gingerbread carving that decorated the top and sides of the caravan, she climbed unsteadily onto the top slat of the seat back. "My legs aren't working so well."

When he came out of the caravan with a pair of quarrel cases, Aleytys leaned over the edge and called, "Shouldn't we have some wood up here to keep the fires going?"

"I thought you said fire wouldn't keep them off."

"Well, it will for a little while. Besides we need the light to see."

He handed her the cases. "How long before they attack?"

"Not long. I can feel them working up nerve to come in."

"Then we won't need wood." He swung up beside her. "Try getting through to them."

"I don't think it'll work."

"Try."

Aleytys stretched out on her stomach and closed her eyes. Breathing rhythmically, she stilled her throbbing nerves and reached out for the minds of the prowling predators.

Like knobs of glass they slid away from her touch, impervious, unreachable. She tried again and again to find an opening, then gave up. "They're protected too well," she said quietly. "I can't reach them."

He cocked the crossbow and slid a quarrel in the slot. "What about the diadem?"

"I wish—" She pushed herself up until she was standing. "Give me that thing."

A crimson feline paced slowly into the ring of light cast by one of the fires and stood staring up at them. Edging along, a careful distance from the fires, amber eyes glaring at them, the cat circled the caravan, looking for a way to get at them. Aleytys fumbled with the bow. "Oh damn," she whispered. "Go away, cat."

A second cat stalked into the light. Then a third. And another. And another. Until five redly glowing rock cats paced restlessly around the ring of fire.

The first one loped away suddenly then came running back through the gap between the fires, in one side and out the other after circling the caravan inside the ring. "They're going to jump any minute now."

"Then you better get your magic working." He armed the second bow and knelt by the front where he could see the circling cats.

Bracing herself, Aleytys closed her eyes. "Rider," she muttered. "We've got trouble. I hope you can use a crossbow. Come, you who share my body. Take it."

A feeling of alertness pulsed through her. The diadem chimed. As the time squeeze began the first cat gathered himself, raced at top speed past the fires, and leaped. The chime raced downscale, freezing him in midair as the timespell came full on.

Beside Aleytys Stavver sat frozen. Her body moved with calm control, lifted the bow, and sent a quarrel snapping toward the leaping cat. The spell affected it, slowing it. The Rider's aim was a bit off also. The quarrel slid smoothly along the cat's side and ended up hanging point downward a few centimeters above the ground. The Rider slapped a second bolt in place, aimed, fired. This time the quarrel bit into the rock cat's eye. The diadem chimed.

Falling, writhing, howling in agony, the big red cat clawed at the bolt protruding from his face. Then he stiffened, jerked, stiffened, lay stretched out. Dead. Stavver moved, too late to do anything.

Two other cats fanned out and came leaping toward the caravan.

The diadem chimed, freezing them in mid-leap. Aleytys' body moved smoothly, calmly. Once, twice, the trigger clacked and bolts snapped out, thudding home into the topaz eyes. The diadem chimed.

The cats fell heavily to the ground, squalled, writhed, stiffened, in bloody wasteful death. Yellow eyes opened, closed. The influence of the diadem drained rapidly from Aleytys' arms and legs as the last two cats fled into the night.

Slowly, carefully, she laid the bow on the flat roof and crouched beside it, holding herself, rocking back and forth on her knees. Beside her she heard Stavver yell and jump to his feet. He stared into the darkness a minute then came back to her. "You all right, Leyta?"

"I don't feel so good, Miks."

"Reaction." He settled beside her. "Come." He held her against him until her chilled body warmed and the trembling stopped. "Poor baby. Better them than you. Or me." He chuckled. "Or me."

"Such a waste. Such a damn unnecessary waste."

"They're predators, Lee. Born to a short and dangerous life."

"I know. Why me, though?"

"You need the answer to that?"

"No. Dammit, no." She pulled away from him. "I keep thanking you, Miks. Once again."

He shrugged. "You only got three of them. Where're the others?"

She pushed up, caught hold of the carving and swung herself down onto the seat. Her voice muffled by the effort, she said, "Gone off. They won't be back."

He swung down beside her. "Any other little surprises?"

"Not now."

He jumped to the ground and strolled over to look at the dead cats. "In the eyes. Every damn one of them. Leyta."

"What?"

"Looks like the diadem's a weapons master. Handy . . ." He caught hold of a back leg and dragged the cat out of the light. Aleytys stood and watched, tears gathering in her eyes.

He came back for another. "What about the horses?"

"I don't know."

"Hadn't you better go see? We need them, you know. Unless you think you can walk Maissa down."

While Stavver dragged the last body away, Aleytys walked down to the stream where she'd tied the horses. They were wild-eyed and stamping about, one tangled in the rope so badly he had come close to strangling himself. She calmed them and untangled them, the healing work helping her to regain her own balance. She ran soothing hands over neck and barrel, crooning softly to them, feeling warm with affection.

"Leyta!"

"Coming." She walked back to the fire. When she looked around she saw Stavver had smothered the other fires, leaving the one by the front of the caravan for their evening meal.

"The horses?"

"Scared. But all right now."

"You're a handy thing to have around." He poured water in the bucket and splashed it over his hands and face, wiping them on a rag.

"Thing!"

"Haven't we had this conversation before?"

"Probably." She shiffed at her hands. "I smell like horse."

"Why not a bath. It's not cold."

"You know me too well. Come in with me?"

"Why not." He dropped his arm over her shoulders. "As long as we don't have more visitors."

She leaned against him. "The other two cats are long gone. Heading back for stone." She yawned. "Miks?"

"What is it?"

"Hold me tonight. Just hold me. Pretend I'm an ordinary girl you picked up on some Star Street maybe who came with you because she was glamoured by the stars."

Chapter II

Aleytys pulled back the curtain and stood sleepily in the doorway. The orange sun hung low in the east, the top of its curve already covered by the unwinding clots of bacteria. The brilliant naked rays glanced across the dew settled on the sparse grass, granting a fleeting loveliness to the stark landscape. The air was cool and fresh. A small, dawn breeze wound through the grass, stirring it here and there, making the dew drops sparkle and shimmer.

Miks slid off the bunk and moved to stand behind her, his hand resting lightly on her shoulder. "It's a different world."

Aleytys tilted her head to watch the bacteria spread in rivers of beauty drifting with slow grace across the cornflower blue of the sky. "Ahyi, Miks, it's . . . magnificent."

They stood a minute in silence. Then Aleytys pulled free and stepped down to the ground, flinching slightly as her bare feet touched the cold dewy grass. "Miks?"

He pulled the batik tight over his hips and slapped the belt around to anchor it. As he buckled the belt he said, "What is it?"

"Could you fix breakfast today? I've got to do some heavy thinking."

Stavver chuckled. "Good thing I'm not a Lamarchan male."

"You're much too sensible to worry about your masculinity."

"Flattery, child?"

"You think you need it?" She grinned up at him, hands caressing tender breasts.

"Go about your business, Lee. I'll have the water hot and the bacon frying when you get back. Figuratively, at least."

Aleytys' mouth twitched into a brief smile. Then she picked her way through the drying grass to the hollow where Stavver had piled the bodies of the dead cats. A stinking, black cloud of scavengers lifted reluctantly from their feast, hooked beaks and massive talons stained with blood. Aleytys shivered. She sat at the top of the slope, legs crossed, turned aside so she didn't have to see the plundered corpses.

"So," she murmured, anger rising in her. "Look down there. To punish me, see what you've accomplished." She stared at the earth, bent over, and placed the palms of her hands flat against the pale gritty soil. "The waste . . . stupidity!"

A hot pinch of anger rippled up her arms. She jerked her hands away, then flattened them again, letting her own rage and disgust fight what was coming up at her. "Your people," she hissed. "You don't give a damn about them. What are you, a clutch of floating egos? Are you so completely irresponsible? Is Karkys such an itch in your hide? Ahai, my friends, you drive the Karkiskya from Lamarchos and you'll soon know what an itch feels like. There are companies who would come in here, rape this world until it was a ball of sterile rubble. Ahhh, listen, I told that Karsk to do you honor, build a shrine. Won't that do? Or do I battle you across the breadth of Lamarchos, wasting life after life. Like those." She jabbed a thumb at the three carcasses. "Let it go. Let me go."

Thunder—tentative, uncertain—rumbled faintly. Beneath Aleytys the earth shifted, bouncing her up and down. She frowned, chewing her lip in a fit of frustration. This was worse than trying to communicate with the diadem. She rested her hands on her knees, searching her memory for the methods the nomad witches of Jaydugar had used to talk to the R'nenawatalawa.

After a while she pulled grass out, tossing aside the rooted clumps until she had a clear space about a foot across. Then she smoothed the earth until it was a flat even surface like a mirror of dirt. After contemplating her work with a burst of satisfaction she took the discarded grass and shredded the blades until she had a pile of green confetti.

She caught up a handful of grass fragments. "All right, talk to me. What do you want from me?" She tossed the fragments into the air and watched them drift down on the cleared space. They twisted and turned, falling into a pattern on the cleared space, a glyph from the Lamarchan syllabary.

"Two? What. . . ." She frowned, then brushed the green off and threw up another handful. "Two?" With an irritated exclamation she brushed the grass aside and for the third time dropped the green. This time the pattern was another glyph, a complex multiple. She bent intently over the pattern, tongue caught between her teeth, and traced the lines with her finger. "Duty . . . things to come . . . question slash. Ah! I understand." She straightened. "Finally. You had four things for me to do. Two have been done. More or less. Two left to do. Question slash? Will I do them?" She sat back on her heels. "All right, what are they?"

She brushed the space clear and tossed the grass. The new glyph was simpler. "A swarm . . . no." She tapped a section of the figure. "Strange . . . determinant for man . . . a large number of men?" She shrugged. "You'll have to do better, Lakoe-heai."

The next glyph was even simpler, expressing one single major idea. "Stop," she murmured. "Command mode. I suppose that means I've got to stop a whole bunch of men from doing something."

She glanced over her shoulder at the sun. "Hurry it up, will you. I want to get after Maissa." She pushed the grass shreds aside and let more fall, grunting with satisfaction as two glyphs formed this time. Once again she bent over the complicated signs, trying to make sense of their assorted meanings.

"Someone . . . something will be there . . . no . . . coming . . . is in motion toward a definite destination . . . from a distant point to a nearer one. Hm. The other . . . there will be—future curl there—yes . . . there will be . . . telling of tales." She frowned. "Lies? No. I don't think—no! Explanation. Ah! Someone comes to me bringing information that will explain these words." She rocked back on her heels. "I wonder . . . Loahn? Mustn't read too much into this . . . all right. I accept that. I suppose that's the third task you have for me. What about number four?"

She brushed the grass aside and tossed the pieces into the air again. "Later . . . a telling." She shrugged. "So. I accept." Her mouth twitched into a rueful smile. "Not much choice. One last thing. Call off the harassment."

When the dirt was clear again, she let the grass fall. "Ah. Agreement." She leaned back on her heels and yawned. A monitory rumble of thunder made her frown. She inspected the glyph again. "Oh. Conditional mode. Temporary agreement conditioned upon the performance of required actions." Her mouth twitched into a one-sided smile. "I get your point. Agreed. Conditionally. There are things I can't and won't do. As you know." Thunder rumbled like lazy stones across the circus tent sky. Laughing she staggered to her feet, brushing the dry grit from her legs.

As soon as she had taken half a dozen steps away from the cat bodies, the hovering carrion birds were gliding down.

"You took your time." Stavver slipped her batik to her and tossed the pin after it. "Much as I appreciate the view, Lee, we're on a public way."

Aleytys chuckled. "How much more does this bit of cloth cover?" She drove the pin through the triple layer of material.

"Local mores, my dear. What you bare and what you don't. Here." He handed her a mug of tea. A frail curl of steam carried the delicate flower scent to her and she smiled with pleasure.

"Thanks." She took a small sip. "It's hot."

"That's the point." He laughed, then sobered. "Did you get your thinking done?"

She cradled the cup between her palms taking more pleasure in the gentle warmth. "I think so. There are some complications, though."

He set pieces of leathery waybread on two plates then dumped strips of broiled meat beside them. "Aren't there always, Leyta."

It wasn't a question. She looked at him startled, then

smiled involuntarily in response to the sudden grin that lit his worn face.

"What's the worst," he said, handing her a plate.

She sat down on the steps. "The worst. Hm. I don't know that yet. It seems they have some other uses for me. Someone's coming sometime today with information for me that will clear up the confusion in my head." She began eating.

"Someone. Sometime." He settled himself on the step above her, stretching out his long legs, resting the plate on his thigh.

Aleytys sipped at the tea. "Might be Loahn."

"They say so?"

"No, but it'd make sense. I think Maissa ran into something she couldn't handle. He'd come back if that happened."

"You know him better than I do." He set the plate down and emptied his mug in one long swallow.

"It still bothers you." She shook her head. "I don't see why."

He shrugged, his face rejecting further comment. "Do we wait here or go on?"

Aleytys stared at her toes. Slowly she wiggled them while she rubbed the palms of her hands over the batik. After a rather strained silence, she said, "No. I can't just sit here."

"Worried about Sharl?"

"How can I help it? Until I hold him again . . . " Her hands rubbed restlessly back and forth over the batik.

"Then I'd better hitch up the horses. Smother the fire, will you?"

"What about cleaning the plates?"

"Your problem."

As Stavver moved off, Aleytys grimaced at the plates and prepared to scrub the grease off them.

Chapter III

"Loahn."

Grinning, the young man brought his horse to a prancing halt. The glow from the orange sun struck flickering highlights from his brush of reddish-mahogany hair. "Ayyi, gikena." He pulled his mount around and held him close to the wheels of the caravan, ignoring his jerking head and dancing sidesteps.

Aleytys wrapped fingers around the edge of the seat, tightening her grip until her knuckles gleamed yellow under the dark-stained skin. "My baby. . . ." She croaked. The words were lost in the rumble and creak from the caravan. She closed her eyes, licked dry lips. "Loahn." Though her voice cracked again on the word, at least the sound was loud enough for him to hear. He leaned closer.

"My baby, did you see him, is he all right?"

He nodded. "I saw him. He's fine."

"Ah." She cleaned back, closed her eyes. "Well."

He rode silent for several meters, his eyes searching the low hillocks ahead. "No. Not well, Lahela."

"You said . . ."

"Oh, the boy's all right." He smiled reassurance, sitting casually confident on the powerful roan, controlling it firmly as it shifted nervously about. "The horde is moving out of the south."

"Horde."

"We need to talk." He looked quickly around. "I've a lot to tell you."

"My baby. . . ."

"Keon!"

Stavver frowned. "What?"

"Stop a minute, will you? Danger ahead."

Stavver grunted skeptically, but he turned the team and pulled up at the first flattish spot beside the road. He glanced at the sky. "Several hours before sun's at zenith."

Loahn leaned forward to pat the roan's neck. "Much further and we chance running into the horde."

"Miks." Aleytys rested her hand on his arm. "It's impossible to talk like this."

He looked down at her hand. "You're the one in a hurry."

"I know." She shifted around on the seat. "Loahn, would it matter if we went a bit further. There's no water here."

"About a kilometer ahead there's a pull-off. Trees. A well."

"Miks?"

"I heard." He kicked the brake loose and started the horses trotting down trail.

Half an hour later, a small fire crackled busily with the teapot nestled close to keep the water hot. Aleytys leaned against the large back wheel, sipping at her mug. The three horses moved over the swelling in the ground beyond the trees, cropping greedily at sun-cured grass. Stavver stood beside her, leaning against the caravan, his face remote, chill, the forgotten tea cooling in his mug. Aleytys glanced up at him, then across the fire at Loahn who sat on a rickety bench, back propped against the trunk of a tree whose loose ragged bark rattled like dry paper in the breeze. "You said the horde was coming out of the south. Horde?"

"Mmm, yes. Leyilli ran into its outriders."

Aleytys pinched her lips together, fighting down the fear that ate like acid at her. She put the mug down and shifted onto her knees. Smoothing out a patch of earth, she said, "Loahn, come here. Write the sign for horde."

Looking puzzled he came round the fire and knelt beside her. He drew the glyph hesitantly, finishing with a grunt of satisfaction.

"I thought so." She rubbed her hand across the lines with a nervous energy that sent a layer of dirt flying out. With both men frowning at her in puzzlement, she chewed at her lower lip, staring out across the low rim of the hillock toward the rising waves of ground swells. "That's the third task," she murmured. "The third. My god . . ." She picked up the mug and gulped down the rest of the lukewarm tea. "Loahn, your feeble-minded Lakoe-heai want me to stop the horde. Horde. How many men?"

Loahn touched her shoulder. "Gikena?"

"How many?" she repeated impatiently, pushing his hand away. "In the horde. How many?"

"Men, women, children . . . several thousand . . . say . . . mmm . . . five or six thousand."

"Madar!" She dug in the earth with her forefinger then flipped little bits of dirt into the air. "I've got to stop that?"

"Stop them?" Loahn stood up like a spring set free, glared down at her. "Impossible. One woman? Ridiculous. You must have heard wrong. It has to be a mistake."

"Oh no, Loahn." Her laughter bubbled with shocking loudness into the tense scene. "No. That's exactly what I have to do." Ignoring his protests, she stood and leaned against the caravan resting her forehead on her crossed arms, her back to the fire, shutting out both Loahn's continuing vehemence and Stavver's sardonic silence.

Loahn's hand closed on her shoulder, but Stavver pulled him away. "Let her alone."

Loahn glared at the long, thin man. "If you don't care about her . . . "

Stavver slapped him with an open hand and jumped back. "Let it lay, boy," he whispered.

His mouth curled in a tight smile, Loahn snarled, "I'm not afraid of you, old man." His hand went to the hilt of his Karkesh blade.

Stavver's lips parted to show his teeth. "Come on, then, boy." He drawled the last word turning it into an insult.

Loahn growled low in his throat and circled, then leaped when he thought he saw an opening. Pain flashed through his body as he found himself sprawled helplessly on the ground. Stavver's face hung over him. Stavver's laughter mocked him. "Boy . . . "

"Stop it, both of you." Aleytys thrust herself between them. "Talk about stupidity! What are you trying to prove? You. Miks. My god, you know I feel about you. But I don't belong to you. I don't belong to anyone. And you. Loahn." She watched him get stiffly to his feet. "What the hell do you think you're doing? Me, I'm none of your business. None!" She threw out her hands, exasperated almost beyond words. "Fool! Attack a man who's forgotten more about combat than you ever learned! Both of you, forgetting you're thinking, reasoning beings! Acting like a pair of rutting bighorns. I will decide what I'm

going to do. I will. Not you, Miks." She sighed. "At least
you haven't tried to run my life. Thanks. And not you,
Loahn. Have you forgotten that Maissa has my baby? Do
you think I would abandon him?"

Loahn bowed briefly toward her, then Stavver. "My
apologies," he muttered. Breathing heavily he strode to the
fire, wrapped the felt square around the handle and tilted
some of the hot liquid into his mug. When he straightened
his face was quiet. "Anyone else?"

Stavver grunted. "Let me get my cup.

Aleytys said quietly, "Bring mine also, will you, Miks?"

Loahn filled the cups then went back to the bench. He
leaned against the trunk and sipped at the biting hot liquid. He looked at Stavver who stood beside Aleytys. "I
don't like making a fool of myself . . . ummmm . . .
Miks."

"Nor do I. Go easy on that name, Loahn. Too many
people know it. Make it Keon. You too, Leyta."

Aleytys sighed. "I simply cannot remember to call you
that."

"Practice," he said dryly. He sank onto his heels, frowning intently at the ground. Then he lifted his head, fixing a
cool measuring glance on Loahn. "We know a little. From
Puki. Fill us in on what happened yesterday."

Loahn swirled the tea in his mug, looking thoughtfully
away from them toward the horses grazing peacefully on
the slope beyond the halt. "When I woke that morning
. . . yesterday? Tchah! Yesterday. The two of you were
snoring louder than a pair of mating buzz-beetles. The
baby was gone and the speaker dead. I got curious. Of
course. I went outside to find out what was happening.
Leyilli was sitting on the driving seat, reins in hand. I
didn't see the other anywhere. She called me over. Well, I
knew she was Firstman of our little group, so I went. She
told me you all had decided to send her out first with the
stones to get them free while you stayed . . . " He looked
from Aleytys to Stavver, then back at his cup. "While you
stayed behind to ward off suspicion."

"Plausible enough," Stavver said thoughtfully.

Loahn pinched the end of his nose, a sour look on his
face. "Yeah. I didn't argue with her. Not that one. Nothing wrong with my memory. The time she went for me
. . . " He shivered, gulped a mouthful of the hot tea.

"Women. Besides, I knew you wouldn't want a lot of noise because of the stones."

Aleytys nodded. "What about Kale?"

"He came back with the other pair of horses. After taking in the scene, me standing there, her with her sweet smiling face, he tied the pair to the wheel of your caravan and climbed into his." Loahn sighed. "Even without the dead speaker the look on his face was enough to keep me thinking in ways they didn't want. So I came back and tried to wake you, Lahela. By the time I gave it up, they were gone."

"Puki told us." Aleytys hesitated. "She said you were going after them. She brought us the horses."

"Good girl." He ran his tongue around his lips. "I was going around in smaller and smaller circles. Before I got to biting the back of my neck I decided the best thing to do was follow them, get a line on where they were headed, and get back to you."

Aleytys clenched her hands into fists, then straightened her fingers and spread them out on her thighs. "You saw Sharl?"

"Heard him crying last night. Loud and healthy. And mad as hell."

"Crying . . ."

"He was hungry. She fed him from a bottle. I saw her sitting by the fire with him on her lap." He grinned. "He's fine, Lahela. No sick baby would sound like that."

Aleytys pressed her hands against her eyes. "Miks, she had a bottle. Milk."

He touched her hair. "So she planned it. Relax, Lee. Use your head. She's taking good care of him."

Aleytys pulled her hands down and sucked in a wavering breath. "Go on," she told Loahn.

"Not much more to it. I followed until they made camp. She was in some kind of hurry."

Stavver chuckled suddenly. "She's finally found someone who scares hell out of her."

Loahn nodded. "Lahela." He took a mouthful of tea, swallowed, sucked in another, visibly reluctant to go on. After another minute, though, he spoke again. "They only camped three hours, long enough to rest the horses and let them graze a little. They argued a lot. I don't think Leyilli wanted to stop."

"Don't read too much into that," Aleytys said impatiently. "I told you. She doesn't like men."

He shrugged. "They started on again about an hour before dawn. Right now, she's only a couple hours ahead of you." He shook his head as Aleytys jumped to her feet. "Sit down, Lahela. I haven't finished." He waited until she sank onto her knees and sat leaning tensely forward wanting him to speak, willing him to speak. "The outriders from the horde came on them about an hour after sun-up. Three men. Kale recognized what they were as soon as he saw them. He dropped the reins, dived into the back, came out with a crossbow, had three bolts through them before they had time to react. He tumbled off the bench, caught one of the horses, slapped the others into a run, and was off to the north like fire rode under his tail. Leyilli's mouth was still hanging open when another pair came over the hump. They saw the dead, the woman."

Aleytys passed her hand over her face, again and again, wiping at invisible flies, staring numbly at nothing.

Hastily Loahn went on. "The boy's all right. They take boy babies to raise in the horde."

"Ah." Unable to sit still any longer Aleytys jumped to her feet and began pacing back and forth beside the fire, rubbing unconsciously at her milk-laden breasts. "Loahn," she said, her voice harsh and staccato under the stress of her emotions. "I'm off-worlder, remember?" She thrust the hair back off her face. "Tell me about the horde."

"Bad news." He sipped at the tea, frowning at the ground.

"Tell me. Don't dither, man!"

"We don't know much about them.

She kicked at the damp earth, dislodging a few pebbles. "However little, it's more than I know."

"Hmm." He licked his lips, glanced briefly at Stavver. "They come out of the south."

"So? Where from?"

"Who knows." He shrugged. "They come when they will, with no set pattern to their swarming." For a little while the only sound was the crackling of the fire. "What are they?" He brooded then raised his head, a wry grin wiping the seriousness from his face. "Let me quote. One of our lesser song smiths. Destruction incarnate. A plague of locusts. Demons gone mad. Blowing across the lakelands like fire, killing and being killed, burning and destroying what can't be burned. We fight them. We kill them by the thousands." The passion in his words infected his body and he too leaped to his feet and joined her, pacing rapidly beside her. "They keep coming. Overwhelming us with numbers. On and on, city after city. Gutted. Burned. What won't burn knocked down. On and on until they burst out the other side of the lakelands into the quaking hills, leaving a burnt-out swath behind them where scarcely stone stands on stone, and everything that lived is dead."

Aleytys shuddered and broke away from him. She leaned against the caravan and folded her arms over her breasts. "You lakelanders never tried to follow them? To find out where they went or where they came from?"

Loahn shrugged. "My grandfather, for one. They came last the year after his blooding when he was a wild young savage." His face turned bland. "Like me."

Aleytys dredged up a smile. "So?"

"He followed them. By the time they crossed lakelands there were only about a hundred of them left. Along with the horde master. They staggered into the quaking hills, looking like qaf smokers in withdrawal. One by one, the last survivors began falling out. He followed a trail of dead and dying. Finally he saw a lot of black smoke. The master's wagon was burning. In the distance about a score of riders, each one with a captured boy sitting before him, rode toward a cliff that rose like a wall, grey-green stone veined with thick tarry black streaks. They rode into the cliff. One minute there, he said, the next, not a sign of them. Horses, riders, kidnapped boys. Gone. My grandfather said it scared the stiffening out of his bones. Nonetheless he went up to the cliff. It was as solid as any rock he'd ever seen, he said, so he gave it up and came back home."

Aleytys closed her eyes, feeling a sour sickness in her mouth and stomach. "All that for no reason except the taking of a few boys?"

Loahn strolled back to the bench and dropped onto it. "None we know. What reason could there be for the massacre of thousands of your own people?"

"You said they took boys into the horde?"

"Right."

"What about Leyilli?"

"They're not in the lakelands yet."

"That makes a difference?"

"It seems to. They didn't kill her. They took her with them, she drove the caravan. In the lakelands they would have slit her throat, slaughtered the horses, and burned the caravan."

"Then she's probably dead now."

"I don't think so." He dug at the earth with his heels. "Since they didn't kill her immediately. Maybe the horde-master needs a woman."

Aleytys shivered. "Miks, what'll that do to her?"

"Keon, Lahela." He smiled at her. "Don't worry about Maissa. She's tough and resilient. She's survived a lot worse than a little rape."

"Still. . . . Loahn. You said they change when they come into the lakelands. How?"

"Hm. No outriders. They don't defend themselves. Don't bother about the wounded, leave them to die where they fall, man, woman, or child. Like there's a single brain controlling the whole mass of them that considers the dead like falling hairs, worth no more concern than that."

"The horde master?"

"Probably."

Stavver broke in. "What happens if the master is killed?"

"I don't know. It's never happened."

"Never?" The word was heavy with scorn.

"Never." Loahn stood slowly, a spark of anger glowing in his eyes. "We're not stupid, starman. We've tried. Each time we've tried. There's no way to get to him. There's a kind of aura . . . something . . . over the horde. Raiders get caught in it. They stop, fall asleep. And never wake up. The master's guard slits their throats."

Stavver glanced up at the glow spot. "About how far away from us are they?"

"Judging by where they took Leyilli, about two-three hours ride.

"We've been here about half an hour. They coming this way?"

"I didn't hang around to see which way they were moving."

"So if we stay here, we're reasonably safe for an hour or so."

"Could be."

Stavver turned to Aleytys. "We've got a problem, Leyta."

"You tell me?" She sat down again, wrapped her arms around her legs, and rested her chin on her knees. "If we don't get Maissa back, we're stuck on this world."

"Perhaps." Stavver brooded a minute. "It wouldn't be easy. We might manage to get on a trader's ship. I don't see how right now."

"Well. That's for later. Beyond getting my baby back and freeing Maissa, the Lakoe-heai have a little job for me. Turning the horde." She rubbed her fingers hard against the firm smooth skin of her forehead. "Given their present feeling about me, I suspect I won't be allowed to avoid doing what they want."

"How the hell. . . ." Stavver moved impatiently away from the caravan. "He said it and I agree." He jerked a thumb at Loahn. "It's ridiculous."

"Have I got a choice? Besides, I think I see how to do it."

"How?"

"Miks . . . sorry, Keon, Don't you see? Of course you do." She shook her head. "I have to kill the master. I can do it, you know. That aura isn't likely to overcome me."

Loahn opened his mouth, closed it, looked at Stavver, flung out his hands, turned his back on both of them to stand staring at nothing.

Stavver nodded slowly. "I see. Think you can manage the killing itself?"

She leaned back against the wheel, brushing her hand across her face. "No. This will." She tapped her temple.

"Your hands do it." The lines in his face deepened.

"I know. I'm not trying to duck responsibility."

"Aren't you?"

"NO. I haven't the skill. You know that. The Rider does. It can do what I can't."

"You've decided."

"Yes."

"Will you take a piece of advice from a thief?"

"Who better?"

"Find a way out before you commit yourself."

She laughed, relief from tension turning her muscles weak. "That I'll do, Miks, That I promise you."

"Since you obviously plan to let yourself be taken, have you considered what will happen to you?"

"As long as I'm left alive, I don't care about the rest."

"You'll probably be raped. Can you handle that?"

She lifted her shoulders, let them fall. "Leave that till it happens. I'll do anything I have to get Sharl back."

He knelt beside her, touched her head with the tips of his fingers. "I wish. . . ."

She tilted her head so that his fingertips trailed over her face. "I know."

Loahn came back and stood before her. "What now?"

She stretched and yawned. "Eat, I think."

"Tchah! I don't mean that and you know it."

She smiled up at him. "Well, you and my friend . . . Keon . . . you two stay here a while, then head north and warn your people the horde is coming."

"And you?"

"With your permission, Loahn, I take that roan of yours and ride out to meet the horde."

"No!" He wheeled to face Stavver. "You were ready to break my back for her less than an hour ago. Don't let her do this."

Stavver snorted. "You try stopping her."

"Lahela . . ." He held out his hands to her. "It's suicide."

"Not quite."

"Then I go with you."

"That IS nonsense. You'd be killed at sight."

He flung himself away, then wheeled back, catching Stavver by the arm. "Tie her up, beat her, do something. She's your woman."

Stavver quietly freed his arm. "Lahela has the right to determine what she does with her life."

"A woman! She hasn't the capacity."

"Hah!" Aleytys stood up and brushed the crumbs of earth from her legs. "I know damn well I'd never make it on this world."

Stavver chuckled. "Relax, Lee. I'll cook some meat and fruit for you." His eyes twinkled as they swept over Loahn's disapproving face. "By the way, when you decide to break away from the horde, I'll be waiting to the east of it for you. Think you can find me?"

"You know I can." With a forefinger she tapped twice at her temple, then grimaced as the diadem chimed in answer. "I don't mean you," she said. "My other talents, Miks."

His hand curved around the back of her head, then moved down to her shoulder. Pulling her against him, he said softly, "Make sure of the bolt hole, Lee."

"You be careful too, you hear?"

He laughed, his breath stirring through her hair. "You've got the easiest time."

"Waiting. It's hard, I suppose."

He looked over her head at Loahn's face. "Our native friend thinks this reversal of roles is obscene."

"He can go sit on a thorn bush. I'm tired of his conceit."

Chapter IV

Aleytys shifted restlessly, glanced up at the glow spot of the sun, then ran her free hand uneasily over her bare shoulders. For the first time she was riding alone on this alien world. The strangeness hit her suddenly like a blow in the stomach.

The land reeled around her, parts leaping at her in exaggerated clarity, other parts blurring. Her stomach knotted, heaved until she spewed its contents alongside the trail.

Feeling the absence of a strong hand the roan shook his head vigorously, snapping the reins from her blind uncertain fingers. The gathering of his muscles punched her out of her shock. She snatched at his mind, stiffened him into a rigid statue. Breathing hard she bent forwards and recaptured the reins, swaying as the motion brought back her dizziness. The stallion settled into a punishing walk while Aleytys splashed water on her face and stared deliberately around, mouth compressed in a tight line, forcing herself to acknowledge and accept the otherness of this place.

Overhead, fugitive patches of blue slipped momentarily through the spiraling streaks of pastel colored bacteria that swarmed across the bowl of the sky, obscuring even the face of the sun. The sun. A single sun, orange, the color of hullu-fruit. A single sun, small and meek. Her birth sun Hesh glittered blue with a cutting light like a steel blade. And Hesh's sister bride Horli. Horli's great red bulk covered a quarter of the sky. Here the horizon was closer, surprising her again and again, whenever she forgot where she was, distracted by events or her companions. The horses here made it doubly difficult to realize she was on another world. Horse. One of the beasts that followed man to the stars. When she looked out across the bobbing heads of the team, she might have been home on Jaydugar rather than on an alien world Madar knew how far from home. Until she looked up and saw the sky.

It hit her now because she rode alone, duplicating her ride under Hesh and Horli, twin suns that would have the hide off anyone foolish enough to ride uncovered. This knowledge etched into her mind, into the unconscious ecology of habit, woke to sudden life as she rode alone under this gentler sun, making her continually uneasy. She rubbed sore breasts and reminded herself that this sun was not Hesh.

Impatiently she dropped the reins letting the roan speed up. He had a mouth like leather and a stubborn objection to control that defeat after defeat never diminished. According to Loahn he was the fastest animal on his horse-run, with a phenomenal endurance, but Aleytys still had not found a gait that was comfortable for his rider. She shifted in the saddle, groaning softly, regretting her black stallion, left behind when she left home. She bent forward and stroked the muscular neck, its reddish hair softened by the blue-grey bloom that made him a roan. "It'll be a relief to get captured, boneshaker." She straightened. "Dammit, horse. When you want a ravening ravisher, there's none around."

The roan kept tugging at the bit until her arms protested each movement she made. After a few more minutes of his jolting trot she sighed wearily, swore, spat out the blood from a badly bitten tongue, and wrapped the reins around her fists, pulling him back to a broken-legged walk.

The rutted dusty road slid backwards under the big

iron-shod hooves as the glow spot of the sun slid down the sky behind her and the fuzzy shadow ahead of her grew proportionately longer. Aleytys slipped into the roan's mind and locked him into the walking gait. Letting out a sigh of relief she wound the reins around the saddle horn and flexed aching fingers, clucking over the deep red pressure marks from the reins. She unhooked the water skin and drank deeply.

When she lowered the skin she saw two men in the road ahead of her, watching her. They were broad chunky figures, sitting their shaggy mustangs with a casual mastery. They wore full trousers and copper studded vests. Long hair whipped about savage grinning faces, held out of their black eyes by red scarves knotted about their brows, fringed ends fluttering among greasy black strands of hair. Their full lips were stretched in wide grins that somehow were not at all reassuring to the watching woman. She lowered the skin slowly and hooked the strap over the horn.

She shook the reins free and forced the animal around. Another rider topped the rise to the left of the road. The roan turned further. Two men sat on their mounts in the center of the roadway, grinning at her. She turned the roan again. On the rise to the right, a sixth rider was a black silhouette against the sky. She finished the roan's prancing circle and pulled him to a halt facing the first pair.

"What do you want?" She would not give in to the tremble at the bottom of her stomach. Lifting her head with fierce pride she stared coolly into the savage grinning faces.

"Come." One spoke, then kneed his mount so that the animal sidled nearer to her.

Aleytys backed the roan a few steps. "I'm gikena, fool."

He laughed, small eyes almost disappearing in the creases of his flesh. "Liar."

"I'm gikena. I heal, but can curse, man of the south. I obey Lakoe-heai."

"Hah!" He leaned over and snatched the reins from her. "Obey the master now. Shaman'll pull your fangs. Gikena!" He shouted with laughter.

Aleytys glared at him. "Let me go."

"Sure. Go with us."

"I won't." She set her face in an icy mask, pleased with her strategy and at the same time terrified. "I'm on an urgent quest, man of the south. I seek my son and what was stolen from me. I lay geas on you to aid me."

He grinned again and brought his hand down hard on the roan's rump, startling him into a quick trot. The others rode off on whatever errands they were pursuing before she interrupted them.

Soon she heard a growling muted thunder that brought a vivid memory to her of the placid days following the herds on Jaydugar. They topped a rise and looked down on a black, moving mass that crept across the rolling land at a slow walk. For an instant she saw them as the ugly armor-plated beasts that the nomads lived off, then she blinked and pulled the corners of her mouth down, jerked back to reality. What darkened the earth was hundreds, thousands of riders, sex indeterminate from this distance.

As her captor plunged into the mob Aleytys felt a sense of helplessness and frustration. One person to turn this— this avalanche of humanity? She looked around, curiosity flaring, dominating for a time her growing anxiety. Women as wild and unkempt as the men stared at her, hate strong and cold in their flat weathered faces. Children rode by, sitting bareback on their shaggy little animals, their faces old and evil. She blinked. Not evil, just wild. It was the distortion in her that changed them into small demons rather than the children they were. She turned away.

With the shriek and rumble of the crude wooden wheels, the multitude of other sounds blending into one vast cacopheny of ear-splitting noise dinning in her ears, beating through her head, Aleytys found it difficult to think, to know what she wanted to do or should do or could do, so she let her tired brain idle, sat slouched in the saddle, hands holding onto the saddle horn, enduring the punishing pitch and roll of the roan's gait.

In the center of the mass they came to an impossibly wide wagon whose flat bed clung with equal impossibility to the contours of the land it crept across. The wood was jointed by dozens of flexible leather hinges, each small section mounted on individual wheels so that the whole moved over the land like a multi-legged creature on hundreds of wheels. Around the sides of this monstrous construction was a hedge of swords, edges glinting in the diffused light. Inside the hedge rose a rounded mound the size of a small hill whose outermost layer was pihayo hide tanned with the hair left on so that the mound fluttered with what looked like limp white grass.

As they rode nearer, the typical stench of the pihayo soured the air. Aleytys wondered how the horde master managed to stand the smell of his dwelling.

She stiffened as they passed one of the last wagons near the great one. The somber black caravan with its glinting gold and crimson scrollwork confirmed for the first time that Maissa had indeed been brought here. Whether she was alive . . . or Sharl. . . . She wrenched her thoughts away as her hands began to tremble and tears hung poised to fall behind her eyelids. Concentrate, she thought. You are gikena. You have power.

She straightened her back and looked boldly at the pair of guards barring the gate to the master's wagon. Make them respect you, she told herself . . . at least . . . she broke into the argument being conducted in the slurred nearly unintelligible dialect of the horde.

"I am gikena." She projected the words with a potent overlay of anger, menace, and power that left both guards and her captor open-mouthed. She slid off the horse and stepped briskly up the crude ladder to confront the startled guards. "Take me to the master."

Chapter V

The stench was incredible. Aleytys found it difficult to think, difficult to do anything but breath as shallowly as possible, blessing the tendency of the sense of smell to burn out fast. She gathered her strength, stilled the trembling of her knees, and snapped her head erect.

The master was a pallid mountain of flesh perched on miscellaneous hides spread over a spongy mass of some kind of vegetable fiber. Aleytys dragged her eyes back to the master, fighting a continual urge to look away from him.

He was naked. As grossly male as he was grossly huge. Aleytys suppressed an inclination to gape and contented herself with wondering what sort of woman could receive that bulk into herself.

Reluctantly she raised her eyes to his face. His head was outsize even for the mountainous bulk that supported it. If he stood his head must nearly brush the rounded top of the tent where the groaning ribs were tied together by a complex knotting of smoke-stained rope, though that point was nearly three meters from the spongy floor. He must never leave this place, she thought. Ahai, Madar! Never to leave this hole! She examined his face again, a tinge of pity overlaying the disgust he raised in her.

His mouth was firm and delicate, even beautiful, showing a strong tendency toward smiling. His nose was strong, a long straight blade of bone and flesh. His eyes, dark fringed and well-shaped, were milky white without iris or pupil, ostensibly blind, though he seemed to be aware of everything around him. This eyeless sight sent shudders running up her spine, the first intimation of the nature of the horde master. If this creature had power that could swallow hers . . . she remembered the diadem and quieted.

His hair was pure pale white, curling closely about his bulging skull. The skull . . . it swelled out from the gentle, even beautiful face. . . . like the bottom of a pear turned upside down. . . . the thick coiling hair masked some of the grotesqueness of its shape, but not enough. Not enough.

The silence stretched on and on. Aleytys refused to be intimidated, either by her own emotions or by the aura of the man.

A thin meager figure came creeping around from behind the master, swinging a censer with black, strong smelling smoke pouring from the holes pierced in the top. Muttering a guttural chant he circled her, throwing the smoke into her face, letting it roll over her skin. She stood, unmoving, a scornful smile mocking his efforts.

Then the drug began to blur her sight, distort her senses. She swayed. Fought her way upright. Then met the glittering eyes of the shaman, his ferret face wreathed in clouds of the drugs' smoke.

Closing her eyes, she fumbled for the black river, fighting back panic as her mind-reach dissolved again and again. Terror was cold . . . cold . . . cold . . . paralyzing. Then she managed to shape Vajd's mandala of peace, simple, pure, the circling triangles drawing her in and out of the center until terror retreated, faded, was gone. She gathered her forces and sank into the mandala, the stable three-pointed figures swimming past her, calm . . . smooth . . . untroubled. . . .

Relaxed, calm, quietly sure of her power, she reached again. The black water spilled over her. With an exclamation of triumph she lifted her arms above her head, glorying in the racing current of power caressing her skin, cleansing her body of the greasy smoke, flushing the drug from her system, leaving her mind clear and sharp. She tossed her hair back over her shoulder and laughed aloud. "I am gikena!"

As she faced the horde master with her new clarity of vision, she saw that his facade of power was hollow; it had a rotten dying smell, a taint of decay. Is this why the horde moves? she wondered. Because the master dies? She set the thought aside to pursue later. "I am gikena," she repeated. She focused cool denying eyes on him. "Out there you have what belongs to me."

"All here is mine." The master spoke for the first time, his voice startling her with its flexible resonant beauty. When she closed her eyes she could see him tall, triumphant, even handsome. Grimly she faced him and rubbed aching overladen breasts to remind herself of her reason for being here.

"No," she said firmly, countering his voice magic with her own. "My son is not yours. My servant is not yours. My caravan is not yours. Like all on Lamarchos, master, you dwell in the house of Lakoe-heai. In the name of them I say restore to me what is mine."

The milky orbs slid over her, blind but preternaturally knowing. "Shaman."

The evil little man sidled around Aleytys, eyes flickering venomously over her before he turned to face his master.

"What happened to the gahane leaf, shaman?" The marvelous voice lashed at the cringing little creature. Aleytys closed her eyes and indulged her imagination momentarily, smiling as the beauty of the master's voice charmed her.

He spoke again, as sharply as before. "Is she what she claims to be?"

Aleytys heard the bedding weed rustle as the master shifted position. She opened her eyes. He was arched over the bent form of the shaman like a great wave threatening a shore.

"I can't say so soon," the wretched creature whined. "She must be tested."

"How?" Grunting with the effort he settled back on the leather and examined Aleytys' slender figure, a light beginning to glow behind the milky white.

The shaman glanced over his shoulder at Aleytys. There was no mistaking the light that shone in those pouchy eyes. He wanted her dead, preferably after suffering great pain. "Gikena be healer, master."

"Could she heal one born deaf?" There was a shrill instability about the voice now that puzzled Aleytys, walking a chill up her spine.

"If this one be true gikena."

"Can you make deaf hear?" Aleytys saw in the master's face a quiver of anxiety.

She shrugged. "I've never done so."

"You failed?"

"No. I never had to try."

"You'll try now. And succeed if you want to live." He slapped huge hands on his meaty thighs. "Bring the boy Ramaikh." As the shaman reached the small arch leading from the tent, he snapped, "Wait!"

The little man fidgeted impatiently in the arch, fingers fluttering the leather doorflaps.

"Send guards for the woman and the male child brought me this morning."

"Master." The shaman hesitated, frowning, smoldering eyes on Aleytys. "Is that wise?"

"What do you know of wisdom, viper?" Gargantuan laughter filled the tent, massive, overwhelming, yet with that taint of hysteria that continued to puzzle Aleytys. "Move!" he shouted, the blast literally blowing the little man out of the tent.

Aleytys seated herself on a pile of hides.

"Did I say you could sit, woman?"

"Do I wait for any man's pleasure to do what I want?"

She laughed her scorn, tossing her head to underline her independence. "There. A question to answer a question."

There was real interest in his face as he moved blind eyes over her. "You forget your place, woman." He stressed the last word to remind her of her status in this man's world of Lamarchos.

"My place is whatever I have strength to take."

"You talk strangely. Where did you find these unnatural thoughts?"

"I say what many women feel. Only, being what I am, I have the power to do rather than merely feel."

"You get before yourself."

"No. I don't need to prove to myself what I am. Only to you."

He grunted then gazed down at his bulging stomach, seeming to turn inward to mull over the outrageous things Aleytys had said to him. The silence deepened in the malodorous tent, but the tension between them was held in abeyance. Aleytys studied him openly, unnoticed, wondering what had made him the monster he was, pitying him deeply, awash with curiosity. Born or made? Born? Made?

The shaman thrust a tall thin boy ahead of him through the door curtains. The boy straightened from his crouch and stood calmly facing the master. There was a strong resemblance between the two males, feature by feature the faces were the same. But the boy had a normal curve to his skull, a thin wiry athlete's body. He stepped away from the shaman and knelt before the master, his head dipping to touch the floor.

"This is my son Romaikh. I have protected him from the fate of the maimed till this time. Do you understand me, woman?"

"Yes."

"You will heal him. This is your test, gikena."

"Even if it wasn't," she said proudly, "I would heal. It is my nature to heal."

"What do we do?"

"Make him understand he is to lay his head here." She smoothed her hand across her lap. "And to be still when I touch him."

"Show the boy."

Mouth pinched into a spiteful line, the shaman led the boy to Aleytys and settled him according to her instructions. When she touched the boy, he flinched, then lay quietly.

Aleytys touched her fingers to his temples, stroking them gently until he relaxed. Smiling warmly, feeling a surge of maternal tenderness, she cupped his head between her palms. She drew in the power making herself a conduit for its flow. It gushed through her and poured out around and around the narrow head. Not understanding in any real sense, she saw the bony growth that closed his ears, saw the dead shrivelled nerve ends not knowing what they were but recognizing their deadness. In the flood of black water the bony growth dissolved and the endings healed, grew, expanded like the desiccated roots of a drought-caught plant at the beginning of the rains. When the thing was done, she freed herself from the river and gently pulled her hands from the boy's head. She looked up and met the master's eyes.

"Well?" The word was a thundering demand.

The boy jumped up, clapping his hands to his ears, his face contorted with fear.

"As you see. He hears. I suggest you keep him apart from all but a few while he learns to cope with this new thing in his life. I suppose he'll have to learn to speak too." She rubbed her forehead wearily. "You ordered the woman brought here. And the . . . " She swallowed. "The child."

The master turned his heavy head to the Shaman. "Where?"

"Outside."

"Bring them." When Aleytys heard these words, her body slumped as she blurred out, nearly fainting. She laced her fingers together, straightened her back, stared intently at the archway.

Maissa came in at a stumbling run, shoved along by a brawny guard. She drew herself erect before the master, her eyes madder than ever, glittering with a hate beyond reason. She stood with a painful awkwardness unlike her usual catlike grace. Aleytys looked from her to the master then back again, suddenly understanding. Maissa was so tiny . . . she stared blankly, swallowing, swallowing . . . he had . . . ahai, he must nearly have split her in half.

Behind Maissa two guards ducked through the door. One held a bundled small shape that wriggled and wailed.

"Sharl." Aleytys leaped to her feet, her hands reaching for her son.

Maissa shrieked and threw herself in front of Aleytys, fingers curling into claws.

The second guard swung his boot brutally, kicking the squalling woman half across the tent. Then he jabbed an elbow into Aleytys' stomach, knocking her off her feet onto the pile of leathers where she had been sitting. She gasped, struggled to suck in the air that had been driven from her body.

The master frowned toward Maissa. "You. Black viper. Move from there and the guard will spit you on his spear." He nodded to the grinning man who moved immediately to stand beside Maissa. She was beginning to hemorrhage, the splotch of blood on her batik spreading like a slow blooming flower. Aleytys staggered to her feet.

"Sit, gikena. Or the guard will pin you to the leather."

Alestys looked with anguish at her baby, then at Maissa. "Let me heal her. The blood . . . "

"That one." The master shrugged his massive shoulders, setting rolls of fat and rippling sagging skin into motion. "Has too much blood in her for her own good. Let the surplus leak out. You claim the child is yours?"

"Yes. My son."

"How'd she get him?" He lifted a meaty hand and jabbed a thumb toward Maissa. "That one."

"She was my servant. She stole the baby from me. While I slept." She spread out her hands. "I must sleep."

"Why would she take him?"

"You don't need me to tell you she's mad."

"Hunh. What do you say, black serpent?"

"She lies." Maissa's voice was suddenly cool and controlled. She smiled sweetly, sat up, and brushed the fragments of rotted weed from her shoulders. "She's barren and sought to take my child from me. I was afraid of her and ran."

"It happens. How do you answer her, gikena?"

"The child is mine." She glared at Maissa. "I doubt if she's ever had one."

"If I decide in your favor, small one, what do you want done with gikena?"

"Kill her. She's dangerous alive." Maissa smiled at him,

then pulled her hands down over her small shapely body, invitation rank in her eyes and posture.

"And if I should decide for you, gikena?"

Aleytys glanced from him to Maissa and back. "Give her to me. she's my servant. Let her serve."

"If she should kill you, what are her services worth?"

"She wouldn't dare. I'm not easily killed, master." She projected scorn at him. "Nor do I give my trust easily after betrayal."

"Come here."

Aleytys stepped closer to him, straining to ignore the rich aroma of urine, sweat, and years of accumulated filth billowing out from his gross body.

"Closer."

She crawled up onto the leather and knelt beside him.

One meaty hand closed on her shoulder, pulling her up against him. He bent over her, taking her nipple in his mouth. His tongue licked over the tip briefly, the he began sucking the milk from her breast.

Aleytyts closed her eyes, struggling to contain her disgust.

He tongued her breast again, nuzzled the other a minute, then pushed her down on the bed with a quick shove. "Dward, your dugs are dry as a well in drought while this one is heavy with milk. The child is hers." He closed his eyes and let his hand wander down to touch himself, a smile growing on his face. Aleytys glanced at him then swallowed a newgrown lump in her throat. She began shaking as apprehension chilled her.

Still fondling himself, lids hooded over his strange eyes, the master said slowly, "Take that dwarf out, tie her so she can't leave the black wagon. Take the baby also. Put it back in the caravan. The rest of you get out. Not you, woman." He closed his hand over Aleytys' shoulder.

Blood trickling down her legs, Maissa found strength enough to turn and smile maliciously at Aleytys before she ducked through the arch. Aleytys could hear her laughing shrilly as the guards prodded her along.

Aleytys tried to push the huge hands off her. "I'm gikena. No."

Breath whistling hoarsely, hands trembling, face furiously intent, he ignored her protest and drew her onto his lap.

Chapter VI

Aleytys slid off the stained leather and stood staring down
at the gross bulk of the master as he lay deep in satiated
slumber, handsome mouth dropping slackly open, lips vibrating to the hog snores that shook his jowls.

Should I kill him now? It would be easy and oh, my
god, I would like to do it. She looked around the malodorous blood-warm interior of the tent, more like a womb
than a place where a grown man lived. No weapons in
here. They made sure of that. She spread her hands out
and smiled down at them. Except these. She closed her fingers into fists and opened them again. No, with the diadem to help her, she could not be disarmed.

She sighed. No. It's too soon. I don't know enough
about these people. Loahn said they change when they enter the lakelands. Like the master is the brain and they're
the fingers of his hand. He's dying . . . why. . . ? She
shook her head . . . no . . . besides, I haven't got my bolt
hole set yet. No use going through all this to get myself
killed. And Sharl. Oh god, Sharl. No.

A waterskin hung from one of the ribs. She unhooked it
and splashed the water over her soiled and aching body.
Rape, she thought. He didn't care what I was feeling. A
hole. That's all I was. She shivered. Then glared angrily at
the master. Gritting her teeth, she splashed more water between her thighs, trying to wash away the humiliation. I
won't feel clean again until I soak a week in a hot bath.

She tugged the batik from under the master's huge leg,
not caring whether she awakened him or not. After shaking out the damp crumpled folds she wound it around her
waist then kicked through the debris until she found the
twisted brooch where the master had flung it. Holding the
cloth around her with an elbow she struggled with the silver wires, straightening the brooch as best she could. With
an exasperated sigh she shoved the pin through the
material and slipped the point under the guard. When she
turned, the master's eyes were open, glowing palely in the
dim light. Grunting, he pushed himself upright.

Aleytys dropped on the heap of leather and stared at him. "What do you get out of that? Poking yourself in me."

He looked surprised. "I don't understand."

"I could be any woman."

He shrugged. "To arouse, no. After that . . ." He spread out his hands. "A woman is a woman."

"It doesn't matter what I feel?"

"A woman is a woman."

"I see. Nothing to bother about."

He nodded, pleased to find her so reasonable. For a minute Aleytys felt like throwing caution away and attacking him now, gross lump of conceit, then she caught her breath. "Why do you go into lakelands?"

He pursed his lips, moved them slowly from side to side. After a strained silence he decided to answer her. "It's time to make a new master."

"Because you're dying?"

He winced. "You're blunt, woman. Never mind. Yes. Because I die."

"I heal. You saw. Why not let me heal you?"

His face grew grim and cold. "There are things you don't understand, woman."

"Many things." She nodded in quiet agreement. "But . . ."

"I'm tired, woman. I die because I'm tired of living, tired to my soul of being what I am."

Chapter VII

Maissa growled deep in her throat as Aleytys pushed the curtains aside and stepped into her caravan. Ignoring her, Aleytys walked quietly to the drawer where Sharl lay whimpering fretfully. She lifted him down on the bed where he lay kicking his feet and whining his discomfort. She splashed water into a basin, removed his soiled diaper and bathed his dirty body, healing the small bruises and abrasions while she cleaned him. At the remembered touch Sharl stopped his uncertain wailing and reached for her with waving clumsy hands. Then he began to howl in earnest as certainty returned to his world and hunger demanded satisfaction. Aleytys tickled his stomach, laughing herself as his face reddened with wrath; she pinned on a clean diaper and lifted him to her breast. As he sucked eagerly at the breast, small fists kneading her soft flesh, Aleytys climbed onto the bunk and sat facing Maissa.

"Well. That was stupid."

Maissa pulled at the leather thongs binding her wrists. Animal eyes, shallow and mindless, flickered over Aleytys and then away, conceding nothing.

"You see where you got us. I have my baby back in spite of you. Soon, I'll be getting both of us free from these savages. However, as you well know . . ." She chuckled, smoothing her hands gently, possessively over Sharl's back. "As you well know, as you are counting on now, we need you to get us off this world. But I'm taking no more chances with you, my friend. If I worked at it, I could probably figure out a way to have one of the traders take me offworld." Maissa's eyes glared suddenly, and Aleytys chuckled. "You see. Convince me."

Maissa shifted on the bunk, wriggling around so her back was against the wall. Intelligence crept back into her narrow face. "How?"

"Good question." Aleytys looked down at the nursing baby; her mouth tightened. She looked up with a jerking abruptness. "You can't lie to me."

Maissa's face sharpened until she resembled a hunting ferret. "Can't I?" She giggled.

"The tea." Aleytys nodded. "You fooled me easily. But. . . ." She looked silently at Maissa, searching the unresponsive face. "I trusted you. But don't fool yourself. I have no more trust left where you're concerned, Maissa. If I lose my alertness when you're around, then I deserve what I get. You can't lie to me, not when I'm watching for it."

Maissa shrugged "So?"

Aleytys lifted a sleepy Sharl across her shoulder, rubbing and patting his back to bring the air out of his stomach. "Stavver says you keep the letter of your word if not the spirit. Dredge up your sincerity, Maissa. Make me believe you."

The small woman met her eyes a minute then looked away sullenly. "Cut me loose."

"Not just yet."

"What do you want?"

"Your word you'll do no more harm to us. Me. Stavver. Sharl. Your word you'll do what I tell you with no argument. That's only sensible, by the way. I know a lot more than you about our present situation."

"When I'm on my ship I don't take orders from anyone."

"I wouldn't be stupid enough to give any. What do I know about starships? Will you swear?"

"Since I keep to the letter, as you say, what do I swear to?"

"Think." Aleytys settled Sharl back in his drawer. When she straightened, she said quietly. "Mean what you say or I'll know."

"What?" Maissa snapped. She thrust her bound wrists forward. "Do I have to stay like this?" When Aleytys ignored her, she let her arms fall into her lap. "Do you expect me to love you, witch?"

"No. Simply mean what you promise and stick to it. First, this. You won't leave us on this world. Sharl, Stavver, and me."

"What if I get to the ship alone?"

"You wait there until we show up. No time limit. Just wait."

Maissa licked her lips. She sat staring at Aleytys with blank dreaming eyes. Then she nodded. "I'll wait. Not that I expect to have to."

"Right." Aleytys closed her eyes and sought the emotion behind the words. Then she looked at Maissa, surprised. "No reservations?"

"You tell me."

"I wonder why. Never mind. Second, this. You will in no way, and I mean NO way, bring harm to Stavver, Sharl, or me before we get to the ship."

"You don't want much, do you." Maissa laughed. "I swear."

"No reservations again. You make me uneasy, woman."

"Do I lie?"

"No. But it puzzles me."

"Exercise for your marvelous brain, witch."

"Third, this. You will deliver Stavver, Sharl, and me to any world he names, without argument, trick or other treachery."

Maissa tipped her head forward, hiding her face behind her masses of blue-black hair. Then she tossed the hair back, a crooked smile on her small face. "All right. I swear."

Aleytys slid off the bunk. "You mean these things. But I sense there's something I've missed. I'll keep thinking and poking at this, that I promise you. Hold your hands out. I haven't anything to cut with, so I'll have to work on the knots. It'll take a while."

Chapter VIII

The bands of color were contracting into towers as the sun rested on the eastern horizon, painting the air vermillion. On the master's wagon the guards hacked away at the entrance to the tent, enlarging it so he could come out. Near the edge of the huge wagon behind the hedge of swords six men sat with tall drums clutched between their knees.

"What's happening?"

Aleytys turned when she heard Maissa's voice. The small woman stood just behind the bench, hands resting on the top slat.

"Getting ready for some kind of ceremony, it looks like. That's the road into the lakelands just ahead there."

Maissa fidgeted about, her fingernails scraping repeatedly across the weathered surface of the wood. "I know that. Look around. All the wagons driven back. Somewhere. Except ours. That makes me nervous, witch." She laughed suddenly, eyes gleaming with malice. "You should know, you're close enough to that monster."

Aleytys shuddered. "Don't remind me." She watched the wagon in frowning silence. Five boys scrambled up the ladder herded by a pair of sober-faced guards. They stopped before the mangled entrance to the tent and formed up into a ragged line.

As the last tip of the sun slipped away the master emerged, dipping through the broken arch to stand blinking in the misty twilight, his white curls glowing like a halo around his grotesque head. He nodded briefly to the

line of boys as he walked past them. While he eased himself down on a leather mound, the boys moved in a wob-
bly line to sit on the wagon floor in front of him, facing
outward, legs folded into full lotus, hands resting on knees.

"The making of a master," Aleytys muttered. "It begins."

"What?"

"Hush. I'll tell you later."

The master's wagon was drawn up on the summit of a
low rise with the caravan parked close on the sundown
side. The thousands of beings in the horde stood packed in
a wedge-shaped mass that began at the foot of the rise and
continued on up to the rim of the three hillocks beyond.
The standers were silent, so still they were like a forest of
statues. Waiting—there was a tension in the air—waiting.

With a great burst of sound the drums began beating.
At first they throbbed wildly with no perceptible common-
ality, then, slowly, out of the chaos of sound, a thrumming
double beat rose triumphant.

Aleytys heard a low murmur, a whispering wordless
sound that fluttered across the crowd. Behind her she
heard a faint echo. When she looked back Maissa was
staring glassily at the master, moaning very very softly in
a cadenced whisper that matched the double beat of the
drums. Aleytys swallowed, closed her eyes and pressed her
hands tight against them, then forced herself to watch,
locked into watching by the pressing need for knowledge.

The master bent slowly forward, planting his elbows on
his knees. He lowered his massive head onto his hands.
The chant intensified, merging with the beat-beat of the
drum.

The shaman came from the tent to stand erect beside
the master, his head barely reaching the top of the meaty
shoulder. He crossed his arms over his skinny chest and
looked around, an absurd little figure with a clattering kilt
made from strips of leather threaded through small polished skulls that danced about and clicked mightily whenever he moved.

The chanters began to sway rhythmically, shifting
weight first to the right, then to the left, then back, over
and over. So tightly were they packed, the slightest break
in the rhythm would have thrown knots of them into confusion. But there was no break. As if they shared a single

nind the horde swayed right then left without stopping. The drums beat the double beat unchanging monotonous hard calloused hands caressing the tough hides with mechanical exactitude.

Ah . . . oh . . . ah . . . oh . . . the shaman circled the master and the boys, feet moving in unison with the great groaning cry of the multi-tongued beast that covered the hills. Behind her Aleytys could feel Maissa's body sliding back and forth in exactly the same rhythm, murmuring the same ah . . . oh . . . ah . . . oh . . . over, over, over.

The drum beats trembled in Aleytys' blood, striking against her will like hugely amplified blows. Her breathing came faster and lighter, a haze drifted across her eyes and her mouth opened to join the chant, the seductive compelling join join join, share the ecstasy—one in many, one of many, one out of many, no more pain loneliness tension difficulties . . . come come come. . . .

"No!" For a minute she thought she shouted it then knew the word had trickled from her lips in a barely perceptible whisper. "No," she repeated softly. "I deny you. I am I." She stared at the shuddering straining master. "I will not join."

As the compulsion retreated, she laughed, eyes sparkling with her victory. She looked at the mob with disgust, sickened that a single reasoning being should allow himself to surrender his will in a kind of beast ecstasy to the monster on the wagon. Now she knew what a master was, and knowing this, the last unwillingness to destroy him washed out of her.

One of the boys jerked suddenly to his feet. A candidate, she thought. Has he passed or failed his test?

The shaman strode into the tent, the skulls clacking about his legs. He came back with a knife in one hand and an ivory white bowl in the other. A huge bowl, vaguely hemispherical with a rough rim and odd bulges. Aleytys came close to vomiting when she realized it was the sawn-off top of a master's skull.

The boy stood swaying from side to side, chanting, blind, lost, unaware of what was happening. The sound, she thought. Ramaikh. It's too much for him. He can't cope. I cured him. My god, I cured him of life. She pressed her fist to her mouth as the shaman stroked the knife expertly across the throat, catching the flood of blood in the bulbous bowl.

He handed the bowl to the boy next to the tumbled body. The surviving candidate drank deep and passed the steaming mess on, wiping the red stain from his lips as innocently as a child wipes off a milk moustache. When the bowl was empty the shaman set it with the knife between the master's feet then continued his endless circling around and around and around. Waiting for the next to succumb.

In the east the moon drifted up over the rim of the earth and sailed in silver silence between the false thunderheads. The chant went on . . . and on . . . on. . . . Oh . . . ah . . . oh . . . ah. . . . The chant and the drum beats . . . on . . . and on. There was no sign of fatigue in the chanters as if they had stepped outside of the needs of their humanity, tapping into another source of energy.

Another boy leaped to his feet.

Aleytys swung past Maissa and dived into the caravan.

Sharl was pushing against his blankets . . . right . . . left . . . right . . . left, whimpering in pain and fear, his small cry echoing the ah . . . oh . . . ah . . . oh . . . chant from outside.

Rage flared in Aleytys, an anger that settled into a cold intensity that filled her with strength enough to slaughter the lot of them if she had to She snatched Sharl up, cradling him against her breasts. "No," she whispered. "No, baby, he can't have you." She let the strength pour out of her into his small body. "My little one, my dream singer. Remember your father. Remember him in your blood and bones, my Sharl, my baby, be strong and wise and warm, remember, little one. You have his gifts, I know it, I know it, my baby, my baby. . . ." She continued humming softly as she rocked him gently back and forth. He relaxed against her, curled up like a kitten, warm and purring.

Aleytys settled onto the cot, shivering as the chill of the night air coiled around her. Tucking Sharl into the curve of her right arm where he would lie safe between her and the wall, she stretched out on the cot, pulling the quilt over her.

Outside, the interminable unchanging chant the interminable unchanging beat of the drums went on and on. As she grew warm and drowsy and eventually drifted off to sleep.

Chapter IX

Warm. Content. Sharl lay beside her, his head propped on her arm, kicking peacefully and waving his arms about while he gurgled and murmured an outpouring of wordless sounds as if he lectured to the air or to the feet he was too young to recognize as his own. Aleytys lay quiet a while, enjoying the sense of well-being, then she pushed up one elbow and tickled Sharl into giggling hysterics. She fluffed up the blankets in the drawer and set him down. "We're moving baby. Going somewhere." She stroked his cheek affectionately. "Sleep, little one. I'm going to stick my head out and see what's going on."

She yawned, stretched, and smoothed the crumpled batik. "Maissa." There was no answer. "Where're we going?" Silence. She slid off the bunk and thrust her head through the curtains. "Leyilli?"

Maissa sat stony still as if she heard nothing except perhaps some daylight echo of the night's chant, reins firm in her hands, holding the team to a steady slow walk that kept the back edge of the master's wagon a measured distance from the horses' noses. Aleytys stepped onto the narrow ledge behind the back of the driver's bench and scanned the horde.

They were in the lakelands. Not on the road. No. They were moving across the gently rolling fields, tearing up fences as they came to them. Aleytys shivered. The faces she could see were set like masks with glassy lifeless eyes, moving with the stiff regimentation of automatons. Licking dry lips she caught hold of the carving at the edge of the caravan and leaned out, looking behind to see what was happening there.

Off to one side there was a break in the dark flood of riders. About twenty of the horde—men, women, children, were mechanically slaughtering a small herd of pihayo. As she watched a gap opened between the standing figures and she saw a stone-faced boy slit the throat of a shaggy beast and thrust his mouth into the warm stream of spurting blood. Beyond him a girl not more than four stabbed

repeatedly at the throat of a calf. Aleytys wrenched her
eyes away only to see black plumes of smoke rolling up
the slant of the morning breeze. She closed her eyes, unwilling to see more. Unsteadily she swung around the end
of the bench to sit beside Maissa.

In eery silence the front edge of the horde swung axes
and clubs, levelling fences and hedges. Ahead, thrusting up
over the tree-interrupted line of the horizon she saw a
delicate scarlet thread. Loahn, Loahn, she thought. I hope
you warned them. Then, over the rumble-crunch-shriek of
the wagons, she heard the musical metallic voice of the
bell calling out the danger beat, triple threes repeated over
and over.

A small band of riders came galloping past, loosing a
cloud of bolts. The horde ignored them, ignored the bodies
of their own dying and dead. And the wounded rolled as
silent as the dead off their mounts, rolled as silent as the
dead under the careless hooves of the horde. Maissa drove
stolidly over the trampled fragments of men. And not only
men. The off-side horse shied suddenly, Aleytys looked
down into the unmarred face of a child, a girl, hair
streaming out over the ground, ragged bloody shreds of
flesh, rubbery white tubing where her neck should have
been. There was nothing in her stomach to void but
Aleytys hung over the side of the caravan racked with dry
heaves, the acids from her stomach burning in her throat.
She wiped a trembling hand over and over her mouth.

The raiders came again. And again. Their quarrels
found easy targets. But it was not enough. The sheer bulk
of the horde defeated them. Ten died, fifty, a hundred.
The loss was scarcely perceptible in the mass of riders.
Ahead the crimson thread rose higher and higher. Aleytys
stumbled around the seat and plunged inside the caravan.
She reached through the back curtains, pulled the waterskin inside. Without caring where the water fell, she
splashed handful after handful of the warmish liquid
across her face and arms, then took a mouthful, sloshed it
around, and spat it out the back. She swallowed more, letting it slide down her burning throat to rest uneasily on
her stomach. She looked at the sleeping baby, her face
relaxing into a tender smile as it always did. She let the
waterskin swing out again, wiped her damp hands on a
rag, then touched the wispy curls haloing his small face.

She pulled the corners of her mouth down, pressed a hand against her stomach. "Eating doesn't really appeal to me, baby," she muttered. "But I have to feed you, little leech." She rummaged through the drawers until she turned up a resin paper packet full of hard greyish-umber chunks of dried meat. She took two pieces of meat, twisted the paper together again and dropped it in the drawer. After slamming the drawer shut she climbed back on the bunk. She glanced at Sharl curled up in his nest of flannel. "Huh, baby. I'll stay in here. No use wasting the effort I'm going to put into chewing this leather."

With her free hand she touched her temple, welcoming the chime with a strong feeling of relief. "Well, Rider," she murmured. "Though you fool around with my body, at least you leave my mind alone." She closed her eyes, rubbed her back against the side of the caravan. "All this is exciting. I wonder what fantastic things you've seen. You know, I think I'm actually enjoying most of this. In a funny kind of way. Still. . . ." She sighed. "I used to hate the thought of having something in my mind, snooping into what I thought and did. Right now, it's kind of friendly. Though . . . to have you watching when I. . . ." She shifted on the bunk and frowned at the soreness in her body. "That elephant . . . left me sore as. . . ." She sighed again and swallowed the last hard lump of meat. "Does this stuff really have any value as nourishment? Maybe it'll fill the hole inside me. I wish you could talk to me. I don't even really know if you can understand what I'm saying."

She lay down on the bunk and laced her fingers together below her breasts. "Rider. . . ." Closing her eyes she sank herself into the deep trance where at the utmost stretch of her mind she could feel the presence she called Rider. Once again she spread out the image of the still black pool. Amber eyes flickered there, amber light flashed over the surface. "Hello," she thought. "I need your help, Rider. Do you know what has happened to me?"

Feeling of affirmation. Amber eyes blinked then vanished.

"Ah. Good. Do you know what I plan to do?"

Affirmation.

"Good. I have to kill the horde master. I don't have the skill or the stomach for it. So." She let her mind rest a minute breathed slowly to dissolve the tension. "So. Will you use your skill, your experience, and do this thing for me? Will you help me?"

There was a strained silence. A feeling of impatience. Amber flickered then black danced across amber then violet thread spun through the fragmented colors . . . like a war . . . black against amber against violet. Aleytys waited. The flickering colors faded, returned as the breathing exercises stilled the turbulence in her body. Then the pond of still water was there again. "Will you help me?" she whispered.

Image of stern black eyes coming through more powerfully than ever before. Feeling of reassurance and agreement.

For a minute she floated disoriented then she babbled. "Thank you . . . thank you . . . thank you. . . ." Tears of relief slipped from under her eyelids and rolled across her face to wet the hair above her ears.

The black eyes crinkled into laughter. She felt warm acceptance glow through her. Then she drifted into a deep, deep sleep.

The baby's crying woke her. She slid off the bunk and changed him hastily, then put him to suck as she pushed through the curtain to find out why the caravan was stopped.

Maissa was gone. Ahead the city was a massive block of grey stone surrounded by the attacking horde like ants around a dying animal. From the walls archers poured quarrels into the mass of the horde swarming below. In front of the gate two sets of bearers swung wagon tongues they were using as battering rams against the iron studded gates. The carriers died and died and died but there was always more to take their places, kicking the dead and wounded aside when they got in the way.

Around the walls as far as she could see the horde was clawing at the city. Some drove up against the walls, unhooked wagon tongues, tied ropes to them and heaved them up the walls with an unnatural strength that sent the tongues three times out of five flying over the top, dragging a knotted rope behind. Again and again the defenders cut the ropes, shot the climbers, speared those of the horde who reached the top. But each time more of them got into the city. In spite of the hundreds who died. More got into the city. And the bodies of the horde piled higher and higher along the walls in a pouring out of life that left Aleytys too shocked to tear her eyes from the waste. And horror piled on horror, it made no difference whether that life belonged to man, woman, or child. Without thought to age or sex the horde poured against the city, expending itself with a prodigality that defeated walls and defenders alike.

The gates boomed open at last, sections of the wall were cleared of cityfolk. Lines of horde beings like trails of ants poured over the walls and through the gate into the city. Aleytys looked up at the sky. The sun was halfway between noon and setting. Three hours. She leaned back and closed her eyes, shutting out the scurrying silent horde, swarming over the city's carcass. Maissa among them. Running wild through the gate, arms and knife splattered with blood. An orgy of death where attackers and attacked joined in a crazy drunken deadly embrace. Three hours to kill a city.

Opening her eyes she stared with hostility at the master's wagon. Sitting there like a spider under that hairy white mound, she thought. How much death does it take to make a master?

Behind the hedge of swordblades twenty men stood, eyes alert, bodies under their own control, separated out from the rest of the mindless horde, wearing helmets of a silvery metal, the shaggy black ends sticking out like coarse grass from under a rock. Aleytys rubbed her forehead. Those helmets . . . but there was still no chance to kill the master, not really . . . there was too much confusion . . . she didn't know enough yet . . . not yet. . . .

She looked out over the lake, frowning at the steeply rising rolls of earth. Miks, I hope you're out there. Somewhere, somewhere. Ahai, Madar. I wish I was there with you.

About an hour later the horde came staggering out of the city, ignoring the dead, ignoring the silent wounded, still locked in that unnatural stillness where men suffered and died without a sound. Having killed and burned in that same eery silence.

She smelled burning. Rolls of smoke came puffing over the walls followed by leaping red and yellow tongues of flame. The crimson minaret tottered uncertainly, then toppled suddenly to crash on the patterned pavement.

The city burned.

Aleytys squeezed the last water out of the skin and splashed it over her face. Holding Sharl pressed against her shoulder she hooked the strap of the skin over her arm. Then she slid cautiously down from the caravan and picked her way through the dead-eyed, reeling death-drunken beings of the horde. A feebly waving hand fumbled at her. She swallowed a scream and winced violently away, repelled by the thought of those bloody dehumanized creatures touching her.

At the lake she filled the skin and left it lying on the springy grass at waterside while she waded out into the lake, slowly, enjoying the feel of the clean white sand under her feet, the lapping of the brilliant, clear water against her legs. She sat down. With her free hand she splashed water over her face, her shoulders, over Sharl.

He laughed and wriggled in her hold, reaching out to pat the water, driving his hands into the mysterious coolness, struggling to get hold of it, complaining loudly as it ran away from his small hands. Aleytys used a corner of her batik to gently rub the water over him while he splashed about on her knees, slippery as a fish.

But the sun was low in the west and the air was beginning to cool. She stood reluctantly and waded back to the shore, slipped the waterskin's strap over her shoulder and trudged back through the sprawling horde, walking with exaggerated care to avoid touching any of them. She glanced briefly at the guards on the wagon, tossed her damp hair back with a scornful twitch of her head, and walked briskly around the caravan and up the stairs.

Still isolated within the gentle idyll she had built to separate herself from the violence and insanity of the horde, she laid Sharl on the cot and rubbed him dry with a soft rag. Then she put a clean diaper on him and settled him back among the soft nest of blankets, pulling one of them over him, tucking it around him to keep him warm.

While she was busily washing the crumpled stinking diapers Maissa had shoved into a drawer, Maissa came back from the city. Aleytys felt the shifting of the floor and went to the front of the caravan to see what was happening.

Maissa sat stolidly on the driver's bench, leaning forward, elbows on knees, hands hanging limply between her shins. Arms and legs were thickly crusted with newly dried blood. Large splatters marked her face and breasts. As if she had thrust her face into blood. As if she had walked through blood. Had crawled through blood.

"I suppose I don't have to tell you to stay out there." Aleytys fetched out the bucket and some rags and began washing the blood off Maissa. She undid the pin and stripped the stiff batik off, dropping it over the side with a grimace of distaste.

Maissa sat like a rubber doll, letting herself be prodded and pulled without the slightest spark of interest, even after Aleytys pinned a clean batik around her.

Aleytys sloshed the rag in the bucket turning the water into a thick red sauce. She wrung the rag out and hung it over the seat then threw the bloody water in a crimson arc across the trampled grass, splattering a number of dull-faced bodies. She refilled the pail and dunked the rag back in. The water turned pale pink and the rag lost its last tinge of red. She wrung it out again and hung it back over the seat to dry. Picking up the bucket she looked down at the water, looked at Maissa, then smiled grimly. "Worth a try . . ." She swung the bucket and arced the water into Maissa's face. There was not a single flicker of reaction. Aleytys sighed.

Drumbeats throbbed in the leaden silence. Maissa stood up.

Aleytys started to speak, then shook her head. No use. The jumble of noise was the same as before but quickly beat itself into the monotonous double beat. The horde gathered, stood packed shoulder to shoulder to shoulder, chanting the endless unvarying ah . . . oh. . . .

The master came out of the tent, sat on the mound of leather clutching his head with the last survivor of the candidates seated between his massive knotted knees, staring out bright-eyed at the swaying crowd, his thin, handsome face glittering with an enormous pride.

The shaman darted from the tent prodding a shambling dull-eyed lakelander ahead of him. Stumbling and swaying, the captive approached the master and fell to his knees under the pummelling hands of the hysterically exultant shaman. He buried his fist in the captive's hair and jerked his head back. The boy jumped up, knife in one hand, bowl in the other.

Hastily Aleytys wrenched her eyes away and stared down at the ground shuddering at the suddenly silenced shriek that cut through the rumbling tamm-tumm of the drums. When she looked up, the boy was lowering the bowl, wiping the red from his laughing mouth with the back of a slim strong hand.

The chanting and the drums went on and on, until Aleytys thought she would go screaming out of her mind. Then a thin wail came from the caravan.

"Sharl!" She plunged into the caravan. He was kicking his feet, waving his arms about, whimpering fretfully. She watched a minute before touching him, then smiled with weak relief as she saw he was not under the spell of the drums. She touched his diaper and laughed aloud. Wet. And he was mad about the discomfort.

When she had changed him, he murmured drowsily and then went back to sleep with a concentrated intensity that please her immensely. She flipped his curls about with a forefinger. "My son. . . ."

She pushed the curtains aside and stood leaning against the seat back, her body aching for sleep. But she was determined to last the night if necessary to find out what happened when the chant ended. If it ever did. After an hour she stretched stiffened limbs and moved around to sit beside Maissa.

The drums stopped. Aleytys glanced at the moon. Only two hours. But it felt like years. She stretched and yawned.

Maissa tilted farther and farther forward until she reached a point of instability and began to topple off the seat. Aleytys jumped over and caught at her then manhandled her back on the seat. She was completely limp, mouth hanging slightly open, eyes closed, a ragged doll with the sawdust running out. Aleytys scowled at her, startled by this new manifestation.

Maissa was drowned deep in sleep. As if drugged. "What next," Aleytys muttered. She looked around. On the battered grassy field, silvered by the moon, the creatures of the horde lay tossed around, lying where they fell in a tangle of limbs and bodies. She turned towards the master's wagon. The silver-helmeted guards were back, moving about in front of the tent, alert and dangerous.

"Damn," she growled. "We're stuck here in the middle of the horde."

Shaking her head in disgust, she hauled Maissa off the seat and pulled her into the caravan, stretching her out on her bunk. Then she stepped out the back and looked around. All over the ground lying one on top of the other, the horde slept, a few of them twisted into painful contortion against the wheels of the caravan. She unhooked the limp waterskin and slipped the strap over her shoulder to have a ready excuse if anyone challenged her.

Stepping carefully over the bodies, trying to avoid stepping on out-thrust arms or legs . . . or worse, into a half-hidden stomach . . . Aleytys picked her way around the edges of the horde. As she walked, several of the guards came to the hedge of blades and stood watching her move, but none of them said anything. Distracted, Aleytys stepped suddenly on a pile of arms and legs. Tottering, arms flying about wildly, she found her feet again and straightened, struggling to control the nausea that wrenched at her.

None of the sleepers moved. They might have been dead except for occasional snores and the rise and fall of chests marked by shifting gleams where the moonlight slid over taut skin.

She filled the waterskin and came back, circling widely to avoid the bulk of the sleepers. As she pulled herself up onto the seat, she glanced casually at the master's wagon. "I can do it," she murmured. She tapped her temple and smiled grimly as the diadem chimed its answer. "We can do it." She lifted her head and laughed, brilliant eyes measuring and dismissing the guards. "Mighty fighting men. We'll get through you."

Chapter X

Aleytys woke with her stomach clamoring for food. But she forgot momentarily about her hunger when she felt the shake and shimmy of the moving caravan. She tumbled off the bunk and thrust her head through the curtains.

The sun was crawling over the eastern horizon. The air was cold and damp with a bright freshness that whipped the sleep from her mind. In the sky the false thunderheads were unknotting and starting to stream across the vivid blue. Around the caravan the fields were empty, stock driven off before the horde could slaughter them. Aleytys sighed with relief. The warning had been passed on. She pushed through the curtains and climbed up on the seat beside Maissa, scanning the horizon ahead of the horde. No sight of one of the minarets. Not yet. There was time. She lowered herself carefully and went back inside the caravan.

Sharl woke and demanded attention. She changed him, dug out more of the dried meat, found a cache of dried huahua, scooped up a handful of the wrinkled purplish brown fruit. Dumping her gleanings on the bunk, she lifted Sharl from his nest. Then she climbed on the bunk and settled herself comfortably, back leaning against the side of the caravan. While Sharl sucked greedily at her breast Aleytys chewed the rock-hard meat and the rather too-sweet fruit, feeling a remnant of the contentment last night had produced. After a while she chuckled, then chuckled again.

"Sharl-mi, look at us. You, little one, thank the Madar, are too young to know what's happening. Me, I should be feeling sunk in the pits. . . . I don't. You know, right now, I can't even feel very bad about all those killed, like they're there all right, but not real . . . ghosts. . . . Oh hell." She lifted Sharl to her shoulder and began to pat the air out of him. "Only a little while longer . . . tomorrow night, I think. We'll do it then, and be on our way. On our way."

She settled Sharl back in his blankets, then stretched out on the bunk. "Miks . . . to the east . . . you said you'd be there. . . ." She closed her eyes and let her empathic sense flow out and out, seeking the cooly green touch like the color deep in the heart of winter ice.

Glowing red spots circled to the east, hot with hate, hot with anger, hot with frustration. She reached beyond . . . beyond . . . sighed with relief . . . cool pale mint green glow . . . on a hill . . . waiting. She opened her eyes, smiling, knowing she could find him whenever she wanted. She rolled off the bunk and went back outside, too nervous to sit still any longer.

To her left a section of the horde swarmed around an isolated horse run. The buildings were already blooming with fire, smoke starting to roll in black greasy puffs from the mossy roof. She looked away. Up ahead a speck of red thrust up over the treetops. She ran her hands through her sticky hair. "Damn . . ." She glanced at Maissa then at the horses. "Time to get to work."

After considerable struggle she got the reins away from Maissa. Gradually she maneuvered the caravan toward the eastern side of the marching horde.

Yelling screaming riders galloped from behind a grove, stringing out into a line as one by one they let off a spate of crossbow bolts. One buried itself deep in the wood by Maissa's head while a second burned a slight groove in Aleytys' shoulder. She jumped to her feet, cleated the reins, then swung up onto the seat, holding herself steady with a deathgrip on the gingerbread carving.

"Hey!" She leaned out and waved her free arm in vigorous protest.

The lakelander lowered his bow and waved the others back. He turned his mount and rode along with the marching horde, keeping a wary eye on the dull-faced riders and a prudent distance between them and himself, his young face puzzled and intrigued. "Hey what?" he yelled back.

"Quit shooting at me."

"Why should I?"

"I didn't say stop shooting at them."

"What's so special about you, woman?"

"You know Loahn Arahn's son?"

"I know him."

"He'll tell you about me, what I'm doing here. Lahela gikena. Meanwhile, could you aim your quarrels in another direction?"

He frowned at her. "You tell me. What're you doing with those?"

She slapped her forehead in exaggerated disgust. "Look, friend." Her voice broke. She coughed and spat. "I don't plan to scream the story of my life. Besides I don't know how much these zombies take in. Get to Loahn, will you. And tell him Lahela said tomorrow night."

"What?"

"You heard me."

He flourished the crossbow in a wide sweeping gesture, pulled the horse around, and galloped off ki-yi-ing at the top of his lungs.

Aleytys settled back on the seat and retrieved the reins. The band of lakelanders rode past again and again, killing . . . no slaughtering . . . slaughtering beings of the horde who fell and were lost under the plodding hooves of the shaggy little mounts. The horde fought back in one way . . . only one way . . . with its numbers. It ignored the flea bites, death was its purpose here . . . the more that died, the quicker its purpose would be accomplished.

In a little while she put the reins in Maissa's stiff hands and closed her fingers around them. Maissa sat stolidly, keeping the horses moving steadily along the eastern edge of the horde. No more quarrels came their way. That was good too. Aleytys leaned back against the slats, waiting to see if she could trust the zombied woman to stay at the side rather than working her way back to the master's wagon.

"Hey, Lahela!"

She jumped up onto the seat clutching at the carving. "What?" she shrieked.

"Loahn says good luck." He waved the crossbow at her then rode off, shooting into the horde as rapidly as he could slap in new quarrels.

"That's nice," Aleytys muttered. She climbed down, holding tightly to the carving as the caravan rocked and swayed over the uneven ground. She frowned thoughtfully at Maissa, opened her hands, stared down at them a minute, then went inside.

"Rope . . . need some rope . . ." She began pulling

open the drawers and rummaging through the jumbled contents inside. "I know Kale had rope. He cut off a piece for Miks ... "

She rested on her knees in the narrow space between the two bunks frowning and chewing on her lower lip. Still frowning, she wriggled around, carefully avoiding the drawer where Sharl slept. Leaning forward, she explored the panel shutting in the Vryhh-box, scratching at it with nervous impatient fingers. After a frustrating struggle costing her two torn fingernails, she pulled the panel free and pushed it behind her, then teetered back on her heels and shoved the sweaty strings of hair off her hot face.

The Vryhh-box was still there, cold and hard against her fingers. She passed her hands over the box, explored the rest of the cavity, "Ah." She pulled out a coil of rope, sissal around a monofilament core. Alien artifact, so put away out of sight. She relaxed and rubbed her forehead, suddenly tired to death, weary of this world, weary of trying to deal with all the conflicting needs yammering at her. Stirred by some vague remnant of the curiosity that plagued her off and on, she probed further into the cavity.

Cold metal stung a hand. Cautiously, she pulled the object out. A knife. In a worn leather sheath. "How ... "

She pulled the knife from the sheath, touched her fingers against the cutting edge. Kale? Maissa? Stavver? She turned it over in her hands. Maissa? Why would she? The knife wasn't her weapon. Miks? He had his own knife, had it with him. Not Miks. That left Kale. But he had a knife too. Aleytys remembered him turning it over and over in his hands ... She held the hilt up to the light. There was a tiny engraved figure nearly worn away. A wolf's head. She pinched her lips together. Kale. Before Maissa painted the fakes on ... she ran a thumb thoughtfully over the small roughness ... wolf's heads on his cheeks. Why?

Well. Only Kale could answer that. Aleytys shrugged and pulled herself up, her joints stiff from kneeling so long. She dropped the knife beside Sharl's nearly cleaned diapers and slid the drawer shut. The panel went back in place somewhat more easily than it came out.

Sucking a pinched finger, she settled beside Maissa. The stone walls around the city ahead were a dark mass against the sky. Another half hour ... she worked the reins from Maissa's hands and wound them around the cleat. The horses kept plodding ahead, ignoring the lack of guidance, swept along by the horde around them.

Aleytys put her shoulder into Maissa's stomach and heaved. With the slight body wrapped around her neck she staggered into the caravan. After stretching Maissa on the bunk, she tied pieces of rope around her arms and legs, then used two other sections of rope to anchor hands and feet to the ends of the bunk.

She bent over Maissa. "That'll keep you out of the city, Captain." She shook her head. "You could've been killed yesterday. Then where would we all be?" She patted Maissa's shoulder and went back outside.

Chapter XI

It all happened again. The dying. The burning. The toppling minaret. The drums and chanting. And the sleep-coma.

Aleytys slipped off the bunk and stretched, working out the kinks that came from sitting still too long. She bent over Maissa frowning at the deep bloody bruises where the maddened woman had tried to tear free from the ropes. She touched the knots, frown lines deepening. "Later, Captain. When we get out of this mess."

She touched Sharl briefly, inspected the padding that held him tightly. The ride out would be rough. She plucked at the quilting. No time to get him in a sling. This would have to do. She pushed the drawer nearly shut.

The blue steel blade of the knife shimmered like silk on the coarse ticking of the mattress. She threaded a piece of rope through a loop in the top of the sheath, then shoved the knife home. After tying the ends together in a neat square knot she slipped the loop over her head and one shoulder so that the knife hung beside her hip. Before leaving the caravan she tapped her temple, smiling at the sound of the chime. "Be ready, Rider. When it starts we'll have to be fast." A second chime answered her and sent her laughing out the back.

She glanced around. A few sleeping figures slumped

around the caravan, very few of them to the east. Before starting for the master's wagon she stared out at the rippling rise of land. "See you, Miks. Soon."

The hard-gaited roan stamped impatiently. Aleytys eyed him with distaste. "Boneshaker old friend." She sighed, pulled the reins loose and swung up on his back. She settled herself in the saddle and swung the animal around, keeping him at a slow walk as she circled toward the master's wagon. The big horse picked his way delicately through the carelessly tumbled figures who lay sunk in a sleep so deep it verged on coma. They had to circle wide to avoid places where the sleepers lay packed so closely the horse would refuse to go on.

When they reached the wagon she slid off his back and tied the reins in a half-hitch in a ring dangling among others beneath the back edge of the wagon. "All right, Rider," she murmured. "Now's the time to do your trick."

The diadem chimed. As the several notes ran downscale to a basso growl she felt the influence again spread through her body. She swung onto the wagon and pushed recklessly through the circle of guards knocking them down like slow motion pins. Her body plunged into the tent.

The master sat with his head resting on his hands, elbows on knees, the boy sitting in front of him echoing his posture. The shaman stood bent over beside the boy staring intently into his face.

Black eyes glinted, narrowed and thoughtful, in Aleytys' mind. It seemed to her they smiled briefly at her . . . somehow . . . then turned back to measure what must be done. Then her body leaped forward.

The knife was in her hand. Her free hand grabbed a handful of springy white curls, hauled the master's head up. The knife slashed once, twice through the neck. Then a third time. Then the boy. His throat was thinner. Much thinner. Her hand lowered the head onto the floor between thin legs. Finally the shaman. He started to topple as her hand jerked his head up. The knife slashed twice and the body fell, cut loose from the head. Her hand loosed its grip on the head, then her body wheeled and ran from the tent, through the still falling guards, trampling on flesh and wood indiscriminately. Her body leaped from the wagon onto the horse, snatched the reins loose, and sent the roan back through the sleepers.

Aleytys felt a strain behind her eyes that grew and grew. Breath sobbing into her body in great gasps, she kicked her heels into the roan's sides, driving him across the cold bodies, slipping, sliding, struggling to keep his feet as he rushed headlong toward the caravan.

A moan whispered across her brain. The low rumble celerated upward and the tightness went away. She shook her head, dashing away the fragments of possession from her brain. Around her the horde creatures were stumbling to their feet, a dazed uncertainty in their faces. Muttering incoherently they took a few steps in one direction, then turned another way, bumping into each other to stand motionless the moment they were in physical contact, then twitching away again in a frenetic outburst of movement.

Aleytys forced the roan through them across the half-kilometer between the master's wagon and her caravan. Fumbling hands clutched at her legs, then moved away, clutched at the bridle only to forget what they were doing, clutched at the horse until the roan's speed threw most of them off. She kicked the others away.

At the caravan she leaped recklessly for the driver's bench, snatched at the reins as she tumbled past them. "Hi-ya!" she shrieked, slapping the reins hard against the horses' rumps, startling them into a run.

Aleytys nearly fell off before she managed to seat herself. She screamed again at the team. The caravan leaped, bounded, threatened to overturn, teetering precariously as it rumbled over confused horde beings. Somehow it stayed upright. The roan ran free behind the caravan, head held high and to one side to keep the dangling reins from under his feet.

They raced across the bumpy flat outside the city and rolled onto a winding rutted road that led vaguely eastward. Aleytys let the team settle to a rapid trot and managed to look behind.

There was no pursuit. She couldn't even see the town anymore. It was down behind a fold of earth. There were no sounds—nothing—except the harsh grinding of the wheels and the rattle of the hooves. She saw the roan stumble then snort, lifting his head high, one of the reins snapped in half.

"Ahai, Madar!" She pulled back on the reins, kicked in the brake. "He'll break his neck." The roan pranced up beside her. "Haiyi, boneshaker, I'm a fool." She slid down from the seat. "If Loahn wants you back, he can go look for you." She rubbed his nose gently, then scratched behind his ears as he whuffed his pleasure. Then she stripped off the saddle and bridle, throwing them beside the road. She used the blanket to rub him down, then slapped him on the rump. "On your way, boneshaker."

She climbed back into the caravan. Sharl was whimpering his fright. The two quilts padded around him had kept him safe but he was terrified by the rough ride. And uncomfortable. She picked him up and held him against her. "It's all right, baby," she whispered. "It's all right." She laid him on the bunk and changed him. As he lay waving his arms about for sheer joy in being able to move them, she knotted a batik into a sling and laid him in it so he could feel her next to him constantly and be reassured. Then she bent over Maissa.

The woman was unconscious, a dark bruise on her temple. She lay folded against the wall, held to the bunk by the tethering ropes. Aleytys cut them off, then worked the gag out of her mouth, grimacing at the dark scummy stains on the knife blade. She wiped the knife against Maissa's batik, rubbing hard to get rid of that blood. Then she shoved it back in the sheath that dangled on the hip across from Sharl.

Reaching for the power, she plunged into it, let it flow over the mangled wrists and ankles where the ties had been, healing the tears and bruises. She used the heel of her hand to force Maissa's mouth open, touched the swollen bloody tongue, bitten through in several places.

When the healing was finished she let the power puddle momentarily in her hands, ignoring the cold feeling of danger that trembled through her. Maissa's eyes were open, staring at her. They saw nothing, acknowledged nothing. Aleytys shuddered. She bent over Maissa, touched her fingers to the small woman's temples, letting the pooled power flow forth. "Sleep," she whispered. "Sleep, little Captain. Let it all be a dream when you wake. It's over. No more hassle, no more master. Forget, forget, forget. . . ."

She pulled her hands away, breaking with the power.

The small thin body was relaxed, breasts rising and falling in a slow steady rhythm. Her face was peaceful, the dark shadows in her soul sleeping with the rest of her. Aleytys felt the relaxation in her and was satisfied.

Back on the driver's bench, she uncleated the reins and reached out, searching for the mint green flow of Stavver's presence. She found it easily. Ahead. Above. She toed the brake loose and clucked the team into a steady walk. The roan whinnied softly and ran ahead of the team. Aleytys laughed, feeling marvelously lighthearted.

"All right, boneshaker, we'll go together."

Chapter XII

"You all right?" Stavver let go of her and stepped back, running worried eyes over her, frowning because the moon had set and only the stars lit the rocky slope.

"Good enough, but glad to see you, Miks."

"They hurt you?"

"A little. I'm more disgusted than hurt, though." She shuddered and moved close to him, holding out her arms. "All that killing."

"It's over, Lee." He gentled her against his chest.

"For me. For you." She felt his heart beating strongly under her ear.

He stirred and moved apart from her. "Maissa?"

"In the caravan. Sleeping."

"She sane?"

"I don't know. I tried to make her forget. I don't know if I succeeded."

"It was bad?" He shifted suddenly, his feet making a scraping sound on the rocky ground. "She was raped?"

"Yes." Aleytys searched his face. "You didn't ask about me. No." She held up a hand as he moved toward her. "Don't bother. Yes. The master had me. Phahhh! I won't be clean again till I soak a month in a hot bath. No one's ever treated me like . . . have you ever used a woman, Miks. Used. That's the right word. Have you ever used a woman when you didn't give a damn about what she felt or didn't feel, when you didn't want her to be a person only a convenience, when you would have resented her making you understand she was a human being with rights of her own, when you didn't want to know her in any way but one?"

He laughed dryly, his shadowed face taking on an indifferent cruelty that jarred once more on her feeling for him. "It happens."

"Well, thank the Madar, it's never happened to me before, and, if I have the least thing to say about it, it never will happen again."

"So you didn't enjoy the copulation. That surprises me."

"Don't talk to me that way." She stiffened, suddenly furious. "If you must let jealousy rule your tongue, Miks, save it for when it's justified."

"Jealousy! You flatter yourself."

"You . . ." Suddenly unable to go on, Aleytys ran up the back steps of the caravan. "I'm tired. Take care of the horses." Ignoring his angry exclamation, she pushed through the curtains and dumped herself on one of the bunks. "Hunh!" She brought her fist down hard on the mattress. "Bastard."

Sharl stirred in the sling and yelled his hunger. The anger drained out of her. She lifted him to her breast and sat dreamy-eyed while he fed. When he was finished she made a nest for him in a drawer and tucked a blanket around him. Then she stretched out on the bunk, feeling warm, weary, aware of the noises around her but not really listening to them.

When Stavver came into the caravan, she was nearly asleep. She felt him bending over her.

"Lee, I'm a fool."

She blinked heavy eyes, smiled drowsily. "You are, aren't you."

"I didn't want to admit anyone had this much hold on me."

"I know."

"Was it really bad?"

"Mmmm." She fought against coming awake. "I don't want to remember. . . ."

"Lee. . . ." His hands touched her face lightly, moved

down, cupped over her breasts. "Are you too tired? We could make a good memory."

Aleytys felt warmth surging through her. She caught his hands and brought them to her lips. "I'm not too tired."

Chapter XIII

Stavver was shovelling dirt over the campfire. Aleytys came out of the caravan with a pail of murky water and damp diapers hanging over her arm. She dumped the diapers over the back of the seat and flung the water away in a soapy arc that splashed noisily against the pile of boulders nestling like a clutch of stony eggs against the steep slant of the hillside. Dropping the pail she smiled at Stavver. "Maker of magic memories."

He grinned at her. "Bring the horses in, witch."

"Let me hang out my wash first."

"How much longer does that go on?"

"Forever!" She chuckled. "You don't know much about babies."

"Only how to make them. I never hung around longer before."

"Poor Miks. Another year at least."

"Good god."

The sound of hooves pounding at speed along the road cut through the peace of the morning. Stavver came leaping onto the driver's seat then onto the caravan top. He teetered there a minute then straightened and stared downtrail.

"What is it?"

"Who, you mean." He swung down. "Your boyfriend."

"Idiot!" She poked her elbow in his side. "I suppose you mean Loahn." She sighed with exaggerated weariness.

"You got it." He slid off the seat and strolled toward the road where it curved past their campsite. Aleytys sat kicking her heels against the box.

Loahn brought his mount to a sliding stop, a grin almost splitting his face in half. He jumped down and bounded exuberantly to her, dropped to his knees and banged his head against the dirt in front of her dangling feet.

She slid down beside him. Catching hold of a tuft of hair she pulled it sharply. "Get up, you clown."

Loahn came up onto his feet grinning at her. He shuffled a little dance, too full of nervous energy to stand still. "Lahela gikena, worker of miracles, turner of the horde. Hi-yi, you did it. I didn't think you could. But you did. Only two cities!"

"Two cities," Aleytys repeated grimly. She turned away. "If I hadn't wasted so much time. . . ."

"No, no, Lahela." Loahn caught her in his arms and danced an impromptu triumph around Stavver's silent figure. He spun her away from him so that she stumbled into Stavver. Then he fidgeted in front of her, grinning, eyes beaming. "Only two cities, Lahela. Last time we lost twenty and half the people dead."

"Calm down, Loahn." She climbed back onto the seat. "I know what I did. What happened after I left?"

"Well . . . mmmmm . . . what with this and that, I managed to collect a lot of men willing to follow my lead."

"This and that?"

"Didn't hurt having your shadow wrapped round my shoulders."

"And?"

"Kekio brought your message to us. We were waiting to attack. So we waited a little longer. Saw you take off like someone set your tail on fire. We went down then, not knowing what to expect. They were like new-born babes, Lahela. We went through them. Through and through. Their minds were gone. Except for a few with funny silver helmets on. We stopped trying to fight them then and just gave them merciful death. Who could hate such lost things? And who could let them go on the way they were? The death pyres will burn long around wahi-Usk."

"Dead."

Loahn hooked his thumbs behind his belt and shifted from foot to foot. "Most of the adults." He turned his back on her and stared downtrail. "It's not finished yet. So many of them. But . . ." he brightened. "The children are coming out of the daze. We'll divide them among the families that lost men. They'll grow up lakelanders."

Aleytys frowned. "If they've lost kin, won't they . . .

mistreat the children?" She stared down at her hands. "I know what it's like being a cuckoo in the nest."

Loahn looked shocked. "No. No, Lahela. Never. These little ones are gift of Lakoe-heai. One does not mistreat a blessing."

Aleytys tapped her fingers on her knees. "Listen."

Loahn sank back until he was sitting on his heels. "What Lahela?"

"You should know what I learned about the horde."

"The horde is finished."

"Is there only one horde?"

Loahn looked startled. "I don't know."

"Then listen. The reason the horde moves out of the south is this—the horde master is dying. Somehow a traverse of the lakelands and the resulting orgy of death forces the peculiar physical and mental development that results in a master."

His bright lively eyes were locked on her face. "Weird."

"Understatement. Have you ever tried watching them for a pattern of action?"

Loahn scratched at the earth with a finger. "Not that I know of. It's all so irrational. Another thing. It's dangerous going near them, especially when the drums beat."

"Right. They've got courage, these young raiders who dash past shooting into the horde."

"They don't hang around long or come too close."

Aleytys swung her legs, kicking her heels against the side of the caravan. "Still . . . never mind. When the drums stop, they fall in their tracks deep, deep asleep. The roan stepped on one and he didn't even stop snoring. Except for a ring of guards on the master's wagon. The ones with the helmets. What happened to those helmets?"

"I don't know. They're around somewhere."

"Better collect them. Carefully. They're more valuable than just about anything else you can have. At least when the horde comes. The drum rite is held before entering the lakelands and after that as soon as sun goes down on a plundered city." She frowned over his head, staring blankly at the far horizon. "It always begins as soon as the sun is gone and ends . . . when it ends. The sleep lasts for several hours. Then they pick themselves up and move on. As far as I saw they never bothered to eat."

"So?"

"So this. After the drums stop, if a small raiding party . . ." she slapped a hand on her thigh for emphasis, "Wearing those silver helmets, slipped among the sleepers and jumped the guards, they'd have a good chance of getting at the master and stopping the whole thing. Like I did. You'd have to lose one city."

"One city. Ah! Wonder worker."

"Idiot." She rubbed at her knees. "I only serve Lakoe-heai. You don't owe me anything."

He flung out his hands, his mobile face animated. "Lakoe-heai. Ha! Our songsmiths shall sing of Lahela gikena and her gift to the people. Our children and their children and their children as long as tongue lives in mouth." He caught her hand and held it against his face.

"Loahn, you awe me with your capacity for nonsense! Talking of tongues, I think you open the floodgates and let the words flow like water downhill."

"Looks like I'm fated to be a famous leader then."

"If hot air qualifies one to be a leader."

"Have you ever seen one without a large supply?"

She chuckled. "I'll miss your impudence, Loahn."

"I couldn't persuade you to stay?"

She shook her head. "Loahn, heroes are only an embarrassment when the emergency's past. You know that."

"I'd better know it if I want a peaceful life." He sighed and didn't look all that happy about his future. He walked away a few paces. "So. I ride out of saga and back into the pettiness of ordinary living."

"Mountain tops can be just as boring."

"But harder to forget. Good faring in your quest, Lahela." He caught up the reins of his horse, sprang in the saddle with a barely contained explosion of energy, and started to ride away. Before the horse completed two strides, he pulled him around and came back to Aleytys. "What'd you do with my horse."

"Nothing. He came along. Over there somewhere." She pointed beyond the caravan to a sparse tinting of green in the rock.

"Where's the saddle?"

"I threw it away somewhere beside the road."

"Threw it away . . ." Loahn burst out laughing. "Threw it away!"

Aleytys stood and stretched. "That animal," she

screamed after the retreating Loahn. "That boneshaker has the worst gait of any horse I ever rode!"

Loahn waved back. "I know," he bellowed, his voice echoing hollowly around the embracing hills.

She watched him until he vanished behind an outcropping of granite. Leaning back against the slats, legs stretched out in front of her, she looked up into the sky where the streaks of color nearly covered the blue. "That's three."

"Three what?"

She sat up. "Four things to do for Lakoe-heai."

"And this is the third. Getting rid of the horde."

"Like I told you."

"So what's number four?" His hand was warm on her knee. One eyebrow twitched up in humorous mockery.

"I don't know. I'm almost afraid to find out. How's Maissa?"

"Still asleep."

Aleytys frowned. "She was still under spell when I killed the master and you heard what Loahn said about the others. I tried healing her. I don't know . . . damn . . . there's so much I just don't know. Better let her sleep."

"Right. You ready?"

Aleytys glanced at the sun's glow spot. "How long to the ship from here?"

"About two days." A wide smile lit his dark face briefly. "Then you can have your bath."

She twitched her shoulders, laughing. "Ay, Miks. Will you still like me as a redhead?" Eyes dancing; not waiting for his answer, she rubbed her stomach. "I'm starving. What about some food? The cupboard's bare over there."

"I'm stocked. Loahn took care of that." He stretched and yawned. "Didn't you just eat?"

"I can barely remember that."

"The fire's out, Lee. Chew on a piece of waybread."

She wrinkled her nose. "All right. If I have to."

He strolled away looking around for the horses. Aleytys chuckled and summoned them so that they brushed past him in an uneven three-legged gallop. They clattered to a stop in front of Aleytys sidestepping nervously, rebelling against the hobbles' restraints.

"Unfair, witch."

She chuckled. "True."

"No time for games, Lee. You want to hitch your own?"

"No."

Stavver snorted and strode off to buckle on the harness, a job he disliked more every time he did it.

The morning passed with unaccustomed placidity. They had to go slowly because the way was little more than a wild goat track leading vaguely south to meet the road that skirted the lakelands. A little before noon Stavver pulled up at a flattish spot and waited for her to join him.

"Time to eat?" She looked around at the desolate rocky hillside, her nose twitching with distaste.

"See those trees?" He pointed. "Down there where the land flattens out."

"Why?"

"That's where we hit the road. It's a couple hours yet. You want to stop now or wait till we get down there?"

"Maissa's still sleeping. I'm beginning to worry about her."

"You want to stop here?"

"No . . . I don't think so." She scanned his team, then her own chewing thoughtfully on her thumb tip. "This downhill work is tiring the horses. They need fodder and water."

"Nothing here but rock, Leyta."

"Right. It's not that much further."

She nodded.

The slope went on and on, down and down, the caravans rocking precariously over the rugged track, friction brakes spealing continuously.

"What's that noise?"

Aleytys jumped, nearly dropping the reins. She looked around. "So you're finally awake."

"Stupid. Obviously I'm awake."

"Well, what does one say?"

Maissa settled herself beside Aleytys. She looked around briefly, eyes glinting with a touch of malice as they swept over the caravan ahead. "How'd you break us loose?"

"How much do you remember?"

"Not much. More like a nightmare you forget as soon as you wake up. You do that too?"

"Hm. I killed horde master and some others. The horde fell apart."

"Filthy beast." Maissa shuddered, looking suddenly old.

Aleytys concentrated on the horses for a while. The trail led downhill in a series of long lazy s-curves.

"Where are we?" Maissa sniffed at the barren landscape.

"Nearly back to the road."

"Road?"

"The one we came in on. We'll be stopping to eat and rest the horses. After that it's about a day's journey to the ship."

Maissa kicked petulantly at the splashboard. "I'm sick of this ball of mud." She sank into a brooding silence. Aleytys let her alone and concentrated on getting downhill in one piece as the gradient suddenly steepened.

"Can't you do without that damn noise?" Maissa pressed trembling hands over her ears.

"No." Aleytys kicked the brake loose as the trail flattened for a moment. "If it bothers you so much, go inside." The trail began to dip, the caravan picked up speed, and Aleytys slammed the brake on again. Maissa winced but shut her mouth in a stubborn line and folded her arms across her breasts. At intervals she flicked an ominous angry glance at Aleytys.

When Stavver pulled his caravan into the shade of the grove, Aleytys silently blessed the break. Without a word Maissa jumped down from her seat and strode to the road where she stood staring toward the east.

Stavver touched Aleytys' shoulder. "There's a well over there. I see sleeping beauty's awake."

"Beauty! Awake and in her usual sunny mood." She sighed and leaned back against him. "You trust her, Miks?"

He rubbed his hand slowly up and down her neck, his eyes on the meager form in the roadway. "Is there a choice?"

"I suppose not."

"We'll take turns sleeping." He laughed and dropped a kiss on her hair. "We can take a week off and relax on I!kwasset. I've got friends there."

"If we get there."

"We will. If she doesn't strip her gears first."

She sighed. "I'm tired of all these complicated plots. Let's get back to simple things for a while. Like watering a lot of tired horses."

Chapter XIV

Maissa slapped her hand against the tree trunk. The camouflage sheeting peeled apart and began shrinking until the ship gleamed a silken gold in the diffused orange light. Aleytys saw it with relief tinged with a growing trepidation. She was tired of waiting for the last task to appear. Three times she'd tried the grass. Nothing, not the slightest hint of a pattern. Even now, with the ship waiting to take them away, tension tied her stomach in knots. What was the fourth thing?

At Maissa's impatient call she drove the caravan under the trees and halted it beside the ship. Stavver stopped the other beside her.

"I don't believe it."

He smiled. "Help me with the horses."

Maissa came out of the ship. Ignoring them she ran up the stairs into the caravan. Aleytys jumped down. "You start, Miks. I'll be out in a minute. With Sharl."

In the caravan Maissa was on her knees clawing at the panel. Sharl's drawer was nearly shut, muffling his angry and frightened yells. Aleytys scowled at Maissa then sighed as she pulled the drawer open and lifted out the crying baby. Maissa was what she was. No use expecting her to change.

Sharl's yells quieted. Picking up a quilt, she carried him outside. Fluffing up the quilt, she arranged it into a nest and laid the baby down in the folds, pulling a corner over him. "Sleep, my little one. . . ." She touched his cheek, then went to help Stavver strip the harness from the horses.

"Stavver! Get in here." Maissa thrust back the curtain and stood in the doorway, radiating explosive energy.

Inside, the panel was tossed onto one of the bunks. Maissa jumped onto a bunk, coiling her legs under her.

She jerked a thumb at the cavity. "I can't move it. You try."

Stavver moved past her and knelt. "Hard to get a hold on this thing."

Maissa shrugged then turned her head to glare at Aleytys. "I didn't call you."

Aleytys shrugged. Leaning against the doorpost she watched Stavver tug at the box. He managed to shift a corner of it into the space between the bunks but no amount of effort could move it further.

"You'll have to empty it," Aleytys said quietly.

Maissa scowled. "I don't want to."

Stavver snorted. "Then you move the thing."

"Ah god, if I only had a man."

"Or an ape. Make up your mind."

"Go outside. Both of you." Maissa slid off the bunk to stand between Stavver and the box. "I'll call you when I want you."

Silently Aleytys climbed down the stairs. She looked back at Stavver and opened her mouth.

He shook his head and led her away under the trees. "You're right, Leyta. She's back to her sweet original." He sat down, leaning against the trunk of a tree. "Come here."

Aleytys sank down, settling herself against him. "You argue too much with her, Miks."

"She knows me, Leyta. So I walk a tightrope with her. Too much independence and she shoots me out of pique. Too little and she shoots me out of suspicion."

"Ahai, Madar! How long to I!kwasset?"

"Three weeks." His mouth tilted into a one-sided smile. "Ouch."

"When Maissa's on her ship. . . . That's her territory. She'll calm down once we're in space."

Aleytys watched the grazing horses move between them and the caravans. "You hope."

"Think, Leyta. You saw her on the ship coming here."

Aleytys sighed. "She's been through a hard time."

"Forget her a minute." He pushed her from his shoulder and turned her so he could see her face. "Stay with me, Lee."

"Miks. . . ."

"Don't jump. Think a minute before you answer."

She put her hands on his arms. "I want to. No. . . ."

She stopped him, shaking her head. "Would you come with me?"

A muscle twitched beside his mouth. "Where?"

"To Vrithian. I think I should go there. For Sharl's sake. For me too."

"That's your condition?"

"No." She dropped her eyes.

"Well, Lee, I've always wanted to see Vrithian. After that I'll show you. . . ." He pulled her against his chest, rubbing a hand up and down her back as she shuddered, laughing and crying at the same time.

"Stavver!"

"Damn."

Aleytys giggled damply then jumped to her feet. "Our master calls."

Stavver grunted. He raised his bony length from the ground with deliberate slowness, narrow face fixed into a heavy scowl.

"Stavver! Get over here. You too, witch."

Wiping her eyes Aleytys followed him to the caravan. Maissa waited for them inside.

"Get in there and clean it out. I'll lower the sling for the box when you've got it empty enough to move." She ran scornful eyes over Stavver's thin body. "Yell if you need help." She ran with quick nervous strides down the back stairs and into the ship.

"It's going to be a long three weeks," Aleytys grumbled.

Stavver knelt beside the box. "Let it slide off, Leyta. She can't hurt you now." He plunged his hand in and pulled out one of the sacks then the other. Tossing them to Aleytys, he said, "Shove the rocks in there. Easier to carry."

Aleytys nodded.

When the box was empty Stavver tipped it onto one side and maneuvered it out of the cavity. With Aleytys' help he hauled it out of the caravan and set it down beside the ship beneath the slowly descending sling.

Aleytys straightened, groaning. "My back. It'll never be the same. Miks, I was NOT meant to be a pack mule."

"Come on." Stavver started back for the caravan. "We've got another load to haul."

"Fun, fun. I thought thieving was supposed to be an adventure. All I can see, it's damn hard work."

He grinned. "No magic in thieving, Leyta."

When they came out of the caravan carrying the sacks, Maissa was standing beside the sling waiting for them. "Hurry it up," she snapped. "I want to get out of here."

Kale stepped from the shadow under the trees. "Stand quiet," he said calmly. "All of you."

Behind him other Lamarchans slid like hunting cats from the shadows, bows cocked and aimed, the wicked points of the quarrels glittering in the sunlight.

Aleytys stared. The underlying sense of barely controlled despair and rage was gone out of him. He radiated pride and self-confidence. Whatever it was that made him bitter, futile, a man acted on rather than acting . . . this intangible thing was wiped totally away . . . how? Then she saw that the false tattoos were gone. The wolves grinned on his face, loped along his arms, slanted up his chest. He held a crossbow casually pointed at the group, leaving the active menace to the men supporting him. "Move away from that box, Captain. I see you wanting the weapons inside."

Maissa glared at him. For a minute Aleytys was afraid she'd ignore the warning.

Kale lifted the bow. "I'm very good with this, Maissa. You aren't fast enough to dodge."

Maissa balanced on her toes, her muscles taut and poised to leap. Her eyes swept from Kale's face to the point of the quarrel, over the stern faces of the men behind him, flicking at last to Stavver and Aleytys. As she read their unwillingness to act, she sighed, relaxed and moved to lean against the tailfin of the ship.

"Gikena."

"What?"

"We could take you with us. If you want."

"If I don't want to go?"

"We could take you anyway. Have you a choice?"

"Yes." Aleytys nodded at Maissa. "You can't control me like that. Have you forgotten?" She smiled. "Be careful, Kale."

Still relaxed and feeling himself in command of the situation, he nodded. "You were given four tasks, gikena."

"I never told you that."

"My father knows. Three are done. This is the fourth. Lakoe-heai used you, Aleytys. To bring the Soul-in-Flight back to the people."

"That poaku?" She glanced at the two sacks.

He nodded. "Captain." When Maissa refused to look at him, he repeated the word. "Captain. Come here. You're standing on my home ground here. I tell you what to do. Not like on your bridge."

"No!"

"Come. Or die."

Maissa straightened, watching his strong cold face with considerable puzzlement, wondering where he had got the force to do this to her. The madness Aleytys feared in her spurred her toward sudden violent action, but shrewd instinct recognized the demands of the real world. What she had to do to survive, she would do. Under Kale's direction she backed against a tree and extended her arms behind her. The youngest of the anonymous guard loped around the tree and roped her hands together with swift efficiency.

Kale jabbed a thumb at Stavver. "You next." He grinned. "That huahua there. A long man needs a long tree."

The boy tied Stavver's hands around the bole, then stepped to the next tree.

"Now you, gikena. Carefully. You see?" He stepped aside. A white-haired man held a quilt-wrapped bundle in one arm, a knife in the other, point just touching the skin of the baby's throat. Sharl. In the confusion she had forgotten him. "I don't think even you could keep the knife from his throat, gikena."

Aleytys backed against the tree, felt the smooth narrow hands of the boy moving over her arms and wrists. "What happens now?"

The white-haired man brought Sharl to her and laid him at her feet, where he lay sucking contentedly at his thumb.

Kale lowered the crossbow. "My brother used a different knot on your arms, gikena. On time you'll be able to work yourself loose. Captain." He met Maissa's furious eyes and smiled grimly. "Don't try following us. We'll be scattered and we'll turn the world against you. One man's hard to find on the surface of a world. I've learned that much in my own faring."

Black eyes burned out of a greyish pallor. She said nothing.

Aleytys pulled gently at the ropes around her wrists. There didn't seem to be any give to them. She left it for the moment. "Didn't you intend to take me with you?"

"I'd like to." His eyes moved over her body, then he shook his head. "I've seen too much of what you can do, gikena. You're an uncomfortable companion for an ordinary man."

Maissa's hoarse voice stabbed at her. "Do something, witch!"

"What? I'd welcome any workable ideas."

An ugly growl tore from Maissa's throat as she twisted wildly at the ropes.

Kale laughed at her and walked away. He knelt beside the bags of poaku, dark shapeless lumps on the paler earth. "Makuakane, the Soul-in-Flight is in one of these. The honor is yours, my father. Bring the soul forth." He moved backward and knelt again in respectful silence, holding the crossbow in front of him, stock snugged against the ground.

Ignoring the three roped to the trees, the brothers gathered around the old man, kneeling beside Kale. Aleytys watched with interest. The white-haired man was an older edition of Kale, the resemblance startling as they knelt side by side. The others shared the elusive similarity of family likeness. She realized with a shock of surprise how very little she knew of this world. Immersed in its problems she had begun to accept her role here as an element of her own personality. Somehow it was easier to deal with this world if she thought of it as simply an unexplored section of Jaydugar. But occasionally one thing or another jarred her from her complacency. A triple handful of days . . . not enough, never enough to absorb the whole of a culture.

The old man took the poaku from the bag, unwrapping each and handing them on to a son who reverently rewrapped them and placed them in a growing heap by his knees. When the first sack was empty the old one turned quietly to the second but shot a troubled glance at his son's impassive face. Again he took the poaku out. As the slow quiet process went on, Aleytys sensed a growing impatience in all but Kale.

Then the slanting rays from the setting sun gleamed along the amber and russet stone. She saw the stopping hawk uncovered. The old man's hands trembled. "Soul-in-Flight. It has come home."

Holding the stone at arm's length he rocked up onto his feet. Bowing deeply in front of Kale he took one hand from the stone and pressed it down on the top of his son's dark head. "My blessing, Kale. You have brought honor back to Wolf clan."

"The stones are mine," Maissa shrieked.

The old man laughed. "Nonsense, woman." Kale put a hand on his arm, drawing his father's stare.

"Makuakane, women have a different place where this one comes from. She doesn't understand what she should be."

Maissa glared at them and began cursing in a dozen different languages while she tore futilely at the ropes.

Kale glanced at her then walked over to Aleytys as his brothers tied lead ropes around the horses' necks and prepared to leave. "I'd like you to understand, Aleytys."

"What difference does it make?"

She saw a sheen of sweat dot his forehead. He moved his eyes from her, the tip of his tongue tracing the pronounced curve of his upper lip, looked briefly at Maissa still shrilling complicated obscenities, at Stavver cold and silent, then came back to her. "Nearly a thousand years of history, Aleytys. Gikena. Beat into our heads. Besides I . . . " He hesitated. "I have respect for you, Aleytys."

"Respect!"

"If you can't accept that, say I like you. Or say we share a common appreciation for living things."

"All right." A breeze wandered under the trees and blew a tangle of hair across her face. She wrinkled her nose and tried to throw the tickling mass off her face. He brushed it back, tucked the straying wisps behind her ear, then dropped to the ground in front of her.

Sitting crosslegged, eyes focused on her knees, he said quietly, "There's a lot you don't know about Lamarchos."

"I began realizing that some twenty minutes ago."

He began tugging at the wiry grass, pulling blades free one by one, chewing the tender whiteness at the base, then shredding the green into fibrous strips. "Gikenas come rarely. And even when they come, they stand outside the flow of life." He lifted his head and smiled at her. "You know how women are placed here?"

"I know I wouldn't last long on this world."

"I doubt that." He shook his head, then sat tossing the

bits of green fiber over her dusty toes. "It's as well you're leaving. I can see you turning our calm lives into battle-grounds." The sweat was back trickling down beside his deep crow's-feet. "I don't know how well I. . . . Never mind. Women keep the house altars, but men serve the poaku and keep the shrines of Lakoe-heai. Like my father. Especially the great ones, the numinous stones." He stared into the shadow under the trees, seeing things from his memories that made him move uneasily, shifting the set of his legs.

"The great poaku. They stay in shrines with their own lands, their own clans to serve them. Soul-in-Flight was served by clan Wolf. It was our purpose, the central aspect of our being, to serve the stone, care for the gifts and the lands and the horses sealed to Soul-in-Flight. In return the stone served as conduit between clan-head and Lakoe-heai. I remember times it healed, times it sat in the great hall humming gently to itself spinning webs of power no man but my father could read. Clan Wolf served year on year on year until the years added up to centuries. We owned nothing but used all and had poaku each of us to buy the Karkesh blades for our blooding."

Aleytys looked over his head at his brothers, watching as they led the horses into the clearing and stood waiting for Kale. Kale fell into silence as if reluctant to go on. "Your brothers are ready to leave," she said.

"They can wait." He brooded at the shadows. "My father had a younger brother. He became . . . the ships of the Karkiskya laid a spell on him. He begged the Kapuna . . ." Kale nodded at the white-haired man who was slipping the poaku Soul-in-Flight into a special embroidered bag. "To buy passage on a ship and let him go to the stars." Kale laughed. "To say my father didn't understand is to call a rock cat pretty kitty. Besides we owned nothing ourselves. Everything belongs to the poaku. So . . . " Kale fell silent again. He threw back his head and gazed up at the streaks and strands of color. "I wonder. . . . "

"Wonder?"

"If I can narrow myself to fit this life again." He shrugged. "He stole the Soul-in-Flight and bought his way aboard a starship. That was twenty years ago. I was a boy, the oldest son of my father. When the stone was taken we were cast out, of course. Turned out from service to the stone, the lands and horses given into care of other hands. Driven away to find some bare corner of the land where we might scratch a living if we could. No poaku for our sons, no bride price for our daughters.

"My father sent me after the thief to make him pay in blood for the wrong." A wry smile twisted up a corner of his mouth. "I never found him. No doubt the fool was soon eaten by some shark. So I wandered world to world until I finally met Maissa. Knowing what she was, the thought came to me to use her to break the Soul-in-Flight loose and take it home." He pushed himself onto his feet. "From the beginning I planned this." He began pacing back and forth in front of her, three steps to the east, three steps to the west. "I didn't know about you then." He shrugged. "The thing is done. My people have the curse lifted from them now."

Aleytys sighed, her anger having trickled quietly away in the course of the explanation.

He found her silence disturbing. "Aleytys?"

"I'm sorry."

"Sorry?"

"I see you're much like me, Kale." She nodded toward the laden horses. "You've got a lot of what your people count as wealth there. Take a few of those poaku and buy your way out of this trap."

He shook his head. "I can't do that." He touched her gently on the cheek. "If you weren't quite so deadly, my dear, I'd keep you with me to make the fitting easier."

"Keep a bolt hole open, Kale. Stavver told me that and I respect his shrewdness. I couldn't go back to my own people now. Even if they'd accept me rather than tying me to a stake and burning hell out of this body." She sighed. "Your father is frowning."

He reached around the tree and pulled at the rope end. "I've loosened the knot. Don't pull at it. Try to work the ends loose." He touched her again then ran to his horse and swung up into the saddle. He grinned at Maissa while his mount pranced nervously. The cruel predator's look was back in his face. He enjoyed taunting her. "Captain!" He flipped a hand at her. "Even your instruments won't find us. Good faring and thanks for all your help."

The trees swayed as the earth rocked under their feet. Maissa gasped, looked with anxiety at the ship as it rocked precariously, threatening to topple on its side. Kale laughed, savage exultation in his dark face. "Our world grows impatient for your departure." He pulled the horse around and disappeared under the trees. The others, having said scarcely a single word, kept their dour silence and disappeared after him.

"Work your hands around so I can see the knots." Stavver's voice was absurdly commonplace and calm. Aleytys burst out laughing then subsided as she heard the hysterical note in her own voice.

After about a half hour's twisting and straining, following Stavver's instructions, she managed to work the ropes loose enough to pull one hand free. She stepped away from the tree, rubbing her sore wrists. "I feel like an arthritic old lady." The earth rolled beneath her, sending her staggering. When the ground steadied again, she darted to Stavver. "We better get out of this fast."

"Lee, idiot. My knife. You'll go a lot faster."

"Ay-mi, thickhead." She snatched the knife from the sheath and began sawing at the rope.

"Careful. I need all my fingers."

She chuckled, but calmed down and cut the ropes away with quick efficiency. When she moved on to Maissa, he walked to the box, rubbing his own wrists. He took the tools and chameleon web out, thrust them behind his belt and worked the box into the sling.

When Maissa was free, Aleytys caught up the placidly sleeping baby and followed her to the ship.

Maissa stopped at the foot of the ladder, staring without expression at the trees where Kale had disappeared. Then she slowly wiped her hands together and ran up the ladder. A minute later the chain tightened and the box began rising toward a cargo hatch.

Aleytys moved close to Stavver, slipping her free arm around his waist, nestling close to him. "I scarcely believe it's over.

She felt him stiffen. "Not yet." His voice sounded strange. "Look."

Through the congealing clumps of bacteria a grey sphere somewhat battered and blackened settled with a hum of power toward the ground about a hundred meters from Maissa's ship.

"The Hounds!" Aleytys clung to Stavver as her knees

threatened to give way. "Why didn't I dream them if they were this close?"

"Up the ladder, Lee." He boosted her onto the first rung. "Move!"

On the screen in the bridge they watched the sphere settle to the ground, extruding two pairs of fins to hold it upright.

Aleytys chewed on her thumb, frowning a little as she watched. "Can you break away?"

Maissa shook her head. She clicked the nail of a forefinger against the glass of a telltale. "Damper field. Drains energy from engines. And here. . . ." The finger moved across the face of the console. "Pincers . . . tractors . . . they've got enough hands on me to hold a battleship."

"Then I better get us some help."

Maissa's eyebrows rose.

"Open the lock for me."

"Why?"

"If I can get the earth shifting under them, can you hold this ship from going over?" She glanced back at the ominous grey sphere. "And would it help?"

Maissa laughed, eyes dancing in her dark face. "That should shake the bastards up." Still grinning she tapped one of the lighted squares. "Move your butt, woman. Get your little friends busy."

Aleytys stood beside the foot of the ladder, body stripped nude, hands flung outward. "You!" she cried, projecting demand, anger, scorn. "You called me sister once. You tricked me and used me. You owe me!"

Thunder answered, sounding petulant and unwilling.

She gathered her anger and flung it at them hot as ball lightning. "PAY!"

She felt an answering anger swirling around her. "Pay!" she demanded. "You owe me. Shake that ship over and we'll be quits."

The earth groaned beneath her feet and thunder groaned in the sky. She sensed a grudging acquiescence. "Good!" She broke the contact with the earth and ran back up the ladder.

Maissa turned when she came back into the bridge wrapping her batik around her. "Well?"

"Wait." She moved to the screen. "Look."

They saw the Rmoahl ship begin to rock in gradually

widening arcs as the earth shifted and slipped beneath the landing fins. Maissa worked busily to keep her own ship upright as the outriding waves of the earthquake passed beneath them. She kept breaking into happy little chuckles as she watch the sphere struggle. "They waited too long. Ah . . . ah . . . ah. . . ."

A crack opened, swallowing one fin so that the Hound-ship tilted and swayed, then crashed heavily on its rounded side.

Maissa thrust Aleytys back from the console. "Get down. Hold on. Both of you." She ran her hands rapidly over the sensors, throwing the ship into the air, it seemed to Aleytys, by force of her will alone. The surface of the world retreated until it was a mottled marble hanging against the velvet dark of space. The little ship swam invisibly through the layer of sensory probes, past the circling Karkesh stingships swarming around hunting for the intruder that had ghosted down setting off enough alarms to stir up the security forces of the whole world. Maissa's ship skimmed through them and darted rapidly toward the zone of FTL conversion.

After conversion Maissa swung around and stretched luxuriously, smiling brilliantly at Stavver and Aleytys. "I believe I swore I'd take you two wherever you wanted. I!kwasset, wasn't it?" She raised her brows at Stavver.

He jumped easily to his feet, his dark-dyed face changing as Maissa's had changed. This was his world as much as hers. His grin met and matched hers.

Quietly Aleytys got to her feet, watching them expand, throwing off the world-life like some smothering blanket, both of them growing stronger as if the engines that drove the ship fed them as much as they fed the ship.

Forgotten for a moment, Aleytys moved quietly to the screen and watched the dance of the stars across the blackness, letting the sheer beauty of them heal the hurts in her. Then she turned away. "Sharl's probably wet and hungry. And I need a bath. Oh god, do I need a bath."

Stavver laughed and ran his fingers through her hair. "I like you better as a redhead, Lee. Come on. We can get rid of this dye along with the dirt.

EPILOG

Aleytys woke slowly, a dull ache behind her eyes. She was lying on the floor . . . a floor? She worried at this oddity a moment, but thinking hurt so she quit. She sat up carefully then leaned against the wall pressing the heels of her hands hard against her eyes. The pain retreated.

She looked dully around. The walls were pink. Ceiling, floor . . . pink. Padded until it felt like spongy flesh beneath the firm smoothness of pink skin. The fourth side of the room wasn't there. She was in a padded pink box tipped on its side with the top gone. Why was it so . . . familiar . . . why. . . .

"Madar!" She slid her hands over over over the smooth sensuous skin. I'm dreaming. she thought. It's that damn dream again. Since I reached puberty. Waking up naked. . . . She looked down at herself. Naked. In a stupid pink room. Oh god, I've got to wake up.

Trembling and uncertain, she crawled to the wall and managed to push herself onto her feet. Wake up wake up wakeupwakeup. . . .

She beat against the wall. It yielded spongily with a dull splatting sound. A dull splatting sound? "Ahai! It isn't a dream." Her eyes snapped open. "Maissa!" she shrieked. Then her knees folded under her and she bounced onto the floor. Laughter trickled from her in sudden bursts. "You can't lie to me, Maissa. Ay-mi, what fool. I don't trust you now, Maissa. So I won't give you a chance to hurt me. What a laugh! If I let you do me after this, I deserve it. God, do I deserve it."

Cautiously, hand pressed against the wall to steady her, she got back on her feet and tottered around the room to the open wall, intending to make her way down the corridor visible outside and find some answers to make sense out of this mess.

She slammed into a transparent hardness. Her knees gave way and she tumbled in a heap onto the yielding floor. When the dizziness retreated she reached out and explored the opening with a shaking hand. Some substance harder than glass and far more transparent blocked it. With a whimper of frustration she slammed her fist against it. Sucking at the reddened spot along the side of her hand she sank to the floor and stared hopelessly at the unreachable corridor.

Time passed. Perhaps she slept. She wasn't sure.

"Lee!"

She lifted her head. Stavver stood outside. His voice came to her as if there was nothing between them, adding one more facet to her confusion. "Miks!" She jumped up. "Where am I? What happened?" She flattened her hands against the transparency. "What is this that holds me in here? What am I doing here? What. . . ."

"Hush, Lee. Calm down and listen."

"Calm down?" She brushed distractedly at the red hair tumbling over her face. "Get me out of here!"

He ran a hand nervously across his face. He looked himself again, tall and thin, a mop of moon-white hair tumbling over pale grey-blue eyes. She could see the blue veins pulsing at his temple, webbing the backs of his thin hands. "Aleytys, shut up and listen."

She drew in a deep breath and let it trickle out again. "What about a few answers?" As her hands closed into fists behind her back, a headache pain began to beat behind her eyes.

Stavver glanced nervously over his shoulder. "Leyta, I've bought a few minutes with you. Old I!kuk gets the oboloi where he can. Listen. You're in the slave pens of I!kwasset."

"Slave pens!"

"Don't interrupt. Maissa tricked me. When I was hunting down . . . never mind names . . . she drugged you, hauled you here and sold you, claiming you owed her passage money. When I got back the ship was gone."

Aleytys swallowed, a new fear hollow inside her. She opened her mouth but the words were tangled in a lump blocking her throat. She licked dry lips. "Sharl?"

He rubbed his forehead. "She took him with her," he mumbled. "I'm sorry, Lee."

"Miks . . ."

"He'll be all right. Leyta. He's your son."

She crossed her arms over her breasts. "Get me out of here."

"No way, Leyta."

"You're the best thief."

"No way. Not out of the slave pens." He smiled wearily at her. She could see a faint beading of sweat on his forehead, something she'd seldom seen before. "Don't you think I'd have you out of there if I could?"

"Would you?"

He flattened his palms against the transparency. "I have to, Aleytys. You've hooked me hard. Look. I can't get you out of here. Once you're sold, that's different."

She moved impatiently. "You got in. Can't you bribe someone or something?"

"With what?" He shrugged. "The guards don't take bribes. They'd be skinned alive. And that's no figure of speech, Leyta."

She shuddered. "What's going to happen to me?"

"You'll be put on the block and sold."

"Couldn't you. . . ."

"No way." He looked over his shoulder again. "My time almost up. I can't steal you out, Leyta. And I can't buy you out. Not at the price you'll bring. No. After you're sold, then I can get you away. No owner will have the kind of security they have here. I'll come for you."

"No."

"What?"

"Not right away, anyway. Miks."

"What is it?" She could hear a chill anger in his voice, an anticipation that she was going to ask something of him he wouldn't want to do.

"Morality. Right. I know it's not fair. But, damn it, I don't have a choice. I hope you're right, Miks, about that thing in me that lays claim on you. I'm going to use you, if I can." She twisted her hands together. "Oh god, if I can. I have to. Miks, go after Maissa. If you love me, if you want me, by all we've shared, Miks, get Sharl from her."

He jerked away and took two steps down the corridor, then wheeled and came back his face twisted with a pain that radiated through his body like a cancer. Gasping for breath he banged his head against the transparency. "Stop it!" His voice rose in a tortured shriek.

Her mouth pinched together in a grim line, she waited.

He closed his eyes. She saw the muscles loosen in his face and neck. "All right, Aleytys, you win. I'll go after her and get your son away from her."

She felt the stiffening go out of her spine. Slumping, stumbling, nearly falling, she put out her hands and pressed them against the transparency near his shoulders. "I'm sorry, Miks." She sighed. "I suppose you won't want me around after this."

"Aleytys," he said slowly. "I'm a selfish man."

"Am I less selfish, Miks? Using you? But I have to get Sharl away from that horror. I do care for you, but you're a man, Miks. Sharl. . . . You know Maissa. I wish I didn't have to do this."

He stroked his hand outside the transparency at the level of her face as if he caressed her. "I could promise you anything, you know. Just to get the compulsion turned off."

She smiled tiredly. "That's a chance I take."

"I've a feeling it's not much of a chance. That if I went my own way, the pain would start again."

"I don't know."

He snorted self-mocking laughter. "Miks Stavver. Knight Errant. Ridiculous. I swear to you Aleytys, I will find your son." He frowned. "If I come for you, would you live with me?"

"Yes."

"Before getting involved in that, I'd better leave ·the baby somewhere safe. Who's his father and where do I find him?"

"Vajd is his name. You'll find him on Jaydugar in a vadi . . . a mountain valley called the Kard. Ask for the dream-singer. The blind one."

A dark-faced guard tapped Stavver on the shoulder and jerked his head toward the exit.

"I know that damn world," he said hastily. "I'll find you, Lee."

"Miks, I. . . ."

He waved a hand and strode nervously away down the corridor, leaving the stolid guard far behind before they passed out of sight. Aleytys stayed pressed against that hard transparency that pinned her in the cell until even the sound of his footsteps were gone. Then she sat down in the middle of the floor, wrapped her arms around her legs and stared dispiritedly at the black wall across the corridor.

The next days moved in and out of a dream. Something in the food . . . something in the air . . . she didn't know . . . didn't care . . . didn't care about anything . . . something sapped her will and kept her in a drowsy listlessness that let time slip past unnoticed.

Image . . . white enamel room accented in stainless steel . . . pain . . . jumbled words . . . hurry . . . before she comes out of the fog . . . takes enough ????? . . . the word was meaningless sound . . . to stun a ???? . . . no referent . . . the psi damper . . . silver disc . . . get it in . . . a cold touch on her back . . . blackness . . . feeling of oppression . . . women working on her limp uncaring body . . . oils for the skin . . . oils for the hair . . . callouses gently patiently abraded away . . . massage . . . pummelling her about . . . all the while a dullness like a cap over her brain that was terrifying when she came enough out of the fog to feel it there . . . underlying terror . . . dulled by the drug. . . .

She woke, mind clear and alert. She jumped to her feet and paced impatiently about the cell, anger burning in her and a cold fear under all of it. She found it hard to think, images tended to fragment. Bits of memory came flooding back.

When she looked down at herself, she found many rather startling changes. Her hands were soft and supple, the nails buffed to a subtle sheen. She pulled at her hair. It glowed with life and health, more silken and beautiful than it had ever been. The red-gold color shone like fire. Her body felt pampered and soft, the muscles acquired by hard living gone somehow. She touched her face. "Merchandise. Polished to a high gloss." She laughed suddenly, grimly. "Someone's going to get a surprise."

Outside her cell an odd little being harrumphed loudly. She came to the open wall.

He sat in a floating dish, filled with a reddish fluid. Huge golden eyes surrounded by busily waving cilia. A parrot's beak. A bulbous pear-shaped body. Four limber tentacles branching from each side of the purple body, a double handspan under the beak. "I am I!kuk." His beak clacked as he spoke, his voice was shrill and harsh with little inflection to the words.

Aleytys nodded, thinking that if he let her out she could tip the dish over and run like hell.

The golden eyes flickered. He waved a tentacle. A guard with a short black rod in his hand stepped into her field of vision.

"The rod he holds is a neuro-stimulator. It will cause pain so intense you will find it impossible to believe you could live through it. This kind of punishment has the value of not marking you or ruining permanently your value as merchandise."

"I see."

The cilia went into a convulsion, marking I!kuk's appreciation of her good sense. "When the force field goes off, step into the corridor and walk ahead of the guards. Don't try escaping. There is no escape from the pens. All you gain from trying will be pain. Much pain. There's another thing. I've had an inhibitor planted in your back to damp out your psi abilities. Pity. But you're too dangerous with them in conscious control. Warning. Don't attempt to use your talents. The inhibitor is not as sensitive as we would like. It not only prevents use of your mind talents but it can interfere with normal thought if it kicks on too strongly."

"You think of everything." She fought back her helplessness calling on pride to keep her from crumbling in front of him. Somehow it was important that she handle herself with what dignity she could muster.

"Of course." The odd creature accepted the irony as a compliment, even preened himself a little. With a faint hum, the dish floated back out of sight. His voice came to her around the edge of the cell. "The field is off. Step into the corridor."

She put out her hand. The transparent hardness was gone.

When the procession moved out of the labyrinthine tunnels into the sunlight, Aleytys blinked and stared up at the ruby-red sun. It reminded her forcibly of home and red Horli. She swallowed a sharp pang of homesickness.

I!kuk herded her to the center of the open-air market and made her climb onto a cube-shaped block made of what appeared to be glossy black stone, then he thumbed the forcefield on, shutting her into an impenetrable transparent box.

She stared out over the heads of the incredibly varied throng of creatures parading slowly past the line of living merchandise, reminding her strongly of the horsetraders that came to vadi Raqsidan during the spring meetings. She remembered her father . . . a frisson of cold hatred clutched at her stomach when she thought of him . . . the Azdar, seeing him feeling the legs of a colt and forcing open his mouth to look at his teeth. Although they couldn't touch her . . . eyes stared at her . . . beings circled her, staring . . . measuring . . . commenting in a dozen languages on her physical attributes . . . listened to the recorded sales talk that went on automatically when anyone stopped to look at her . . . bringing angry blood surging into her face . . . sometimes she felt as if she couldn't breathe . . . sometimes she felt like shrinking in on herself . . . sometimes like breaking through the field and killing them all . . . the rage in her so great it threatened to blow her apart. . . .

I!kuk drifted past, turned back and floated, bobbing gently up and down in front of her block. Some kind of favored client beside him, dwarfing him. Over two meters tall . . . thin narrow body with long, long arms . . . more than one elbow joint . . . they hung strangely . . . long, thin legs that also looked to have more than one joint in them . . . thin austere face . . . eyes huge, black . . . multifaceted . . . more like an insect's than . . . short stubby antennas ending in reddish knobs . . . brilliant crimson tunic of some velvety material. . . .

A red curtain slid around the forcefield, cutting off view of the market.

Aleytys sank onto her knees, pride no longer supporting her when the others could no longer see her. "Sold," she muttered. She rested her head on her knees. "Like a piece of meat."

She heard a sound and jumped to her feet. The back side of the box opened out. I!kuk and the goggle-eyed being watched as she walked down the slanting ramp, feeling uncertain and strange.

"Introduce me, I!kuk." The being's voice was deep and musical.

The cilia fluttered wildly around the amber eyes, underlining I!kuk's disapproval, but he backed his dish off and said, "Aleytys, I present the kipu Anesh of Irsud."